Villainous Summer

LINNEA MARCH

Also by Linnea March

Prevalent Notion Series
Faultless Notion
Treacherous Notion
Ruinous Notion

Seasons of Us
Wren's Winter
Villainous Summer

Other Titles
Reckless Liar
The One You Chose

Contents

Notice for readers

This book contains infidelity, revenge pornography, violence and assault

To Rusty, for loving the
beautiful and the ugly just the
same

And to every woman who has
ever been called difficult, from
Rizzo to Rosalie and beyond.
Stay bitchy, my gals

"I support women's rights, but more importantly,
I support women's wrongs."

One

Summer

WITH A BOTTLE OF champagne in hand, I studied the front door of the man who's made me the other woman.

Five blissfully ignorant hours before, I was forty-one thousand feet above Alberta, staring at the picture on my phone.

Despite the past three months of daily video calls, sexting, and exchanging more naked pictures than the ones littering my cousin's nudie magazine stuffed under his mattress, Cory was engaged to someone else.

Cory Thompson. My Cory. Only he wasn't mine.

Someone named Kodi Ann had tagged him in the pictures, proving that. Her heart-shaped face split in a big grin as she held up the halo style engagement ring between her and Cory. Cory kissing her, with her left hand resting on his cheek.

Cory and Kodi.

Bile rose in my throat.

Two weeks before I was to leave for London for my three-month internship with Prescott Hoteliers, I met Cory at a local dive bar, Skol House.

It was trivia night, a weekly tradition I would faithfully attend with my cousin Autumn and our friend Wren. Only, this time, they bailed. Leaving me to sit alone at the bar and watch the fun being had by other teams.

Three Freedom Bay Ales in, I had spotted him nursing a bottle of German beer and staring at the Kraken game three stools down. When his eyes would catch mine, a warmth would flush through my body.

Medium brown hair, light-brown eyes, and a slender build, he was charming and seemed sweet. He had told me he moved to the area a week before for a civilian job in on the local naval base.

As I switched to soda water, he had three more beers. As that night wore on, our knees knocked together, and he brushed strands out of my eyes, his thumb tracing my jaw.

When he asked me to go home with him, I did.

He had no ring or tan line. His phone's wallpaper displayed a Gonzaga Bulldogs graphic.

We had spent two perfect weeks together, laughing and falling for one another.

In his rented house, pictures of his parents, Don and Sheila, hung from the walls. Wallets of nieces and nephews stuck to the stainless steel fridge with a magnet from Kamloops, BC. Sparse decorations indicated he was still moving in.

When he would leave the room to answer calls, I had assumed it was his job. When I would ask him to meet my friends, he would have an excuse, but I would chalk it up to him settling in.

As I tried to leave for London, he kissed me a dozen times. He'd downloaded a new app for us to talk on while I was abroad. Upon landing, I had a dozen sweet messages filling my inbox. After finding out my new address, he had arranged for a bouquet of blue tulips to be delivered the next morning, as he would call me "his blue" for my eyes.

Blue as my heart without you.

I had tucked those flowers between pages in a book and kept with me while I was away.

Every day, we would talk, sending pictures back and forth. It was lonely in London, though the weather was so similar to my hometown of Ridgewood in the Pacific Northwest I didn't have my usual homesickness for rain. Confiding in each other and reading his long, passionate emails got me through damp nights.

At no point did I think there was someone else—worse of all that I would be the one to intrude.

I had dissected every detail. She was tiny, smaller than me, with dark hair like mine. Blue eyes. We could have been sisters. No one could say he didn't have a type.

Gripping the phone, I reread the caption.

Five months of the greatest love story, two months long distance, one big move-in day, a foster kitten, and I finally got that BLING.

Five months.

They, likely, had started dating only weeks before we met.

With the gift of foresight, I could see everything I had missed. All the hints I had ignored.

With social media full of sports memes and beer, he wouldn't let me post pictures of us, claiming that he liked "privacy," that others didn't need to know our business, and that what we had was "too precious to spoil with social media."

I cursed under my breath. I could have stayed in the flat. Shopped and went out to the pub with my new friends and got takeout. Instead, I had paid an extra two hundred dollars to change my ticket and be dumped in the sky.

Not one to process my feelings alone, I screenshot the announcement and sent it to my girlfriends.

Autumn: That complete dickwad. I'm going to egg his house.

Devin: I'll get the TP

Wren: I never liked him.

Autumn: I had a bad feeling about him. When you said he doesn't like animals because they're too messy, I should have known.

Neither Wren nor Devin was close enough to Ridgewood to succumb to petty vandalism, but I appreciated their rage.

My friend's words pulsed under my skin.

Hours after seeing the picture, I found myself standing in his driveway.

With narrowed eyes, I willed myself to walk away. If I acted right then, I still had a shot to get my ride back, and no one would know I was here.

His rented home resembled the one I had spent with him those two weeks, when I had been falling for a liar. Same bright blue siding, a basketball hoop over the garage, and a cooler on the porch. Blue printed curtains hung in a window. An oversized sign beside the front door exclaimed, "Oh, hello!" in gigantic calligraphy. Over the peephole was a fake sunflower wreath, complementing a row of dying potted daffodils on the steps.

Being there was a bad idea. Nothing good could come from confronting him. Maybe it was the three overpriced vodka ginger ales I had slammed after getting off the plane. Maybe it was my friend's vitriol. Whatever it may have been, I was teetering on the edge of an all-too-familiar anger, the same fury that made my high school English teacher cry when she demanded Autumn change her top because she was distracting the boys. The same one that caused a man to back into a tree, who had tried to get away from me when his car door hit mine.

I didn't need to confront him. I could've been mature, the better person, and leave Cory and his cheating ways behind.

Sitting in the spot my car would've been parked, a newer red coupe had a license plate frame infested with rhinestones, a monstrosity. In script letters, it read *His Blue*.

That was it. Red glazed over my vision.

With the champagne bottle, I marched up the drive. The doormat was made of coir with *Probably at Target* painted in red-and-black script letters.

Pounding on the door, I didn't stop until it was wrenched open. The fake flower wreath swung up and whacked the white-painted wood.

Cory stood on the other side. He blinked at me as if I were a mirage.

The bottle's foil seal dug into my palm, centering me as I stared him down. He looked smaller, shorter, and less muscular than when I had left.

Had he changed, or was it the memory of him I had built up in my head?

"Summer?" He glanced behind me, sucking in a breath. "What—I thought you were in London until Friday? I—"

"I guess we were both wrong about things, weren't we?" Sticking out my lower lip, I feigned pity.

"Uh—"

His eyes darted around.

Likely, this fiancée was nearby or would be expected at any minute.

Good, I could only hope she knew what a scumbag her fiancé was.

"I heard congratulations are in order?" I offered a sickly sweet smile, cocking my head. "Locked it down in five months? That's an amazing feat. Good for you two. Where's Kodi? That's her name, isn't it? I should be able to congratulate the woman you've been fooling for the past four months."

Yanking my elbow, he whipped me to the left and ushered me down to the walkway. "You need to get out of here."

Breaking free of his grip, I pushed the champagne bottle at him. "To celebrate with your fiancée. I got it before I caught the early flight. Of course, I assumed I'd be celebrating with you, but you had other plans, didn't you?"

"So, you know." He assessed me, with his arms stiff at his side. "Did you have one of your nosy friends check up on me?"

A laugh escaped from my chest.

"That's your big concern? No, my *nosy friends* did not. She tagged your Instagram. How exactly did you think this was going to go, Cory? Did you think I would never find out?"

"No, I . . ." He sighed, looking up at the sky as if it would give him the answers. "What do you want me to say, Summer? I was lonely, and you were there. I didn't expect to fall for you. Then you were gone in London, and it all felt like pretend, you know."

"No, I don't know."

With his thumbnail, he scratched his jaw, forming a grimace. "Don't make this harder than it needs to be, Blue."

At the nickname, the fire inside me flared red to white.

"Don't call me that. You think I didn't see her license plate holder? Blue. Can you form a single original thought? We even look alike!"

Stepping closer, he set a placating hand on my cheek. "Look, if you leave, I promise I can explain it all later, okay? I'll call you, and we can do dinner soon. But you have to leave now."

I batted his hand away, shaking my head. "I can't believe you. You think there is anything you could say that would make this okay?"

The sign he gave was patient, as if I were a petulant child. "Grow up, Summer. We had fun, but it's over. Now, could you be an adult about this and leave before you get more emotional?"

Emotional? I'd show him emotional.

Sneering, I narrowed my eyes. "You want me to leave? I can't do that before you take your gift, Cory." Once again, I pushed the wine at him, but he didn't take it. "Fine, your loss." I stepped backward and hurled the bottle at his front door.

It whizzed by his head, narrowly missing his ear, where it hit the frame.

Yellow fizz and black glass exploded as it shattered against the *Welcome* sign, showering Cory. Liquid dripped from the wreath and onto the kitschy doormat.

He ducked, his hands covering the back of his neck. "You stupid bitch. What the fuck do you think you're doing?"

As if bombs were falling—not a prestigious cuvée of Veuve Clicquot—he threw his hands over his head.

"Only what you deserve!" I shouted.

In my peripheral, an older lady stepped out onto her porch, narrowing her eyes and wrapping a cardigan around her shoulders.

Swiping away the frothing champagne from his hair, he glowered. "Are you crazy? That could have hit me! I could have been hurt."

"You'd deserve it. I wish it did, you lying piece of shit."

More people popped their heads out of their front doors.

Stalking to me, he reached for my elbow again, but I jerked it back.

"Can you go, before you make an even bigger fool of yourself."

His words were hisses through clenched teeth.

Rage boiling in my veins, I wanted to stay, to scratch and wound him as deep as he had me.

I wasn't going to stand here and allow this man to tell me what to do.

"Me? I'm the fool? You sack of garbage. I ought to—"

From the left, someone asked, "Cory, should I call the police?"

With a glare to the neighbor, I stumbled back.

In the two weeks after I met Cory, that neighbor used to wave and flash a cheery smile at me. Now she was threatening me?

Cory waved, plastering on a customer-service grin. "No need, Mrs. Partridge. My guest is leaving." He turned to me, the placating smile falling away. "Go now. Before this gets worse for you."

A part of me wanted to call his bluff, to see how he would handle the police showing up. His fiancée would find out for sure. But then what? I'd be the crazy gal who threw wine at him? The jealous ex?

I was due to go back to work in days. This community was too small to be starting drama before I even began.

Turning on my heels, I stomped off. I was a block away before the rage simmered lower and the red faded from my vision.

The late spring wind nipped through my too-thin sweater. A glance at the darkening sky told me it would likely rain again in the next hour. Miles from my apartment, I was alone with nothing but my temper to warm me.

Another block down, the first icy drop fell on my cheek. Clouds above me were slate colored and then it was a barrage.

That was the moment the police car pulled onto the street. At first sight of the light bar, I started up the driveway of a small two-story white craftsman. Passing the rows of well-tended irises and hyacinths, I headed for the front porch.

I knocked three times, training myself not to look behind me as the cop car rolled past. No answer came from the other side of the white door, with its stained glass lily window.

I knocked again. No answer.

Rolling down the soaked road, the car's engine faltered as it slowed.

"Fuck it," I mumbled as I tried the doorknob.

It turned, welcoming me inside.

Framed watercolor paintings of bright flowers adorned the walls flanking an ornate gilded mirror. Coats hung under a bookshelf lining the doorway to the end of the peach-painted hall.

In a large frame on the table was a picture of an older woman in a wheelchair and a younger man crouched beside her. His dark locks blended with her salt-and-pepper hair as they leaned into each other. With matching wide smiles, their identical gray eyes sparkled with affection. Judging by the decorations, the woman must have been the owner of the house.

"Hello?" I called down the hall and waited for a response.

A rumbling dryer and a faint scraping filled the silence. As far as I could tell, the house was empty.

On my tiptoes, I peeked out the front window. It looked like the police car was gone.

Maybe waiting a minute or two inside this empty, unlocked house would do me some good. I could call for a ride and stay out of the rain.

As I unlocked my phone, the picture on my wallpaper of Cory and me assaulted my vision. Our hair was the same shade of brown, my blue eyes squinted in laughter as he nestled into my neck. It was blurry, candid, and I had thought it was so lovely in that postcoital moment.

"Foolish," I mumbled to myself.

Some women would have been insulted by being called a bitch. Called crazy. That wasn't what hurt me. It was being foolish.

Being so careless in what I wanted him to be, I missed the red flags. I was weakened by this man, and worst of all, I allowed it.

As if I could shake the thought away, I tossed my head.

Focus. Next step. Get out of this random elderly lady's house and go home.

With the rideshare app pulled up, I tapped on the screen when a door clicked open somewhere in the house. Frozen, I looked up to find a hulking man a few feet away.

Tall and bulky, he took up half the hallway. His thin blue shirt had grease smeared on what I had to admit were amazing pectoral muscles. The shirt's sleeves stretched taut over his wide shoulders and biceps. Dark hair fell in front of his steely gray eyes. A muscle ticked in his strong jaw as he stared at me. He held a dirty blue cloth, wiping his palm with it.

In a deep voice that made my stomach twist, he asked, "Who are you, and what are you doing in my house?"

No simpering would get me out of this. I never was good at playing at the damsel, and I certainly wouldn't start.

As if I had every right to be dripping water on his blue floral rug, I put out my hand. "I'm Summer Townsend. I need a favor."

Van

THERE WERE TWO HUNDRED and fifteen minutes left of my day, and I was counting down each one. I had nowhere to be when I left work. No friends to meet at the local bar. No family dinner with a wife, two kids, and an overly rambunctious golden retriever. All I had was a television in need of replacing and season two of *The West Wing*.

Not for the first time, I wished this job was more demanding, that the hours were longer, and that the expectations were higher. That way, I could distract myself from the dark silent night ahead of me at the house I refused to call home.

Since coming back to Ridgewood after my decade-long self-imposed exile, I tried to keep up with my friends in Seattle. In the beginning, I could manage everything being a ferry ride away. But then there was the fall and the hospital and the guilt. My city friends had attempted to contact me, but over the months, the check-ins died down. Happy-hour pictures no longer featured me and then, slowly, new people were introduced.

As the crow flies, my house in Ridgewood was only nineteen miles from my old apartment at the Harbor Steps. But it might as well have been a world away. From my old apartment window, I could see the ferry coming in from Manzanita. Since then, my current view features Mr. Bishop's rusted-out Ford truck. I exchanged a Brazilian steakhouse in my lobby with a fifteen-minute drive to the grocery store.

After what happened, I never wanted to come back here, but I had no choice. I let down the only person in my life for decades, and I needed to atone for that.

It had been a year since I took this job with SanoTech, and for the bulk of my time, I had spent getting my mom situated at Glenwood Homes on the outskirts of town. Coming back to Ridgewood after ten years away was a hard decision. The last time I saw its familiar Norwegian-themed downtown was the day I caught my sperm donor between the thighs of the woman who was assuredly not my mother.

Then, a year ago, my mom called me and told me the news that brought me home. I took the job, and though it didn't pay as well as the Seattle-based firms, it was enough to pay the taxes on my mom's small home and pay for her care. Since my father took off, I was all she had.

A tap sounded on my door, and I glanced up from a report one of my junior engineers had sent me.

My boss, Mr. Haruki, stood in the doorway, his hands shoved in his SanoTech fleece vest. As a man in his late sixties, he made an impressive name for himself for his ingenuity and diligence in the field of medical technology over the past two decades. He still had a full head of shaggy jet-black hair and trusting brown eyes. Those warm irises hid an innate sense of business acumen and a shrewdness that led into his firm's success.

"Mr. Haruki. How can I help you?" I asked, setting the report down.

"Donovan, I've told you to call me Dennis." He leaned against the door and studied my messy desk. "I was popping by to make sure you'll be at the party I'm having next week."

Every year, Mr. Haruki would invite staff to his Front Street home to watch the annual Fourth of July parade. Between lutefisk eating contests, carnival rides, strong-man competitions, and their own mini Viking village, there was a large parade downtown. As a teenager, my parents would give me twenty bucks on Friday night, and I wouldn't see them until Sunday afternoon, a highlight of my younger years.

"I was planning on it, yes."

While I would have rather watched the parade from the balcony of a local brewery, this invitation would be an opportunity for advancement in the company.

"Wonderful. My granddaughter Devin will be there, too. She's a lovely girl. Twenty-five graduated from UW with a degree in graphic design and had been working in Seattle for that carbonated vegetable juice start-up." He wrinkled his nose. "The stuff is truly awful, but whatever pays the bills, right?"

Trepidation settled in my stomach. No way would I be set up with my boss's daughter. Allowing someone to rely on me would only lead to that person getting hurt. I knew who I was and what I could offer someone, and it would never be fidelity.

Since then, I've found ways to keep my bed warm, but I never let it get into anything close to commitment—or even worse, monogamy. Dating Mr. Haruki's granddaughter would be career suicide.

"She sounds lovely. You must be proud."

"I am. She's good to her Jiji. She's done everything I could hope for. All I need is for her to find the right man."

I cleared my throat, hiding my hand behind my fist, struggling for something to say to get me out of this situation.

I couldn't tell him I wasn't interested. That would be blasphemy.

"Could I bring my girlfriend with me?"

His black brows raised at my comment.

"Girlfriend? I didn't know you were seeing someone. What's her name?"

"Summer," I blurted.

Why I said that woman's name, I couldn't be sure. Had I thought incessantly about the beautiful woman who had broken into my home? Yeah, okay, guilty. It's not every day you find a gorgeous lady dripping rainwater on your mom's favorite rug, staring at you with the deepest blue eyes you've ever seen.

"Summer what? What's her last name? Maybe I know her. I know a lot of people in Ridgewood."

This was true. His company was one of the largest donors to the community, sponsoring softball teams, fun runs, and fireworks on the Fourth of July.

My brain worked overtime as I shuffled through the Rolodex in my mind. Taylor? Torres? Townsend. That was the one.

A week after she broke into my house, an envelope showed up in the mail addressed to "Guy Whatever" with a blank check inside from Summer Townsend of 223 Lindvog Way, Apartment D-4.

Who even uses checks these days?

"Summer Townsend."

Mr. Haruki nodded at me. "Summer Townsend, huh?"

"Do you know her?"

Why are you digging yourself deeper in this hole?

"I might. I just might." He hummed, considering me. "Of course you can bring her. I'm surprised you haven't mentioned her before. You know I like to think of this place as a family, not coworkers."

While many corporations used this mantra to get their employees to work grueling, underpaid hours, that wasn't true for SanoTech. While I wasn't making nearly as much as my Seattle job, the office closed every day at six, and Mr. Haruki would insist we had no overtime work.

With the back of my thumb, I scratched my jaw in thought. That ridiculous lie was a mistake, but I couldn't take it back. It was a small town, and I had the women's address, after all. How hard could it be to track her down? This was foolish, so I might as well go all in to stalker territory.

"I wanted to keep things separate. It's still pretty new and all."

"I look forward to seeing you two on Saturday."

Flashing what I hoped was a convincing smile, I nodded. "Of course, Mr. Haru—Dennis—We look forward to it."

Once he left, I sank back into my chair and ran a hand over my face. What had I done?

Three

Summer

I MOGEN STOPPED BY MY desk. "Boss, I have a huge favor to ask of you."

Taking my eyes off the special requests for the Pryce reservation, I glanced up to find my event coordinator huffing.

Smoothing her thick red hair down with a manicured hand, she clutched a bulging folder. "The school just called, and they can't get a hold of my mom. I guess my brother had been waiting in the office for over twenty minutes."

Up until six months ago, Imogen's mother had been the veterinarian at our local Ridgewood Humane Society. But mishaps in the office led to her taking a leave of absence.

"You better get going, then. If you leave now, you'll beat the ferry traffic on the highway."

A large smile broke across her freckled face, making her look younger than her twenty-five years.

"Thank you so much! I'll be back in thirty, maybe even twenty. He's fourteen, so he should be able to get himself food and all that. I just need to take him back to my parents'."

"Take your time, Genny. It's okay."

With watery eyes, she offered me a smile and sighed in relief. "Oh, and I should be back in time for my prospective wedding tour, but if not, her name is Dakota Lowe. Maybe you could get them a drink while they wait or—"

"I'll figure something out. Angie should be back from her lunch in ten. I'll make sure the future bride is taken care of. Now, go before your brother walks home on the side of the highway."

She left the file with me, which I placed to the side.

My focus now back on the special requests, I pulled out my walkie-talkie to call our housekeeping manager to have chocolate and wine sent up to room 317.

It was a quiet day at the hotel. The historic Sandoval Building, built in 1907, was painstakingly renovated from a general store into forty-seven rooms. With a small speakeasy-style lounge, a smaller gift shop, and the third-floor rooftop garden boasting unobstructed views of Freedom Bay, it's been popular since its opening.

The owner, Lesa Wu, had hired me straight out of high school to work at the front desk at her Manzanita Inn. After a few years, she gave me more tasks, having me work with the assistant manager for scheduling, then promoted me when the assistant manager quit. By the time she opened Ridgewood Inn, she told me I was the only one she would trust to run the place. It was on her recommendation I was accepted into the Prescott Hotelier internship.

Being behind the desk of a hotel isn't every little girl's dream, but I loved it. Its shiny white marble floors, clicking of luggage wheels, the ding of the elevator, and the low chatter of guests. A hotel never really sleeps, and breathing in a part of that was exhilarating.

As a child, my father couldn't take me on trips, as he, often, worked two jobs. I was lucky if he had time off for day trips.

When I was ten, I joined my good friend Devin at the Freedom Bay Resort for her birthday. While there, we swam in the pool, ran through the halls, and stayed up late on blindingly white sheets, watching reruns of cheesy sitcoms from our parent's childhood. That's when I fell in love with hotels. The prepped rooms, the pungent clean scent on the pillowcases. How it could be all yours for the night.

People fell in love and fell apart in hotel rooms. Made love and mourned the loss of it.

Hotels were my refuge.

Until Cory, with my clone on his arm, strolled in, tainting the once-cozy two-hundred-twenty-square-foot lobby.

I cursed the quaint setup.

Faint beeping on the door code rang to the right of me as Angie returned from her lunch break to take over the desk.

Kodi let out a tinkly laugh and swatted at Cory's arm. She was smaller than I expected, a delicate thing, with bone-thin wrists and what had to be size-five shoes.

I flexed my own size tens and frowned.

Her hair was exactly like mine. It was bizarre. Standing beside one another, they looked more like siblings than a couple.

My jaw tight, I moved to my office to avoid his sight.

No such luck.

Cory stopped, his smile faltering. He wore a blue-and-pink striped button-down tucked into pressed chinos. His hair perfectly gelled into a hard helmet. His brown eyes narrowed suspiciously, as if I were the one intruding on him.

He knew where I worked. What kind of idiot would come in here?

In the corner, Angie was setting her purse down to fish through it. My feet tingled with the need to step to the left and avoid Cory.

My ingrained professional training forced me to pull the corners of my mouth up in what should have been a smile but was more of a grimace.

"Welcome to The Ridgewood Inn. Checking in? Angie here can help you."

Angie, ducked on the floor with her purse, was still searching for something. What on earth it could be, I had no idea, but heat climbed my neck as I tried not to glare at her.

Kodi bounded up to the desk and set her left hand on the marble. Under the overhead chandelier, her diamond ring cast rainbows around us.

"We're here to see the wedding planner—um, Ingrid something?"

"Imogen," I snapped, then recovered with a placating smile. "She is finishing up with other business now, but if you'd like to head to the bar, Neil can take care of you while you wait. Complimentary, of course."

Kodi shot Cory a look and frowned. "So, she's not ready for us? That's not a good look for a prospective client."

You're ten minutes early and getting a free drink, lady.

Not that I needed any reason not to like her, but I wanted to think she was some sweet girl being taken advantage of by Cory. But having an attitude about my staff was going to piss me off.

"Free drinks are my favorite drinks," Cory said with that cocky grin I used to find charming.

"I suppose we have some time," she huffed, as if it were an imposition. "One drink, but if she's not here on time, we're leaving."

Good riddance.

As they turned away, Cory rested his hand on Kodi's elbow, steering her. Seeing the familiar gesture made my stomach roll.

Leaving Angie at the desk, I retreated into my office to message the bar about the comp.

Then I brought up the thread with Autumn.

In high school, the four of us came up with code for when we needed each other.

Chartreuse: I am emotionally unwell and might throw up.

Vermilion: I'm about to murder someone.

I was the only one who deployed this one.

Khaki: I'm incredibly bored and need company.

Obsidian: the highest level, only to be deployed in a genuine emergency.

We had used this one only once, when Devin's father passed away two years before.

Autumn didn't read it, being the only one who left the read receipts on like a sociopath. Probably because she always responds immediately instead of forgetting about the message and panic-texting five hours later *OMG, I just saw this*—the way normal people did.

While Angie and a guest discussed the best place to get Italian food, I stayed in my office, comparing the cost of paper products until my eyes blurred. Heels kicked off under my desk, I buried my toes in the plush carpet, trying to center myself, as Autumn instructed.

Tense your toes, then release and feel the ground beneath you, then move up—

The soft alternative music filtered from the lobby. My hands in my hair, I dragged my nails over my scalp, pulling strands loose from the low bun. Brown tendrils fell across my face, and I stared at them.

I was a natural blonde—not platinum, more dishwater ash. Two years ago, some lady at a salon recommended I go darker. That it would play up my blue eyes and make my cheekbones "pop." I had been a faithful servant to 5G-Cinnamon Pecan box dye ever since.

After switching to my texts for the fifth time in the last fifteen minutes, I tried to send a psychic message to Autumn to call her favorite cousin back. Instead, all I had was her daily group chat affirmation.

Autumn: I am fully in charge of my future. I am the only one who can dictate the outcome.

Rolling my eyes, I set the phone on the desk beside my feminist icon of the day calendar.

Easy for her to say. But then again, she always made things look effortless, even while struggling inside. Her eternal optimism was grating at times, but she was so sincere it was hard to fault her for it.

Unlike me. Since returning, it was as if I had a wet cloak over my shoulders, weighing me down and chilling me. Never letting me forget the mistake I had made and how blind I was to not see through his bullshit. That's what happens when they look for the positive; they don't see the flashing lights until they've blown through the multiple stop signs, just to be T-boned by a semi.

Okay, maybe that was dramatic. But, seriously, I allowed myself to put blind trust in that boy, and still, a month later, the memory of his engagement photo haunted me. The living, breathing, tinkling laugh was proof in the bar of my hotel.

Maybe a notification in the group text would get Autumn's attention.

> Summer: I wish the rest of you were closer so we could have a drink together. I need some girl time!!!!

Wren: me toooo!!! Adrian and I will be in town this weekend for the fireworks and the parade? We can meet up then? Beers at Sticky Cow? You can meet our dog, Maizie!

Devin: Yes!!! I have to stop by my grandpa's party for a bit but after that let's get a burger and ride the Zipper until we puke?

Wren: Just looking at the zipper makes me want to puke.

No response from Autumn.

Scrubbing my face with my hand, I fought the urge to scream in frustration. After the champagne hurling and a slight case of illegal trespassing, I tried to put the incident behind me.

I was doing well at work and went back to trivia nights with my girl-friends—but lost terribly. Every Sunday, I delivered groceries to my father, who cooked dinner for us. I practiced the cable stitch for the baby blanket I had promised my cousin Alec, who was due in November. On the surface, everything in my life was practically the same as before I met Cory.

But deep down, something shifted inside me. At the store the week before, the cute guy behind the deli counter added extra spicy honey turkey to my one-pound package. When he winked at me, my first thought was *I bet this piece of shit is married.*

When Wren mentioned she was sick with a cold and that her new boyfriend went to see his friends Penny and Tam, I told her they were probably all sleeping together. She had the decency to demand I take it back, which I did, with a chagrined apology.

I couldn't trust a single man, and worst of all, I couldn't trust myself.

Was I in love with Cory?

In the dreary, slick streets of London, when I had little to lean on, I thought so. But being back home, with my support system in place, all I could feel was wounded pride. How dare he think I would be okay with him cheating?

"Summer, a guest needs to speak with you," Angie called from the front.

As I rose, I shoved my feet back into my low heels. Rounding the corner, I smoothed over my crisp white shirt tucked into my black slacks.

I stilled when I saw it wasn't just any guest.

No, as if I conjured him from my ire alone, Cory was on the other side of the marble barrier, his brown eyes boring into me.

While I wasn't sure what he would say, the chance that my response would be something unprofessional was likely.

On more than one occasion, he would talk on his phone while ordering a drink at the coffee shop, so he wouldn't have an issue saying whatever he wanted in front of my employees.

"Mr. Thompson, why don't I show you our courtyard? The tulips are especially lovely."

Not giving him a chance to disagree, I stepped out the side door and into the small garden area as he followed. Once it shut behind us, I dropped my professional smile.

Arms crossed over my chest, I glared at him and raised a brow. "What do you think you're doing here?"

"Kodi wanted to check this place out for the wedding."

"And you agreed?"

"You said you don't work on Tuesdays."

I tapped my pinky nail with my thumb. "There is no such thing as a set schedule in hospitality. I work when I need to work, which means I'm always here."

"Oh." He kicked the wandering path's gravel.

"Can you not do that? I'll have to get our grounds crew to fix it."

"Sorry." He looked down, chagrined, then back up with big sad eyes. Eyes that used to work on me but had since made my skin crawl. "How have you been?"

"Busy." I trained my face to remain passive.

If I had allowed any of the emotions out, I wasn't sure what I would do. A coiling heat formed in my stomach, my ears getting hot.

I should have sent a code vermilion instead of chartreuse.

"You don't have to be rude. I was only being friendly."

Friendly? Why on earth would I be?

"It doesn't have to be like this, Summer."

I realized I had spoken aloud. Just as well. There was no reason to hide how I felt.

Digging my nails into my arm through my shirt, I glared at him. "Where's your fiancée?"

"Her mom called. She'll be chatting with her for at least ten more minutes." Cory shoved his hands in his pockets and rocked back on his heels. "You haven't responded to my texts."

"Because I blocked you."

Boredom dripped from my words as I stared him down.

What were the pressure points you went for in an attack? Groin, solar plexus, nose, and what?

He tsked at me, shaking his head. "You don't need to be like that."

Instep. That was the one.

The urge to pull a Gracie Lou Freebush overwhelmed me.

He leaned down closer to me. "Things don't have to change that much, you know. We had a lot of fun together. We could do that again." He brushed my hair off my face. A strand wrapped around his pointer finger. "I like your hair like this. The curls never suited you."

"Don't touch me." Slapping his hand away, I leaned back.

He frowned, stuffing his hands in his pressed chinos. "So, you really want to be like that? After everything we had together?"

I snorted. "We had nothing together. We were a mistake."

Considering me, he cocked his head before shrugging. "I guess all I have left of you are the pictures you sent me."

My blood ran cold.

A month into my internship in London, he asked for them. I knew the risk but was so sure of Cory I figured where was the harm? After a few pints of Boddington's at the pub, I had set up my phone against my flatmate's stack of dragon shifter books and set the timer for three seconds. Stripped for the camera. Showed off my body to a man I thought I could trust.

He had promised me no one would see them.

"You need to delete those. We aren't together anymore."

I didn't like the dread rising in my voice.

"Is that really what you want, Blue?"

Swallowing down the panic, I nodded. "Yes. That's what I need. Delete them."

He nodded at me, his lips pursing, as if I had disappointed him. "Fine, I will. But you're making a mistake, throwing us away like this."

"I didn't do a thing." Through the window, I saw Kodi swing the door open and walk in. "Run back to your fiancée and leave me alone."

"Think about it. I know you still have my number saved." He left me alone in the garden, my blood boiling.

The strand of hair he had wrapped around his finger stung as it fell against my cheek, as if radioactive . If I had a knife handy, I would have sawed it off.

Feel the ground beneath you.

I wished the ground could swallow me up.

In my peripheral, Imogen walked in the side entrance, waving at me.

With a steadying breath, I returned inside to Imogen. "Your three o'clock is waiting in the lounge for you."

I didn't wait for her response before stalking back to my office.

I closed the door, something I hadn't done in the month since I had started.

No way was I leaving the safety of my space until six. But I wouldn't be going home. I needed to stop at the beauty supply store first.

Bleach stings. It singes your nose hairs and burns your scalp. That was the first indicator that maybe trying to go level ten blonde was a bad decision. In my teens, I had dabbled with fun, bright colors. Before my senior year of high school, Devin and I had gone to the salon and got matching pink highlights. This was blue slop, piled high on my head.

Autumn stood behind me, painting the acrid mixture into my hair. Devin was on a video call with us, talking us through the process. Because she was the expert, having constantly changed the wild shades in her hair, I deferred to her.

Every few minutes, Autumn would ask, *Are you sure?* I'd respond with a wave to get on with it.

Under the plastic cap, my hair was hot on my head, the orange a reflection of my emotions.

On the video call, Devin leaned closer to the screen. "You know, if you would have asked, I could have cleared this whole thing up for you. Took me three minutes once you gave me his full name to find out everything about him."

"That couldn't possibly be . . ."

"Cory Otis Thompson, birthday June seventeenth," she muttered. "Of course he's a Gemini."

"What does that—"

"Born in Redmond. Parents Don and Sheila. Mother's maiden name Maguire. Went to Gonzaga for two years but didn't graduate, favorite color blue, favorite food . . ."

"Okay, I get it. Stop." I huffed. "God, you're scary sometimes."

"Only when you're hurt."

"I'm not hurt. I'm annoyed. There's a difference."

"Annoyed?" Behind me, Autumn raised a brow. "Should I call the police now or wait until you've cut his brakes?"

Pulling the cap off my head, I scraped a chunk of blue bleach off my hair to see how light it was. "I won't murder the guy."

Arms crossed against her chest, she frowned. "But you're not going to leave him alone."

"He'll get what he deserves." I pulled the cap off and unwound my hair.

The roots were lighter than the bottom, but that was okay. A good purple toner would take away the brassiness.

"Nothing illegal. I don't make enough at the Marine Science Center to bail you out."

"Me neither," Devin chimed.

Although that wasn't the case. Out of all of us, Devin was, by far, the most successful.

I widened my eyes in mock outrage. "I would never."

"Promise me no laws will be broken. Pinky swear," Autumn said.

I hooked my pinky with hers, and on the screen, Devin held hers to the camera.

"Fine. No laws will be broken."

Autumn smiled. "Good, I'm glad you'll do the right thing."

Shooing her out of the bathroom with my phone, I gave her a last coy look. "By whose definition? Just because something is legal doesn't mean it's right. And I plan on being all sorts of wrong."

As I shut the door, she grumbled on the other side.

The shower on their morality speech faded. It had been a while since I had put any effort into my own brand of justice.

Cory thought he could use me to cheat and that I'd be okay with it? That he could come into my place of business and proposition me feet away from his fiancée?

It took one month for me to lose my shit again. Truly, was it right to say it was my fault? A woman can only handle so much humiliation before she is forced to act.

I would stay away from Cory, sure. But not before I let him regret that day he sat beside me at the bar.

All my life, I've fought the fury inside me. I tried to be calm, tried to be cool. But I was livid.

I'd show them just how villainous I could be.

Summer

WHEN I SAT AT the two-top at The Cabin, I expected nothing different other than being there for their sweet potato fries on the happy-hour menu.

Designed with meticulously weathered white shiplap and dark-blue walls, the waterfront restaurant boasted the best views of Freedom Bay.

As a child, my father would take me here on every birthday, allowing me to get the pirate ship meal off the kid's menu. My first legal drink was at the bar, a slippery nipple that tasted better going down than it did coming back up three hours later. The walk from Ridgewood Inn took me across Front Street, past Sticky Cow Brewery, and up a staircase to the heavy cabin door.

The day had been a long thirteen hours at work. When one of my servers called in a half hour before his shift, I knew that the day would be tough. Marnie in housekeeping had informed me that the guests in 221 stole the towels and pillows from the room and that Angie's car had broken down and couldn't get a ride to work until her boyfriend returned from his job.

All I wanted to do was head back to my apartment, but my fridge was as empty as the gas tank in my red two-door Camry. While I could have Nutter Butter bars for dinner—again—I deserved tourist-priced wine.

With my glass of a local Viognier on its way, I opened my reading app, pulling up *A Ladies Guide to Impropriety.*

When the server set my wine down, he winked.

He was cute enough, someone a few years older than me at school. I was pretty sure he had asked Devin out at some point.

As he walked away, I sent Devin a text.

> Summer: Is John who works at The Cabin the guy who sang Ed Sheeran to you in the middle of the courtyard at lunch junior year???

> Devin: It was Coldplay, but yeah

That was a no-go. I added "serenading servers" to my *immediately jail* list. So far, I had cheaters, men who wear deep V-neck shirts, girls who baby-talk in the middle of a conversation, anyone with a beer opener on their sandals, people who hate Taylor Swift and Beyonce based on vibes, and those who tell me I don't understand Wes Anderson movies.

It would've been nice to have a little physical attention, though. The dating pool in Ridgewood was getting slimmer each year. While I've had a few flings over the years, hooking up with a random from the Skol House wasn't an option anymore when they could also show up at the hotel.

Dating apps were a lost cause. Most people who popped up lived across the water in Seattle, and with as horny as I could get at night, I wasn't going to hop on a boat for an orgasm.

Switching from the message thread to my library book, I read the first sentence when the door opened. I glanced up, the street roaring below us, and almost dropped my phone on the table.

It was the guy.

It had been over a month since I had seen him. But somehow, he looked better. In all the heightened emotions of the day, I told myself he wasn't nearly as good-looking as I remembered. But, no, if anything, he was better-looking. A clean gray tee shirt clung to his broad chest, gripping those firm biceps. His beard had grown out thicker, but it was well groomed. When I last saw him, his dark hair was disheveled, but it was neatly combed.

I wasn't sure what I liked more.

He stopped at the hostess stand, his thick forearms flexing as he shoved his hands in his pockets. A sly smile crossed his face as he talked with the hostess. She giggled, then waved him toward my general area.

No. This couldn't be happening.

He wouldn't come over and talk to me, would he? Our exchange was awkward, possibly felonious, and I had done everything to wipe it from my mind. So much so that I wasn't sure I remembered his name.

Taking a gulp of my cold wine, I racked my brain.

Did he tell me his name?

No, I didn't think he did.

Did he?

He looked like someone with a butch name. Jagger or Diesel or Ace. Something like that.

Surely, enough people were there to hide among.

Pulling my blonde hair over my eyes, I picked up my phone, my eyes downcast.

The night before, I had been engrossed in the tale of Viscount Rodolphe as he stole a phaeton to confess his love for Beatrice.

Now, I had to will myself to reread the same sentence repeatedly. My eyes darted to the bar where the mystery man was seated with his back to me. The server was flirting with the bartender, leaning between the row of ketchup bottles and rolled napkins to talk.

Had they put my order in the system yet?

At this rate, I couldn't avoid being seen. I willed my server to stop flirting.

The sooner I could finish my food, the sooner I'd be on my threadbare couch watching *The West Wing*.

Josh Lyman wouldn't do me wrong.

With a shaking hand, I sipped my wine and trained my eyes to stay on my book. Viscount Rodolphe was easing Beatrice's chemise off her shoulder. As this was my third time reading this book, I knew biggest gossip in the Ton would soon interrupt them.

"You changed your hair," the deep voice sounded.

He stood beside my booth, looking at me.

From my vantage point, he was eight feet tall. And big—all over. His crotch was directly at my eyeline. It was difficult to tell whether that bulge was odd-fitting jeans or if he was majorly packing. Judging by his mere size, it was likely the latter. For a moment, I wondered what those strong thighs would feel like between my own.

Don't be thinking about this stranger's dick right now.

Blinking away my lusty thoughts, I craned my neck to look at him.

Those startling gray eyes boring into mine, rimmed with long dark lashes. The kind of lashes that women spent hundreds of dollars on. Life wasn't fair.

"Do I know you?" I feigned innocence.

"Nice try, little thief. I'd recognize you, new hair or not."

"I didn't steal anything." Sending invisible messages for him to go away, I looked back at my phone.

It was embarrassing enough that he showed up here, but did he have to call me out for my terrible behavior in my favorite restaurant?

He slid onto the other bench, set his beer on the table, and folded his hands.

Scratches and white scars riddled his knuckles. Working-man's hands. He was tinkering with something greasy when he found me in his home. I bet he worked in manual labor and that those hands wanted to wring my neck for showing up in his house.

My father had working-man's hands, never clean enough, even after scrubbing them with the orange-scented grit.

"What are you doing? I didn't ask you to join me."

He shrugged. "I was about to place a to-go order for dinner and have a beer at the bar and then I saw you."

"And?" I asked, not bothering to hide my annoyance.

Sure, I had barged in on this man in his home, but the time for him to be upset had long passed.

"You looked like you could use a rescue."

"I don't nee—" Scowling, I set my phone face down. "I was reading a book. Despite what *men* may think, a woman sitting alone is not an invitation for company."

The comment didn't seem to bother him.

"I was going to stop by your house, since I know your address from your check, but here you are." Instead, a glint of mischief flashed in his eyes. "And it felt like fate."

"Fate?" I snorted.

Fate was for my dreamy cousin, Autumn—and for my mother, who flitted around Southern California in her camper van, never knowing where the road would take her and sending me birthday cards a month late.

"That's the stupidest thing I've ever heard. And yesterday, my cheating ex tried to proposition me."

Sitting across from me, he studied my face. "You owe me a favor. I'm here to collect."

Brow raised, I took a tentative sip of my wine and waited for him.

Long stretches of silence never bothered me. My friends would fill up those moments with idle chatter but not me. There was a power in not saying anything at all and staring down your opponent.

Unlike most of the men I would level, he didn't appear ruffled. He chuckled softly to himself, nodding, as if I was confirming something for him.

"Here's the deal. I need a date for the parade. My boss has a house on the route, and every year, he throws a big party at his place. I need you to come with me and pretend to be my girlfriend for the day."

I snorted, cocking my head. "Your date? Yeah, sure, big guy."

"I'm serious. You owe me."

He didn't seem to be lying.

Back flush with the cold wooden booth, I crossed my arms. "You're a good enough-looking guy. I'm sure you could be charming if you weren't so pushy. That's a week away. I'm sure you could find some other random gal to take with you."

"I can't use some random gal. It has to be you."

"Me? Not that I don't think I'm a catch, but I doubt I made that great of an impression that you've been lusting after me dripping rain all over your rug."

This time, he looked away, his mouth turning to a grimace. After grumbling and huffing, he finally looked at me. "Because I already told my boss that you're my girlfriend."

A burst of laughter wheezed out of me.

"Wait, what? Why?" I choked out between laughs.

He leaned back in his chair, studying me, as I tried to contain my snickering. "You done?"

Lips pursed, barely containing a smile, I nodded.

"It came out. My boss asked me to take his granddaughter out, who I'm sure is a perfectly nice woman, but I don't date anyone seriously, and I can't risk my job if I broke the heart of some barely-out-of-college girl. So, I told him I had a girlfriend, and when he asked for a name, I gave him yours."

"Mine? I'm the first person you thought of?"

"Unfortunately." He glared at me with a murderous expression.

I drained the rest of the wine and set the empty glass on the edge of the table. When the server saw it, he nodded at me.

"I still don't know why you would ask me to do that. You don't even know me."

He held my gaze, and for the first time in what felt like forever, I was the first to look away.

Years before, I went on a road trip to California. Autumn had talked me into hiking near Mammoth Mountain to see Rainbow Falls. We saw this towering formation of basalt columns there, the geometric rocks dwarfing us.

His eyes were the same gray of those boulders, striking and enigmatic.

Copying my pose, he crossed his arms, mirroring me. "I have a good feeling about you. It's one night and then you can go off on whatever breaking and entering fantasies you like to conjure up."

"First of all, there was no breaking, only entering. You left your front door unlocked. And second, I told you my ride let me off in the wrong spot, and I was lost."

A smile quirked on his face.

"Sure, let's go with that."

"Why would you trust me? I could be a serial killer for all you know."

"A female serial killer who mails a check *for dry-cleaning your rug* in the comment line?"

My steady gaze faltered.

"Yeah. It's a devious move, obviously."

"Not that I didn't appreciate the gesture, but maybe think twice before sending someone a blank check in the mail. I could have ripped you off." He frowned. "You didn't even write my name on it."

"You didn't give it, and I had better things on my mind than getting to know the man who was about to call the cops on me."

"It's Donovan Logan. Van."

"Van Logan."

The server returned with a second glass of wine and my salmon and avocado tacos. I ordered them overly garlicky, as I wasn't kissing anyone tonight or any other night.

"Anything for you?" the server asked him.

"Yeah, can you have them make my to-go order for here? I'm dining with my girl."

The server's eyes flashed to me in confusion, but he nodded. "Of course. Give me a minute."

I scowled at him. "Why did you do that?"

He grabbed a piece of avocado that had fallen from my taco and popped it in his mouth, a familiar gesture that twisted my stomach. "Because we have loads to discuss. Come on, my treat."

I thought of the hefty chunk taken out of my savings for the first and last month's deposit for my apartment. Of the money, I had to spend on businesslike yet comfortable heels for work.

"No funny business."

"Only serious business." He frowned, his brow furrowing mockingly. "Of course, Ms. Townsend."

"Don't call me that." I flicked my thumbnail against my pinky nail three times.

He pushed his half empty beer to the side and leaned forward, his voice low. "What should I call you? Summer? Because you are the least sunny person I've ever seen."

"As if you're the most charming person yourself," I retorted. "You bull-doze your way over here, ruin what should have been a perfectly pleasant evening of wine and tacos, and worst of all, interrupt my reading when it was getting good. It makes sense your name is Van because you drove roughshod all over my night."

He pressed his full lips together as if biting back a smile. "You done?"

I flipped my hair over my left shoulder and gave him a withering look. "Maybe."

He ran a hand through his dark hair, mussing the styled coif. A lock fell over his forehead as he leaned toward me. "Look, it's one night, great view of the parade, free food—and even better, free drinks. I just need my boss to stop trying to set me up with his granddaughter."

While I had stopped following Cory everywhere, he still viewed all of my posts. Didn't hide behind a fake account or anything. It was possible he even had notifications turned on because he was the first to view each post. Maybe if I popped up with someone else, he'd leave me alone. And suffer a little. I wasn't above wanting him to suffer.

"I have one condition. You will let me take lots of pictures of us together."

"You need to make someone jealous?"

No way was I divulging my reasons for this guy.

I raised a brow and stared him down. "Do you want me to come or not?"

Van nodded, extending a hand. "Fair enough. You got a deal, sunshine."

As I took his hand, a zing of something ran down the inside of my arm. His hands were softer than I had expected, though still calloused. His grip was solid. A man who didn't know how to shake was an immediate turnoff for me. A man with a weak grip for no reason doesn't respect you enough to think you can handle it. This man didn't hold back, his touch firm. I liked that. It was as if he knew I could take it and more.

I tightened my grip, and a sly smile played on his lips.

"Deal."

As he pulled away, his thumb grazed the back of my hand, his touch sliding down my fingers.

A scene in my book flashed through my mind. Viscount Rodolphe pulling off Lady Beatrice's glove. The wantonness of such an innocent move bound something in my chest.

Slipping my fingers around the stem of my wineglass, I needed to steady myself before I took a drink.

The server came back with Van's burger, setting it between us.

Before he could leave, I said, "My guy here is insisting that I take a slice of the peach pie home. Could you box that up for me?"

Van snorted, shaking his head and then nodding at the server. "Of course. Anything my girl wants, she can have. Why don't you make that the dessert sampler? We'll need a treat for later—extra energy and all that—won't we, Sunshine?" He gave me a lascivious wink.

Despite myself, heat flooded my cheeks. If this were one of my books, I'd call him rakish. In our time, it's a fuck-boy look.

The server mumbled his response, walking away.

My smile dropped, and I scowled. "Was that necessary? You look pornographic winking like that."

"Pornographic. My, my. You have an imagination." With his elbow propped on the table, he swirled his thumb over the tip of his pointer finger.

I thought of how that hand felt in mine, the strength of those fingers as they slid over my skin. I had never given much thought to the strength of a man's hands, but it was consuming me.

"It's indecent. I work across the street, and now the server is going to be picturing us in bed together."

Van glanced at the server, who was at the bar talking to the bartender. "That man has been picturing you in bed this entire time."

"You don't know what you're talking about." I scoffed.

"He has, and you know it. You can be my little thief, but don't you dare lie."

"I didn't steal, and I'm not your anything."

Regretting the decision to allow him at my table, let alone agreeing to this fake date with him, I realized I could always stand him up.

"Oh, you're something alright, but that's not important. Now, before you get too far in objectifying me, let's talk logistics. What do I need to know about you before Saturday?" He took a big bite of his burger.

Staring across the table at this gorgeous man, I tried to think of a dozen reasons to leave.

I didn't know him. He was infuriating after fifteen minutes. His face was far too symmetrical to be trustworthy.

All the warning signs were there. This was a stupid idea. But it wouldn't end with me having to get tested at the clinic or with a bottle of duty-free champagne thrown at his door. I was original enough to switch things up, anyway.

What harm could one fake date do?

Summer

E VEN IN EARLY JULY, the weather in the Pacific Northwest can't be trusted. Some years, it rains nonstop through the parade, soaking the pageant queens in their convertibles and melting the scattered crowd candy. Others, it's sweltering heat on the concrete of Front Street, with nary a breeze from Freedom Bay to cool. This year, it was a perfectly pleasant sixty-six degrees on the sidewalk. By noon, people were setting up their chairs in front of the hotel to prepare for the two p.m. parade.

My assistant manager, Lucia, was due to arrive at twelve-thirty to take over for me.

A part of me hoped she would get stuck in traffic or twist her ankle or something so that I would have to stay and miss the parade party. But it was not to be. Lucia arrived, as fresh as ever, at 12:27 p.m. Blast her punctuality and professionalism.

I gave her a quick rundown of the guests. We were fully booked because of the holiday weekend. When I offered to stay, she shooed me to my office to change, reminding me that, since I started, I had been working over sixty hours every week.

With my office door locked, I changed from my white button-down and black slacks to a blue sundress and nude sandals. I styled my hair that morning in a braided coronet. Pulling out the pins, I shook my head until the kinked strands cascaded around my face. If I had more time, I would have curled my hair, but the slightly crunchy wave would have to do.

Using the camera on my computer, I applied a swipe of mascara, bronzer, and watermelon-colored lipstick. I had forgotten a strapless bra, so I would need to go without or risk everyone seeing the thick-strapped dirty-dishwater monstrosity I had pulled on. I needed to invest in a bra that cost over thirty bucks.

Luckily, my small boobs could afford me a braless day. Not that I didn't wish I had the cleavage. Why Autumn got the buxom DNA and I didn't was a crime.

Standing back, I turned this way and that, making sure I looked presentable enough.

Briefly, I wondered what Van would think, but it didn't matter. This was a no-strings-attached occasion. It was obvious he wasn't the settling-down type—even if he didn't explain how he didn't want to find another girl to bring, since she'd think it was more serious than that. It was in the way he flirted. He was used to the short term.

As I walked out of my office, Lucia raised a brow. "Aye, look at you. Está buena!"

I gave a mock curtsy and shrugged. "Thank you, thank you."

"This guy better treat you good."

"Don't worry about that. It's nothing serious. Not even a date."

She crooked a sculpted brow and pushed me out the employee door.

I didn't want Van to see my place, so I had asked him to meet me at work. With over twenty minutes before he got there, my stomach was in knots.

At the bar, Neil was restocking after the brunch rush of mimosas and Bloody Marys.

Never having a chance to try signature cocktails I had been recommending to the guests, I thought a quick drink could help.

On the high-back leather stool, I ordered a cherry fizz and took stock of the bar. It had become second nature to think of improvements at the hotel. Moving the tables in the center closer to the window would allow us to install a second armchair and create a little nook in the corner. The small candlelights were already looking worn; maybe something metal instead would look better than cloth.

On my phone, I pulled up the restaurant supply store and scrolled through options.

Beside me, a stool pulled out, and a man sat. He was slender, with shaggy dark-auburn hair.

Not Van.

The man ordered an IPA and turned toward me. "Summer. Hey."

I raised my head to see Nicolai Evjen smiling at me. He stepped down from his stool and strolled to me.

"Nico. Hi." I leaned forward and gave him a one-armed hug.

He had been good friends with my older cousin Oliver since they were kids, but I didn't know him well. He was at least ten or eleven years older than Autumn and I. In a small town, we had a level of familiarity with each other.

"Ollie mentioned this was your spot." He settled into the chair beside me, pulling it forward by reaching between his legs.

"It is. Been managing it for a little over a month now."

Nico leaned over the bar to grab his beer and pulled it closer to him before angling his body toward me. "It's wild seeing you. I wanted to reach out a while ago but wasn't sure."

I quirked a brow. "Me?"

Nico was handsome, all lean lines and hair a touch too red to be called brown. I remember when I would have sleepovers at Autumn's, when we'd catch Oliver and Nico sneaking back in after a night of teenage debauchery. Nico had a kindness to us Oliver never exhibited.

Growing up, Autumn and I were more like sisters than cousins, and Ollie treated me like a sibling, grudges included. He never forgave us for the time we spilled Sunny D all over his gaming keyboard. Or when we stole all his socks and dyed them hot pink. Yet he was fiercely protective of us. When my homecoming date had left me at an after-party without a ride, Ollie had come to get me and then tracked the guy down and threatened him to tears. Fond memories indeed. But he was still a pain in the ass.

I had a certain warm regard for Nico. I think all four of us had a small crush on him.

We ignored the brief infatuation Wren had for Ollie. Absolutely disgusting.

Nico was a known entity. He wouldn't have been flirting with me if he had a girlfriend; to do so would incur the wrath of his best friend.

Tucking a wavy strand of hair behind my ear, I leaned closer. "What did you need to talk about?"

A muscle ticked in Nico's jaw, and he swallowed. "Look, don't shoot the messenger, alright?"

That didn't sound good. If this was his version of flirting, it was terrible. "Okay—"

"You know how I work with contractors on base, right?"

Nico, like many in the area, worked for the Department of Defense, building torpedoes or ships or something for the military. Between the three bases in our county, it was the largest employer in the area. You couldn't spit a wad of gum without hitting someone who worked on base.

"Sure, yeah."

"So, we have this new guy that started in our code. Cory Thompson. I think you know him?"

At Cory's name, a chill settled in my stomach.

With a shaky hand, I grabbed my drink and gulped half the tart cocktail.

My reaction must have been the confirmation he needed.

"A week or two ago, Thompson started running his mouth. He kept bragging about some chick he had on the side. And he was flashing your picture around."

A bone-deep chill soaked my bones.

"Wha—" I cleared my throat, the question scaring me as the trembling words tumbled out of me. "What kind of picture?"

Nicolai had the decency to look away, his cheeks pink.

"I didn't look at them. Told him to put the phone away. You're a kid to me. I mean, I know you're an adult but not really. At least not to me."

A lump formed in my throat that I couldn't swallow.

Cory was a cheater, but he wouldn't, would he? He told me he'd delete them. My right eye twitched as I tried to make sense of what Nico said.

"Are you sure they were—"

Of course they were me. It was one thing to have my photos on his phone but another thing for him to show other people. Ones I might know.

"It was you. I recognized your birthmark." He coughed into his fist. "I mean, I've seen you in a swimsuit before, so—"

My birthmark. A large brown misshapen daisy mark covering the ribs on my right side.

Bringing my drink to my mouth? I knocked the rest back. This fifteen-dollar cocktail was meant to be savored, but I needed to fuel the fire building in my chest.

"He's a piece of shit. If it wouldn't risk my security clearance, I would have punched him. I won't tell anyone."

It was a kind gesture, but if Nico had seen my boobs, then so did countless others. As if it wasn't bad enough to be the other woman, he was sharing my private photos.

Before discovering this, I had filed Cory under the "shitty boyfriend" column. But this was grounds for an upgrade.

Swallowing the simmering fire in me, I set my empty glass down. "I appreciate it, Nico. I'll handle it." I waved at Neil to get me another drink.

It was far too early to be slamming hard liquor, especially at my job, but if I couldn't dull the wrath, it would fester inside me and make me do something very, very bad.

Doubt flashed over his face. Maybe he could imagine my plans, but instead of offering more insight, he changed the subject, asking about my dad.

After drinking his beer, he wished me well, giving me a second one-armed hug before leaving a healthy tip for Neil.

Why can't a nice guy like that be into me?

"Starting early, sunshine?" My date eyed the drink, a frown playing on his full lips.

Did he have to be so handsome? It was disgusting. He had one of those sharp jawlines, like a model out of a cologne commercial, just the right amount of scruff and hard lines.

"You okay to come to the party?"

Tapping my nails together, I considered his question. This was my out. I could go home and plot the demise alone in my small apartment. Or I could go to this party with a sinful-looking man, get all the pictures I wanted, *then* plot Cory's fate.

Van reached over me, grabbed the drink, and put his lips to my lipstick stain. His eyes never left mine as he sipped.

He set the half empty glass down. "That was a rhetorical question. You're coming whether you like it or not."

Going to a party with this strange man under even stranger circumstances was shaping up to be a bad idea. But I was never one to wallow in my feelings alone. A distraction with a little scheming might do the trick. Plus, free drinks.

"Let's skedaddle, big guy."

Before I could fish money out of my wallet, Van had put a fifty down on the bar, then held my hand to lead me off the stool.

I wished I was wearing my wedge heels. He towered over me while I wore my flats.

Those silver eyes bored into mine. He traced the back of my hand with his thumb before letting me go.

My breath stuttered out of me as I glanced away and waved at the money on the counter.

"That's too much. I get an employee discount and—"

He placed a hand on my back to usher me through the lobby and out onto the bustling Front Street.

Caleb, behind the desk, raised a brow as I passed, but we kept moving.

I should have met Van at a different spot to avoid gossip.

Out in the summer sun, the lines to watch the parade were three people deep, with small children sitting on the sidewalks and their feet dangling into the road, a fortress of lawn chairs, and people standing behind them.

A vendor with light-up wands, bubble machines, and plastic Viking swords zigzagged the street, selling his wares. The parade wasn't scheduled to start for another forty-five minutes, but viewing real estate was precious on the five-block route.

As we moved through the crowd, dodging children with sticky candied apples and adults with dripping ears of buttered corn, Van paused to allow me to catch up, his strides being larger than mine. After we got separated for the third time, he gripped my hand—more logistical than friendly, but I didn't mind the tingle of awareness his touch gave me.

On the corner, crowds dissipated as the sidewalk ended in the residential area. As we approached a familiar house, I tugged on his hand, and he stopped to glance back at me. "Wait, who's your boss?"

"Dennis Haruki."

I laughed. "Haruki? Really? You could have led with that at The Cabin."

"Do you know him?"

"You could say that." I grinned.

At the entry path to the large white house, a small dog rushed toward me.

Taking my hand from Van's, I bent down to pick it up. "Hi, Momo. Hi, my little momsers," I cooed.

Van furrowed his brow.

The two drinks had definitely made me a little loopy, and seeing his confusion was priceless.

"You know his dog?"

Still crouched, I smiled at him. "Mr. Haruki is my friend Devin's grandfather. I practically grew up here."

The man of the hour came walking down, donning a big smile, his arms wide.

Six

Van

S ON OF A BITCH. Why didn't I factor in that Summer might have known Mr. Haruki before I asked her to be my date? Standing in the walkway of my boss's sumptuous yard, I knew there was no going back now.

Mr. Haruki wrapped an arm around Summer's shoulders and pulled her close. "Summer, my dear girl. You've made it. I was so excited when he mentioned your name."

Was he? At the office, his reaction was a little strange when I told him her name, but I had filed it under the oddness of the entire exchange.

Summer beamed at him with a wide pink smile. "I'm always happy to come over. You know that. I can't pass up Baba's brownies. Please say she made a batch for the party?"

"Of course. When I told Tonya that you were coming with Donovan, she made double." His arm still around Summer's shoulders, he grinned. "Now, have you introduced Donovan to Peter yet? I know your father will have a thing or two to say about him."

Summer laughed and swatted at his chest. "Jiji, of course not."

Jiji. She even had a nickname for him.

"What about my granddaughter? Has Devin met him yet? She'll be here in a bit."

"Not yet."

Summer was still smiling, as if this was the most natural thing in the world to be chatting about.

Doom settled deep into me. Despite the early Summer sun, the air was chilly. What had I gotten myself into?

Mr. Haruki glanced at me with a smirk, his eyes bright. "You know, I tried to introduce Donovan to Devin, but it looks like you go there first. Swooped in. If it can't be with my granddaughter, I'm glad it's with you. Or Autumn or Wren."

"Oh, Wren had a fella. Adrian something. They just moved in together. He's a teacher, I think. I'm supposed to meet them tomorrow for a drink."

"No one tells me anything!" Mr. Haruki said in jest.

Still standing on the outside of this conversation, I felt dread creep in. The whole point of this was to avoid pissing off my boss, and I had landed myself in deep with one of her dearest friends.

Summer caught me watching them and shot me a quick wink.

I hoped that meant *Don't worry, I won't get you fired.* But who knew?

"You're such a gossip," Summer teased.

"Guilty, guilty. It keeps me young. Now, you two go enjoy yourself. Drinks are in the cooler on the patio, and, Summer, you can show Donovan where the bathroom is."

"Absolutely. Remember when we accidentally dyed your sink pink with hair dye?"

"Took you girls weeks of scrubbing after school before it came out."

They laughed.

"You two have fun, and, um"—he leaned in conspiratorially—"I'd stay clear of my neighbor Tom's pasta salad. He keeps putting raisins in it."

As he passed, Mr. Haruki set a hand on my shoulder, leaned in, and whispered, "You be careful with this one."

I gulped down the imminent threat between the words. "Of course, Mr. Haruk—Dennis."

After slapping my shoulder twice, he sauntered away.

Summer had been standing at the drink cooler and fishing through the ice.

My head down, I stomped after her, trying to keep the rise of panic and annoyance out of my expression. "What was that?"

She straightened, two cans in her hand. "Do you want Rainer Cherry or Fuji Apple? Or they have beer, too. You had a lager last time, right? They have that or—"

Pulling her to the side, I leaned down, my voice low. "Why didn't you tell me you knew Mr. Haruki?"

She took a languid sip of her hard seltzer, her light-blue eyes steady on me. "You never told me his name. Loads of people have parade parties. How was I to know?"

I slid a hand down my face, the bristles of my beard scratching my palm. "I can't believe this. My career will go up in flames."

She pulled my hand away. "Relax, have a drink. Nothing is happening to your career."

"But you—him. You called him—" I let out a flustered sigh.

"I'm twenty-five years old, Van. Do you really think I'm going to run to him if I got my delicate feelings hurt? I'm not a child."

Delicate and Summer were the unlikeliest of descriptions. In the short time knowing her, I'd describe her as tempestuous, sharp, and confident. But delicate?

She took my silence as agreement.

"Trust me, I know how to handle myself. And I'm not involving emotions with a guy like you. Now, cherry or apple?"

Grabbing the green can, I popped the top and took a big swig.

A smirk playing on her face, she mirrored me. "Better?"

"Why wouldn't you get emotional over me?" I asked.

I wasn't even sure why the statement bothered me, but it did.

Scoffing, she shook her head. "Because none of this is real. When someone tells you who they are, believe them. You don't want commitment. I won't be committed. Easy as that."

"You don't think I'd be worth committing to?"

What was I doing? Why was I arguing for the exact thing I told her I didn't want? Between work and my family obligations, the last thing I needed was a distraction in the form of a pretty woman. One with soft hair that fell over her smooth shoulders. One with blue eyes so light they looked like the edge of the sky on a perfect day. One with full pink lips begging to be crushed in a kiss—or wrapped around something.

Summer tilted her head and surveyed me. "You know, they say skin is the largest organ in the body, but I'm pretty sure your ego is giving it a run for its money. No, Van, I don't think I'll have any issues not going moon eyed over you."

The rejection stung. I couldn't remember the last time I had tried to flirt with a woman and not have it work.

My words seemed to fuel her decision—she wasn't attracted to me.

"Good. I'm glad you understand."

The words sounded hollow, but my worries didn't seem to concern her as she pulled out her phone, angling the camera until the lighting was right.

"Stand on the left side of me so we can get that cool sunbeam vibe for our couple photos."

I leaned in without touching her. The scent of clean floral clung to her. Her head swiveled as she tried to frame the photo.

"Scoot closer."

Still trying not to touch her, I moved in.

The scent intensified.

In the camera's reflection, she frowned. "No, closer. If I were your girlfriend, how would you stand?"

"If you were my girlfriend, I'd be all over you."

As her eyes flashed over to me, pink tinged her cheeks. Her gaze roamed over my body.

"Is that so? With those big muscular arms?"

"Holding you would be so easy." I smirked at her.

She gulped. "Then, do it. Do it like you want me."

Her words were a challenge and all the permission I needed.

From the moment I saw her at the bar in that little blue sundress, I wondered what she would feel like pressed against me.

Sliding an arm around her waist, I dragged her to my side. She fit perfectly under my arm.

Wrapping her fingers around my nape, she turned her face to mine.

She was warmth and sunshine soaking through my shirt and blooming in my chest. It was easy to pretend she belonged there.

Her pupils dilating, she stared up at me, poking her tongue out to wet her lips.

If I were a less composed man, I would want to kiss her. But that would be very, very foolish.

"How's this?" I asked, my voice scratchy.

"G—" She cleared her throat. "Good. Let me just—" Glancing away, she focused on the camera, fumbling to get the angle with her short arms.

I took the phone. "Let me take it."

Just as she said, my head blocked out the sun, creating a halo around us.

I started the timer for three seconds to take a burst, and she flashed a wide smile.

It was happiness and innocence and so damn sweet.

I figured I might as well go all in on this. If we wanted to look realistic, I'd do more, right?

Without thinking, I bent down and kissed the top of her head.

Her scent invaded me. It was a smell I would want splayed over my pillows.

She turned to me, and those blue eyes darkened. As I clutched her waist, she leaned in closer. In my hair, her nails dragged against my scalp, and my chest tightened.

Her smile widened, and I matched it.

"That's probably enough pictures," she murmured.

I had forgotten I was even holding the phone.

"Right, of course." Internally groaning, I stepped back, my arm retreating from her waist.

She scrolled through the new pictures, frowning. "These should work."

Her fingers flitted over her phone as she posted the pictures to her Instagram.

"What's your at?" she asked, glancing at me.

My cheeks burned at the question. I was rarely on social media and hadn't changed my username for almost a decade.

Scratching the side of my nose, I pursed my lips. "It's—um . . . hotrod underscore van."

"Hot rod Van?" She smirked. "Okay, Hot Rod. You've been tagged."

"I like cars, okay?"

She put up her hands, the silver can in her left hand sloshing. "I didn't say a word. I like a man who can work with his hands. Though it's a well-known fact that car guys are just the horse girls of men."

Damn if that wasn't the rudest yet funniest thing a woman had ever said to me. Her innocent eyes barely betrayed how cutting the comment was.

Taking a swig of the hard seltzer, I stepped away from her.

I didn't need this woman to like me. After this party, we would part ways, and I'd be fine never seeing her again. Plenty of women would find me charming and handsome and easy to commit to.

I hadn't realized how easy it had been with women until this one came around, challenging me.

She was absolutely right when she said I could have found someone else to join me. In fact, a woman in my neighborhood would jog around and stop to ask me questions about the plants in my front yard. The gal at the gym would always pick the treadmill beside me. The woman from high school would always send me funny memes.

But it was Summer's name rolling out of my mouth. Summer, I wanted beside me. Even if I wasn't sure why.

Walking across the wide lawn, I stared at the deep gray-blue of Freedom Bay. On the other side of Mr. Haruki's hedge, parade viewers lined the sidewalk. Young girls had tinsel threads braided in their hair, and boys had superhero face-paint. Historically incorrect horned helmets on every other spectator.

My mom would bring me down to the parade when I was a child, setting me up on a beach towel on the curb. I could still feel the rough grain of the asphalt under my thighs. She would get an elephant ear and finish it for me when I would take the three bites, then abandon it. My father never joined us, complaining that the crowd was too big, that the parking was a disaster, and that everything was overpriced.

My mom would wipe my face clean of the powdered sugar, erasing the sticky evidence of her buying me a treat, knowing that he would quiz her on what she bought me. She would show him the bag of snacks she had packed beforehand. The same old carrot sticks and popcorn we had in our pantry.

That was back when Mom could get around by herself, when the world was simple.

The strains of a marching band started farther down the road. The first car was the grand marshal, a local war hero, followed by the navy band.

Beside me, Summer craned her neck to see it. As the leading entries passed us, she waved at Miss Ridgewood in her Bunad and sparkling crown.

"Ah! She looks so cute, doesn't she?" Summer blew her a kiss, which was returned in earnest from the curly-haired girl in the convertible. "I ran for that in high school with my girlfriends. Lost spectacularly. Turns out you need talent to sing in public."

"Or an incredible amount of confidence."

She laughed. "Yeah, well, bravado can only get you so far when you're completely tone-deaf. My cousin Autumn won, though. So, I got to sit in the front seat during the parade, and I wasn't forced to eat lutefisk at the gazebo like she did."

I wrinkled my nose.

As a teenager, a friend and I entered the yearly lutefisk eating contest. I had choked down three pieces of the gelatinous lye-soaked cod before tapping out. Max had five. It took years before I could look at white fish without feeling nauseous.

A local troupe of gymnasts came through, performing flips and rhythmic routines to the radio edit of a hip-hop song. Moms followed them, picking up stray bows and throwing candy into the crowds. A rain of bright sweets flew over spectators and landed at our feet.

Summer bent down, gathering a handful.

"Hold out your hand." She picked out the good candy from the bunch, then dropped them into my hand. "The kids don't care about flavors."

As she was about to toss the rejects back to the children, I stopped her. "Wait, let me grab this one." I plucked the yellow wrappers from her hands.

"Banana? Really?" She raised a brow.

I unwrapped one and popped the small taffy in my mouth. "It's the best flavor," I said through sticky teeth.

She snickered, shaking her head. "You're wrong, but whatever gets your motor running."

Biting off another one, I grinned. "You don't know what you're missing."

After rolling her eyes, she focused on something over my shoulder. "Oh, there's Dev. I'll be right back." She squeezed the inside of my wrist, a strangely intimate gesture.

Heat radiated from her touch, blooming over my skin.

As she walked away to the patio, I admired her backside. Her dress swished around her thighs and hugged her ass. With her so far away, I envisioned what that ass would feel like in my hands, a nice thought I could tuck away.

Behind me, Summer was hugging a woman with short black hair streaked with blue wearing a T-shirt that said *Don't be salty* with a girl under an umbrella logo. With a new purple can in her hand, she rocked back and forth with her friend, their squeals ringing from across the lawn as they embraced. The woman whispered something, and Summer threw her head back in laughter, exposing the long column of her throat in mirth.

She caught me looking, and her smile faltered before she turned back to her friend and laced an arm with hers.

They walked across the yard, then stopped in front of me. "Devin, I want to introduce you to the man Jiji tried to trap in marriage. Van Logan, this is Devin."

Devin was slightly shorter than Summer, with large green eyes behind black-framed glasses.

"Nice to meet you, husband," Devin joked.

I cracked a smile, extending my hand to shake hers.

It was warm, soft, and completely platonic. While Devin was cute, I was not attracted to her.

Summer looped an arm over Devin's shoulders and smiled at me. "I told Devin all about how we met."

Raising a brow, I waited for her to continue. Waiting for her version.

We had concocted a story at The Cabin: she was dropped off at the wrong house and knocked on my door, asking if she could wait out the rain on my porch. My version was finding her soaking my mother's rug. And then there was her own version, the one she refused to explain to me.

Her story never made sense to me. There had to be more.

"Is that so?" I asked.

"Quite the dark knight, weren't you?" Devin asked. "Thanks for saving my friend."

"Oh yeah, the world is flush with knights swooping in today, aren't they? So many gentlemen out there." Summer drained the can, then held it upside down to shake out the dregs.

Summer's phone chimed, and I saw "Nico" flash on the screen.

Dropping her hand from Devin's shoulder, she stepped back. "I'm . . . um—getting another drink."

Devin furrowed her brow before she shot me an awkward smile. "She'll be right back."

Tilting my drink up, I swallowed the rest of the warm liquid.

Summer

MY CELL WAS BURNING a hole in my hand, but I fought the urge to look at the messages from Nico again. It wouldn't help to see his pity. I was a mix of emotions, and there was nothing Nico could say that would change the facts.

With a new can of seltzer in my hand, I glanced around the party.

Mr. Haruki had invited the usual people. In high school, the girls and I would sit on the balcony with our sodas and watch from above, rating our favorite entries.

That was a long time ago. I could begrudge my friends for moving on, but in the midst of what could be a real scandal of my own making, I felt irrevocably alone.

I knew the risks. Hell, I told Wren multiple times not to send nudes to her dipshit ex, Buck. But when I get asked, all reason goes out the window.

A neighbor waved me over to the table where they had set up a shot-ski.

With the one-and-half cherry fizzes alongside the three seltzers, my brain was already fuzzy.

But then my phone chimed again.

I set it face down on the arm of a wicker patio couch and took place between Fred and some girl with short blonde hair.

The red liquor was sweet but burned as it went down. I fought back the cough as people around us cheered, and a new warmth flowed through me.

I grabbed a new can of seltzer and my phone, then headed toward Van, who was standing with a few others.

Without a word, I laced my arm through the crook of his elbow.

He looked down at me with surprise and what seemed to be appreciation.

After a few minutes of chatting, I laced my fingers with his and tugged Van toward the side of the house.

"I want to show you something."

He followed along, his hand in mine.

I tried not to think about how well our hands fit together. On the side of the house was a riot of azaleas that Tonya had cultivated for years.

"Dennis had these brought over from Kyushu about twenty years ago. It's pretty, isn't it?" I rubbed a petal between my fingers, smiling. "I thought this would be nice for more pictures."

He raised a brow. "Really? You're not just trying to get me alone, are you?"

I laughed. "Maybe I am. Come here." I pulled out my phone, struggling to unlock it. Gulping, I slowed down to get the right code in against the blurry digits. "Scooch in, Hot Rod."

He took my phone again, angling it to capture both of us. This time, though, he wasn't holding me as tight. That wouldn't do. A boyfriend would get more handsy as the night wore on, not less.

"Like I said before, I'm supposed to be your girlfriend, right? So, don't treat me like a leper."

"I didn't want to make you uncomfortable." He hesitated as I leaned into his body, tucking a stray hair behind my ear as I gazed up at him. His eyes darkened as he assessed me. "Do you want me to touch you?"

"We would be a lot more believable if you did." I leaned closer, resting my hands on his chest. "So, why won't you put your hands on me?"

Even to my own ear, my words were too low and throaty.

He gulped. "Is that what you want?"

"I'm not saying you have to fuck me under the pergola." I thrilled at the way my words shocked him, toying with his top button, exposing his neck. He sucked in a breath at the motion. Reaching up on my toes, I brushed my lips against his ear. "If I were really your girlfriend, you'd be all over me."

"If you were my girlfriend, would you let me?"

His voice was coarse and brought to mind dirty things in a darkened room.

"Are you really that dense?" I keep the smirk on, trailing a finger over the space between his pecs, his cotton shirt warm under my touch. "You need to get better at reading body language. This is me saying yes."

He held my head, our lips inches from each other, the aroma of sweet banana taffy lingering. In the fading twilight, his irises were molten silver as his gaze flickered from my eyes to my lips. He brushed the hollow of my ear with his thumb, his grip steady as he leaned forward.

The first kiss was a caress, a whisper of skin and breath. Side by side, we traced one another. My mouth tingled from the contact, flushing me with excitement.

He pulled away, his focus on me as if gauging my reaction.

Whatever expression I had must have been the confirmation he needed. This time, his hand tensed on my head as he dragged me to him.

Our mouths found each other, and this time, there was reverence. Whatever qualms he may have had before disappeared as he backed me into the porch rail, the push of his body against mine. The pulsing between my thighs, demanding more. Heat exploded from me as he traced my lips with his tongue. His kiss tasted of the banana taffy. Against my back, the wooden railing held me steady as he bored into me, securing his mouth to mine. The hard lines of him exacted against my own, and his rigid length grew quickly, pushing into my hip bone.

Light exploded behind my eyelids. I had never been kissed like this before.

His hand moved from my head, down my arm to wrap around my waist, then to my ass. Pulling me into his body.

This kiss was everything I wanted. Head dizzy, I ran my nails through his hair. His mouth left mine, then traveled over my cheek and down my throat.

My dress rode up as he stood between my open thighs, grinding his cock against my core. A thin piece of fabric, so easily removed if only we were somewhere more private. As his kiss deepened, he thrust against me, sending sparks through my body.

Holy hell. It always took a long time for me to get off, but kissing Van was almost as good as my vibrator.

"Summer." His words were a blessing against my skin. "I could fucking devour you."

Devoured. That was the word. I was being consumed. This heat inside me, the pulse of wanting more and more and more, all rationality falling away.

Realization dawned on me. We were making out at this party like a pair of horny teens, teetering on pornographic. At any moment, someone could've walked by.

This was supposed to be a silly kiss for Instagram. It's not real, not real, never going to be real.

Pulling my arm out of Van's grip, I stepped back, wiping my lip with a finger. "That was a bit more than I was expecting for the cameras." I frowned at where my phone landed. "You didn't even take a picture."

Van scoffed, grabbing onto my hair at my nape. "Who cares about a picture?"

"I do. That's why you kissed me, right?"

He snorted, shaking his head. "No, I did that for me."

His hands were still in my hair, a pulsing need to close the gap again tearing through me.

His touch should've stung but instead only made my thighs clench harder. The way he was looking down on me, the strength in his grip, showed me he would know exactly how to handle me in bed. How he would take control and wring every last drop of pleasure out of me, taking me to the point of pain before allowing me to crumble around him. Judging by the massive ridge against my aching core, I would have plenty to work with.

This was dangerous. A thudding started in my ears, and the party was fading. It would've been so easy to fall into bed with this man. From how he was looking at me, he seemed willing. But then what? Another foolish mistake? Getting my emotions involved? I couldn't afford to get attached.

Reaching behind me, I traced the back of his hand before pulling away. "We shouldn't have done that. Next time you want to show off, a simple peck will do."

"You think I was showing off for someone else?"

Raising my eyes to his, I inhaled, trembling. "I know you did. This can't be real, right?" When he didn't correct me, I stepped back, wrapping my arms around my waist. "I'm getting another drink." Scooping my phone off the ground, I left him on the side of the house.

I felt exposed again. Cory was making me a fool in love and in the flesh. With the feel of Van's lips still lingering on mine, I washed down the taste of his kiss with a long swig. I didn't need Cory. Or anyone. A toe-curling kiss couldn't distract me from what was important. And at that moment, it was drinking enough to forget.

Eight

Van

TWO AND A HALF hours later, the parade was over. Thin streamers littered the road between candy wrappers and half-melted popsicles. Summer stood beside me, another drink in her hand. I had lost count of how many she had, the colors of the can changing from red to purple to pink to green to green. It wasn't my place to ask her to slow down on drinking, but she was getting less sure on her feet. Her laugh louder, she kept hugging people.

At some point, Summer had disappeared inside the house with Devin, leaving me on the porch to make small talk with partygoers. When she came back, she had a new can in one hand and her phone in the other, a list visible on the Notes app.

Devin trailed behind her, brows furrowed. "Sum, why don't you rest in my room?"

"I'm fine." She waved around the room. "Besides, I can't neglect my date any longer, can I?"

Rather than approaching me, she passed me and plopped down in a chair in the middle of the lawn.

Devin came to stand beside me. "Look, my grandpa obviously trusts you, so I will, too. Can you help me get her home? She won't listen to me."

How Summer had been acting wasn't my business, but her behavior was odd.

"Of course." I hesitated. "I don't want to sound like an asshole, but is this normal?"

Devin shook her head, the blue streaks whipping her cheeks. "No. She—" She grimaced. "It's not my place to say, but just know she never acts like this. She's going through a rough time. Don't hold today against her."

"I don't have much to go on, you know?" I offered.

Devin smiled, brows downturned. "I know you don't. But in the decades I've known her, I've only seen her like this maybe two other times. I am sorry you had to see it, though. Some date, huh?"

Sighing, I glanced at Summer, who was sitting with her face resting on her hand, eyes drifting shut. "Can you give me her address? I'll get her home safe."

Devin nodded, texting me the address.

According to the map, her place was a twenty-minute walk from the party on the other side of downtown.

Getting Summer out of the chair was a feat, but with some cajoling and the promise I'd get her a big pretzel, she stood. Her balance was wobbly, but she could walk.

A block away, I handed her a water bottle from my back pocket. She leaned against a wall and chugged half of it before handing it back to me.

Her hair was a messy riot of blond crimps and what looked like a fleck of confetti. A strap of her dress fell, exposing the swell of her breast. From my angle, a rosy nipple peeked out.

I glanced away, tugging the strap into place as she halfheartedly swatted my hand.

"You know, with your dress hanging off you, it doesn't leave much to the imagination."

She snorted at me, glancing up and down my body. "The last place I need to be is in your or any other man's *imagination*. Keep your trousers on, big guy."

"You're practically flashing the street."

"There you go again, being noble and shit. It's all an act. We both know it."

"It's an act to not want you to accidentally expose yourself?"

"No," she retorted. "Men being decent. It's a farce, made up, cannot be real. You all want something, and when you get it—*poof*—who cares about the consequences?"

This wasn't about me. Whatever had upset her had nothing to do with me and everything to do with the text she got. And I would have bet my left nut that whatever it was regarding had happened before I picked her up.

"You want to tell me what's going on?"

It wasn't my business—nothing about this woman was—but a desperation seized me. I needed to know.

"Summer?"

"I like the way you say my name," she mumbled. "I shouldn't, but I do."

"Summer." I stepped closer.

I pulled the strap tighter toward her body until it couldn't fall again.

Her skin was velvet under my fingers. If only she weren't so drunk.

"I can't tell you. I know I made an ass of myself in front of you today. But if you knew . . ." She narrowed one eye as if she were seeing double. "I can't trust you."

"In the short time we've known each other, have I done a single thing to appear untrustworthy?"

I was standing too close, but I couldn't find it in me to step back.

"No, but there's no way a man with shoulders that wide can be trusted."

"So, I have untrustworthy shoulders." I rocked back on my heels.

This was drunk blubbering but entertaining nonetheless.

"Your biceps are too big, and your eyes are a weird color that reminds me of rocks." Her lip curled. "And I won't even go into your jawline. You look like a bad action villain with a jawline that sharp."

"So, I'm too muscular, and my jawline is too sharp, and therefore I can't be trusted?"

"Yeah." She rolled her eyes. "Obviously, you're too good-looking. And that kiss, whew—" She smiled to herself. "Damn, you have a talented tongue. But men whose hands do what yours do are trouble, with a capital T-R-O—"

"I've never heard that rejection before." I laughed, shaking my head.

With a hand on the wall, she closed one eye as she stared me down. "Men who are as handsome as you are used to getting what they want. They'll take and take and take. And women like me are left looking foolish."

Someone had hurt her.

Anger rose in my chest. I hadn't been protective of anyone but my mother, but the thought of a person causing this level of grief in Summer made my skin feel tight.

"You are many things, Summer, but foolish could never be one."

She closed one eye as if focusing on me. "You have no clue what I'm capable of."

If she were sober, it would have sounded like a threat, but its slurred nature zapped its power.

Hoisting her up, I wrapped an arm around her waist again. "Alright, tough guy, let's get you home."

At her apartment, I had to fish her keys out of her small purse, then open the door with one hand while holding her up with the other.

Inside was sparsely furnished, boxes lining the walls beside a small couch.

Summer stepped out of my hold and stumbled to the bathroom, where she retched beyond the wide-open door.

When I came in behind her, I gathered her hair in my fist as she vomited bright red liquid in the toilet.

As far as first dates went, this wasn't in my top five best but not in my worst, either.

She sat back on her haunches. Her eyes closed, she wiped her mouth. "This has to be one of the most embarrassing days of my life."

"I've seen worse," I joked, allowing her the space to stand at the counter.

Rinsing her mouth, she blinked at her reflection and grimaced. "I look like absolute flaming garbage dipped in dog shit."

"Again, I've seen worse."

"You're supposed to say that."

"Saying I've seen worse is hardly a compliment."

Straightening, she ran a hand over her face. "I need to shower."

"Oh, I'll just—"

Before I could step out, she turned away and pulled her dress straps down.

When the dress pooled at her feet, she kicked it to the corner, stumbled to the shower, and turned the water on.

She was drunk—very, very drunk—and I shouldn't have been standing there, gawking at her like I was thirteen. I had seen naked women. So many naked women. And it was her back and her underwear. Not even a thong or something sexy but regular women's briefs.

"Sorry, I'll um—"

She glanced at me. "Okay."

I stalked into the small living room when the shower door clanged shut.

Remembering I had promised her a pretzel on the way back, I grabbed her keys and left.

For the entire walk to and from downtown, my mind raced. The afternoon had gone completely off the rails. And while it was not how I had planned it, I didn't mind it. Summer was fire, and I found myself, even in her battered state, drawn to it. She was a complex woman, and while another man wouldn't want that level of complication, it only intrigued me more.

I texted Devin that she was home safe and immediately received a heart-eye cat emoji. Whatever that meant.

Back at the apartment, I set the wax paper-wrapped pretzel on the counter.

She was dressed in an oversized T-shirt and tucked under her bedspread. Her room was as sparsely decorated as the living room, with a double picture frame on her nightstand.

On one side was a photo of her with an older man with the same light-blue eyes, and the other was of three women, one of which was Devin.

"I left you a snack," I whispered.

"Van." She held out her hand, and I took it. Her fingers slid across my palm. Warmth crept up my arm. "I am sorry about today. Please, don't hate me."

"I could never."

Covering her with the blanket, I couldn't help but press a kiss to her forehead. Her wet hair smelled of soap and flowers. Something about that drew an ache in my chest.

She rolled over to her side, mumbling, "You might not, but he will." She relaxed, and her breathing deepened.

After leaving her keys on the counter, I let myself out.

Summer

MY MOUTH WAS PUTRID fruit and bitter chalk. I rose fourteen hours later to the unmistakable memories of my terrible decisions the day before. Had I really drunk that much? Eaten anything? I got that message from Nico checking in on me. There was the kiss, the feel of Van's hands in my hair, the desire between us, then a blur. I had several drinks, then someone had passed out shots of something bright red and sweet. Might have been vodka-based, might have been rum. Was definitely a bad idea.

When I was eleven, I was recruited to walk in a fashion lineup at a wedding show. Along with a dozen other kids, I got to wear formal dresses from the local bridal store. I was thrilled to sport puffy pastel taffeta and strut down the runway alongside beauty queens. After three full-skirted flower-girl gowns, the owner placed me in a tight green dress, saying I was modeling for the junior bridesmaid line.

At the end of the catwalk, I performed my trademark twirl as the shrill of tearing fabric let in cold air that hit my bare back and butt.

So, up until last night, I would have said showing off my pink fairy princess underwear to a crowd of hundreds was the most embarrassing moment of my life.

I saw Van in passing as the fading afternoon sun waned in the sky. At one point, Devin found me, dragging me to her room, and demanded to know what had gotten into me. I told her everything. I expected reproach for either the naked pictures or the champagne-throwing incident, but instead, she just asked me what I was going to do about it.

With stumbling fingers, I had created a new note on my phone titled "Operation Super-Villain." I couldn't remember much after that.

I started walking home with a disgruntled Van.

Did I tell him he was too handsome to trust? Ugh, I did.

Flashes of me throwing up came and went, and I couldn't remember if it was on Van. I hoped not. Then I was in bed, wearing my father's old Perth Sailing shirt from his time in the navy.

Van stayed for a bit. I couldn't even imagine what he must have thought about me after my disgraceful antics.

A quick inventory of my apartment showed my keys on the counter beside a hardened pretzel. My stomach grumbled, and I grabbed the solid snack and, with my front teeth, ripped off a section. The starchy carbohydrate was better than nothing.

After splashing water on my face and brushing the terrible tangles out, I picked up my phone to check that it was past my normal 8 a.m. alarm.

For years, even after a night of drinking until the late morning, my body would naturally wake at eight.

A text from Autumn was at the top of my notifications.

> Autumn: Forget the day's troubles, remember the day's blessings.

I groaned and set my phone down.

My hangover was not conducive to my cousin's mantras.

No one responded to Autumn's mantra. We never did anything more than add a heart to it, anyway, but Devin and Wren had been planning for us all to meet at Sticky Cow Brewery in an hour.

Every cell in my aching head and screaming body wanted to skip it, but I hadn't seen Wren in months since she moved an hour and a half away to Icicle Creek with her new boyfriend. And while I got to see Devin the night before, that was a complete wash after my shenanigans. Looks like I was going downtown again.

At the brewery, Devin was at the table, wearing her thick black-frame glasses, a graphic tee with a cartoon corgi that said *Even baddies get saddies*, and a little skirt.

Autumn waved as Wren and Adrian joined us.

He carried four full glasses as Wren walked beside him with her own. A small caramel-colored, wiry-haired dog padded alongside them. Wren must have given our orders at the bar because my normal strawberry wheat beer was placed in front of me.

Even their porters matched, alongside their red T-shirts and blue jeans. Wren's dark curls were wilder than I had ever seen, but a calm happiness radiated from her. She and Adrian were so blissfully in love and glowing in the summer light that it made my stomach roll.

I couldn't begrudge Wren for finding a nice guy who made her happy. She certainly had her share of shitty men in the past few years. But seeing the way he leaned into her and kissed a spot behind her ear was too much for my hungover state to handle.

They exchanged introductions, and I tried to keep up with their tales of their moving escapades.

Thankful that Autumn didn't drink alcohol, I skipped my beer, grabbed Autumn's ginger ale, and took a big gulp, hoping I wouldn't spew all over the oyster shell firepit.

"You don't like your beer? I thought the strawberry one was your favorite," Wren asked.

"It is. But I overdid it at the party last night," I admitted.

Devin snorted into her huckleberry cider. "That's an understatement. She told my neighbor that he looked like Fred from Scooby-Doo and then stole his drink."

I didn't remember doing that but couldn't deny it.

"Whatever. You know I'm right about him. All he needs is an ascot."

"I never said you were wrong, but you still can't say it to my grandparent's podiatrist neighbor."

I feigned a smile, holding onto Autumn's ginger ale.

She grumbled but left and returned a minute later with her own and a small plate of crackers and smoked salmon.

The conversation flowed around me. Autumn updated everyone about the new geoduck exhibit at the Marine Science Center, where she worked. Devin shared that her company would use her graphics for the next orange-kale-matcha tea to debut in the fall. Adrian told us that his students had accidentally set an orange on fire and then dumped it into a trash can in the back of his classroom.

"The room smelled pretty good, actually."

The beers in their glasses went down and then it was time for a second round. Adrian offered to treat us again, and after a few exchanges, we let him.

The moment he was out of earshot, Wren leaned in close to me and hissed, "Okay, what is going on with you? I know you can't be upset about not being with that Conan guy."

"Cory." I shook my head, wondering why. "And it's not about not being with him anymore."

"Tell her," Devin said.

I shot daggers at Devin, who returned my look with equal ferocity.

"It's a long story, and I really don't think your new boyfriend wants to hear it."

Wren nodded, then got up and disappeared into the brewery. A minute later, she came back, holding the new round of drinks but without her boyfriend. "Adrian is going down to the food stands and is getting everyone a Viking burger—"

Devin opened her mouth to say something.

"I know except for you, Devin. He'll grab you a veggie burger." Wren turned to me. "Now, give it to me. What's going on? You barely said a word, look like you're going to be sick, and didn't make an inappropriate comment about the penis fish when Autumn was talking."

Autumn rolled her eyes. "They're not fish. Geoducks are a mollusk, which is the second larges—"

"Aut. Not important right now," Devin teased.

Wren bored her eyes into mine. "Something is very wrong, and you need to spill it."

Same as the night before, I spared no detail, giving my friends the worst of what had occurred. Autumn's face paled when I mentioned seeing Nico and what he had told me.

Wren's cheeks flared red.

I sat back and allowed my friends to process.

Devin was the first to speak, likely because she had a twenty-hour head start on the information.

"Like I asked her last night. What are you going to do about it? Show them the list."

I pulled out my phone and scrolled through the bulleted note from the day before. In the sober light, the spelling mistakes and gibberish entries sprang to life.

Wren studied them, tapping her bottom lip. "Okay, well, as funny as placing glitter inside his showerhead would be, you'd have to get into his house to do that, and I don't think you have it in you for breaking and entering just yet."

"Agreed," Autumn chimed.

I hadn't told them about me walking into Van's house. Not that I didn't think they would support me but because the entire story was bad enough.

"You don't need to maim him. Just make his life a little more miserable," Devin said.

"You could always talk to him, ask him to delete the photos," Autumn offered. "I bet if you asked, he would."

We stared Autumn down in incredulity and humor.

We all loved Autumn's positive spin on the world, but sometimes, she was too naïve.

"Uh, no. Pass," I responded. "I don't want that man to have the satisfaction of knowing he's affected me at all."

As we looked over the list again, the plotting became more concrete.

Wren vetoed my idea of placing valerian root in the vents of his car, citing that if I got caught, it was a class two felony in Washington. Buzzkill.

Devin suggested scattering dried mashed potatoes on his lawn, which, while funny, was more of a harmless prank my cousins used to do to one another, and it was not the vengeance I wanted.

Autumn reminded me that a life well lived was the best revenge, which was not the vibe I was going for.

By the time Adrian returned with a bag of burgers, we had gathered ideas of some semi-legal ways I could make Cory suffer.

I was feeling slightly better once I got the greasy meat and cheese into my system and was able to drink half of my beer before we parted ways.

Autumn and I walked back to the apartments together. She lived on the first floor, while I was in the back corner on the third.

When we got to her door, she turned to me, her face drawn. "Are you sure this is a good idea?"

"No. Of course not. But I can't sit back while that man terrorizes me."

"And you're sure you can't talk to him? I'm sure if he knew how upset you are, he'd . . ."

I put up my hand to silence her. "No. Definitely not. Babes, I love your big heart and endless empathy, but men who show off pictures of their naked exes are not the type you can talk to. I'm already the crazy ex to him. What do you think he'd do if he found out I know?"

"It was one bad day."

I laughed. "Yeah, it was. But when is the ex-girlfriend allowed bad days? No, he deserves nothing but torment for this."

Autumn dragged a hand through her auburn hair, then pulled it from her face. "Promise me you won't let this anger fester in you."

Fester.

What a great word.

Autumn knew me too well for me to argue. I had a tendency to take things too far at times. But I've never struck at a person who didn't burn me first. I wouldn't start fights, but I sure knew how to end them.

"You know me. If I went over there and tried talking, I'd start running my mouth, call him names, maybe make him cry—and, yeah, that would be hilarious. But he'd know he had power over me. No way."

Autumn slid her key into her door, her lower lip between her teeth, letting out a resigned sigh. "Just be—careful, okay?"

"Cross my heart, hope to die. I will be."

The trek up the cement and metal stairs to my apartment had my knees aching. I may have twisted them a bit in my drunken stumbling.

Once home, I flopped back on the couch and stared at my reflection in the hand-me-down TV from my dad. Despite showering the night before, my hair somehow looked lank, and my skin was sallow. My cheeks were puffy and eyes bloodshot.

I looked like shit, but that wasn't my concern in the sweet reprieve of my apartment.

At the brewery, we wrote the broad strokes of a plan, but writing was different from action. I suspected my friends only thought I was joking about this revenge idea. But I was completely serious.

The first ones, I could do at home. All I needed was my internet, a VPN, and his number. I made a fake email address to send all this to corythema n@promail.com. It was a quick search to find multiple companies where I could input his information.

Years before, my father had put his number down for a home warranty service, and he was still getting a barrage of messages from the company, who had even shown up at his door a few times. Cory would get incessant calls about roof repair, life insurance, as well as religious organizations. I only subscribed him to the ones I knew to be the most tenacious. The companies who keep calling and emailing until you send a notarized letter asking for them to stop.

For about fifteen minutes, I worked on a photo editing site, creating haphazard graphics with his profile picture. Then I went on an online classified ad page, posting about free goats. I posted on the dating section, seeking a couple looking to add a third. Free scrap metal and lawn-mowing services for a fraction of the price.

After logging out of my social media accounts, I typed in his email address in the username field. He told me once his passwords were all the same, his birth year and his childhood cat's name. I tried not to dwell on the fact that I knew Fudgie's name the entire time but had no idea about his long-term girlfriend.

One try, and I was in.

From there, I could schedule three weeks worth of posts. I started out with slightly embarrassing things, cartoon memes that our grandparents love and updates about his upset stomach. Every other day, I posted updates of incriminating things he had told me. The time he shit his pants while waiting in line for concert tickets. The way he still called his father "Daddy." The hair plugs he tried to pass off as real. The time he threw a rock through his middle school teacher's window and hit her husband. How he shoplifts candy from convenience stores.

While I was in London, he shared so much of his life with me, and I was able to use it all. Was there a chance he would suspect it was me? It was a possibility. But something told me if he was so flippant with me, he was the same with others. I was likely one of many who had this information on him. Judging by the way he thought I'd still be interested when he stopped by, he had severely underestimated me and what I was capable of.

I changed his password and contact email address, sending it to a fake account I had set up a while back. Knowing what I did about Cory, it would take him a while to notice the updates and even longer to check his email.

I used to tease him about the astronomical notifications he had on his phone, which would work in my favor.

Remaining precautious, I tried to get into his email and found it wide open. Logging into his socials was one thing, but his email could've been another.

Once in, I skimmed his emails but didn't read anything. I'd save my ability to log in just in case I needed it later. I then deleted Meta's and password change emails.

He had no two-party authentication. No security questions. For being such a deceitful man, he was far too trusting.

After setting the laptop aside, I pulled the basket beside the couch over to me. Knitting needles and the Aran yarn in hand, I set to work. Counting the stitches, I brainstormed my next move.

Van

ALL CARS COME WITH an owner's manual. A guide to every feature and how to fix the simple problems. For years, I had thought that the guide to women was as simple as a car.

Yes, every car is different. Some require more upkeep, some a different touch when handling their undercarriage. But there is a guide, a plan.

Before everything fell apart with my father, I used to help him in the garage. He and my mom bought me a '76 Datsun 280Z for my fifteenth birthday. It didn't run, but they promised me that if I could fix it up, I could have it.

For months, I was under that car, scraping my knuckles and pinching fingers. I cleaned the grease off old parts and reassembled them. I would look up videos online of how to replace the timing chain.

All the while, my father was there, monitoring when he could and encouraging me. It was the closest we had ever been as father and son. That lasted only long enough for me to graduate high school until he dropped the bomb on me and my mother.

It took me years before I could as much as check my tire pressure without thinking of my father.

It had been over five days since I dropped Summer off at her place. Five days of meeting friends at the local dive bar for a drink. Of work and home and dinners alone. Of visiting my mom and stocking her fridge with groceries. Five days where I tried to forget the sense of holding Summer's body close to mine. Five days of catching the hint of flowers and soap, only to find nothing there. Of wishing I had done things differently.

Devin let me know Summer was fine—feeling a little rough after her night but, otherwise, back to her old self. Not that I knew what her old self was.

Summer was a mystery to me. Normally, I liked it when things fit together. When the step-by-step instruction tells me exactly which part goes where and how best to optimize productivity.

In the past ten years, my romantic relationships could only be described as simple. I liked nice girls looking for a fun time. Girls who laugh easily and came even easier. Sure, they would come with expectations, and while I didn't like letting them down, I was also never deceptive. I can't do monogamy, so don't expect it from me—take it or leave it, and almost all took it. No strings, no complicated expectations or emotions involved.

There was none of that with Summer. She was complex, a puzzle I could assemble. And despite always telling myself I didn't need complicated in my life, I wanted to know more about her.

At night, when I would go to bed, I would wonder what got her so upset at the party. Who was this ex she had mentioned? What was it about her that entranced me so fully?

Was she thinking about me?

Then, just like months before, she was on my porch—this time on the proper side of the front door—with a bakery box in her hand.

Swathed in the late afternoon light, sun filtered through the fir tree in my yard to cast shadows over her light hair. She wore a light-pink silk strappy top and jeans, her toes painted a bubblegum pink in gold sandals.

"Hey, Hot Rod." She gave me an uneasy smile.

It was the first time since we had met that she looked shy. No, not shy exactly but uncertain. As if she wasn't sure about coming over. As if I wouldn't want to have seen her.

She held up the telltale white box with its blue letter of the local bakery. "I come bearing gifts."

I leaned against the doorframe, taking her in.

Her cheeks were flushed a beautiful pink, and her lips were painted with something shiny. Was she always this beautiful?

I stepped aside, allowing her to come into the hallway.

The first time she was here, I was so shocked I hadn't thought of how the place must've looked to her. But as she walked in, I was all too aware of the decor.

As we moved to the kitchen, her eyes darted around the floral wallpaper and the gilt-framed mirrors.

As she sat on the green-and-white ivy print upholstered stool at the kitchen bar, she set the bakery box on the counter.

"What did you bring?" I grabbed the box and slid it closer to me.

Again, her cheeks stained pink. My fingers twitched to touch her skin to see if she was as warm as she looked.

"A peace offering. I can't tell you how embarrassed I am. Normally, I stick to a few drinks, but I had just got some bad news. And, unfortunately, you're the one who had to suffer for it. It took me all week to build up the courage to come over here."

"But you did. Most people wouldn't. Almost anyone else would avoid the other person, but you're here, apologizing, with a"—I popped the box open and surveyed the contents—"cake?"

She flicked her pinky nail with her thumbnail, making a small tapping sound. "Lemon rose. It's my favorite, and I thought maybe . . . Do you like lemon? I should have asked. An apple or chocolate cream pie would have been smarter, but I wanted to—"

"I fucking love lemons," I blurted.

As if her body had been tense for my response, she suddenly sagged, a grin blooming over her face. "Oh, good. What a relief. It was bad enough that I likely barfed on your shoes—but to bring a dessert you wouldn't eat, that would be unforgivable."

"You're officially forgiven." I grabbed two forks from the drawer and handed her one. "And you never barfed on me. All vomit was strictly where it belonged."

"Praise be for minor miracles." She crooked a brow. "I really am sorry, Van. I told you I'd come with you and act like your perfect girlfriend, and instead, I made a mess of myself."

"I didn't need a perfect girlfriend, or else I wouldn't have asked you in the first place."

She stuck out her tongue as she scooped out a small bite of the cake.

"Besides, Mr. Haruki told me he was glad I was able to see you home safely. I think being the doting boyfriend made a good impression."

Since she had already taken a bite directly from the cake, I followed suit, forgoing plates to cut off a piece with my own fork.

The airy, tart flavors exploded in my mouth as I chewed.

Her brow furrowed, and she drew her lower lip between her teeth as I swallowed. "Do you like it?"

"It's incredible." I scooped a bigger bite, my mouth full of cake.

She set her fork down and tucked her hands under her legs. "You probably want an explanation for why I was acting the way I was." She sighed as if it was hard to offer.

"Only if you want to give it. Or we can just say that you had a very, very bad night. Devin said it was a fluke."

"You talked to Devin?"

Concern creased her face.

"I promised I'd let her know you were home safe. Nothing more."

I wasn't sure why I added that last part. While I wasn't planning on talking to Devin again, I wanted Summer to know there was nothing between us.

"You don't strike me as someone who loses control easily."

She chuckled. "Well, I have been known for my temper. But, mostly, yeah, I have standards for myself, and that night was not it."

"We all have bad days. If I'm getting cake out of every mistake made, screw up more often."

"You really don't want me to tell you?" she asked, her eyes hopeful.

"Not unless you feel like it."

Something about my answer seemed to pass a test because her smile grew wider and brighter.

At The Cabin that day, I interrupted her dinner and told her she wasn't a sunny person. But the expanding sensation in my chest felt like the warmth of an August day. Radiant on your skin as you savored the heat.

"Redo?" she offered. "If you need me for any other work functions, I'm your gal. I'll stick to mineral water the whole night, be your DD, whatever you need."

I didn't have any mandatory work functions coming up, but the offer was intriguing. A part of me ached to spend more time with Summer and get to know her better. What I wanted from her, I didn't know.

Still, the yearning to have her with me had me saying, "I'd love that. This weekend, I was—"

A knock sounded down the hall.

Cursing whoever was on my front step, I excused myself. At the door was my neighbor, Harvey Hubert, who was standing on the porch with a scowl.

"Donovan. I've told you and your mom a hundred times, no street parking on my side of the road. Get your guest to move the car, or I'll have it towed."

While this wasn't an enforceable rule, I wasn't in the mood to have Mr. Hubert calling the police. He was trigger happy with his landline and had called on many of my neighbors before. Most of the time, it ended with a shouting match in the street and shaking his cane at the parking enforcement officer. There was room beside my truck in the driveway, which was easier to deal with than arguing with an octogenarian.

"I'll get it moved, Mr. Hubert."

He grumbled as he bumbled down my walkway with angry little stomps.

When I returned to the kitchen, a big portion of the cake was missing, and Summer set her fork down, eyes averting, tucking her hands under her legs.

"Sorry, I went overboard. I'm not used to sharing it. Is everything okay?"

"Yeah, my neighbor is the parking police today and doesn't like where your car is on the street."

She jumped off the stool, opening her purse to find her keys. "Oh, geez, sorry. I'll go. I don't want to get you in trouble with your neighbors."

Taking the keys from her hand, I shook my head. "He's a crotchety old man who had nothing better to do than stare out his window and suspiciously look for kids skateboarding. You're not going anywhere. I'll move it, but we have more talking to do."

Her keys in my hand, I left her and the half-eaten cake.

Inside her older red sedan, I had to pull the seat all the way back. A clear plastic cup with what looked like melted ice and dregs of coffee was in the middle cupholder. A sticker on the left top corner of the windshield said she was due for an oil change at the one-hundred-fourteen-thousand-mile mark. On the passenger side was a book with a bare-chested man baring pointed teeth at a woman in a red silk dress. Sitting beside the book was a large clear bag filled with small keys. I usually wouldn't have snooped, but I couldn't stop myself from grabbing a key at the top.

Silver, with a plastic name tag attached in precise print, it read *Please return to Cory Thompson 360-555-0128.*

I grabbed another key.

They all had this Cory Thompson and the same number written on them.

It was an odd thing to find in her car, but something told me to reserve the questions for later. It wasn't my business, and how could I ask it, anyway?—*Hey, I was snooping around your car and found five hundred identical keys with some dude's number on them?*

No, I'd file that under the none-of-my-concern category.

I turned on her car, and the odometer read one hundred twenty-three thousand miles beside a myriad of other warning lights. Pulling the car into my driveway, I parked alongside my truck. I climbed out of the driver's seat of her car, popped the hood, and grabbed a rag from my glove box. It took me less than a minute to check her oil level to find it low but not dry.

After putting everything back, I made my way inside.

Summer was standing in the living room, inspecting my mom's collection of vintage teacups on a shelf.

Grabbing my fork, I slid the cake toward me from her side of the counter as she traced a finger over the edge of a teacup.

Since moving back in, I hadn't invited anyone over to the house, opting to meet my few friends in town for a beer. Between starting my new job, tending to my mom, and working on the Datsun, interior decorating had fallen to last on the list.

"They were my grandmother's. She passed them down to my mom. I think Mom wished she had a daughter or a niece or something to give them to, but it's just me. It's my mom's house. I've only lived here for a few months and haven't had time to redecorate."

"Oh, is your mom—around—or . . ." She glanced around in horror. "Oh, God, please say she's still around."

I hesitated. "She lives at Glenwood Assisted Living."

"She has MS. About a year ago, she had a nasty fall. I tried moving in with her to help, but she insisted on moving. She still has her independence, a little apartment with no stairs to navigate, and they have medical personnel there who can help when she needs it."

It wasn't a shameful secret or anything, but to dump my personal issue on her when we barely knew each other felt wrong. In the end, I figured a little information would be okay.

Summer opened her mouth, glancing around the house and then, as if she thought better of it, closed it.

"Are your parents divorced or . . ." She shook her head. "Sorry, that was too nosy of me."

"No. My parents are still married—technically. But my father lives in Illahee with his girlfriend. Has for the past ten years. But they refuse to get divorced. Keeping her on his health insurance is the least he could do." I sighed. "When my mom had her fall, I sold my place in Seattle and moved back here."

"You left a condo and a job you loved in Seattle to help your mom?"

I nodded.

While I wanted nothing more than to bash my asshole of a sperm donor, I couldn't unleash that on Summer. She must have sensed that there was more to be said but didn't pressure me.

She turned to look at the teacups, her finger still trailing over the glass. "When I was little, my cousin Autumn had this beautiful tea set. It had little pink roses on it. I would go over to her house every day after school, and my Aunt Lorelle would make us sweetened tea and toast with apple butter. Once, I snuck one of the teacups home, hiding it under my bed, but my dad found it and made me give it back." She looked back at me, a sad smile playing on her lips. "My dad did the best he could, but there weren't pretty teacups at our house."

"Is your mom not in the picture?"

"She's in loads of pictures." She laughed, shaking her head. "My mother is what I'd like to call a *wanderer.* I'm sure the same things that made my father fall in love with her are exactly why she was never suited for life in Ridgewood. She left when I was two. The last postcard I got from her, she was living out of one of those converted buses somewhere in New Mexico. Her pictures have been published in magazines. She's a wonderful photographer but kind of a shitty mom."

She blinked at me a few times, her cheeks tinting pink. "Sorry, trauma dump. I swear I don't normally blab about myself like that. Boring, right? Wah, wah—crappy parents are a dime a dozen."

"Doesn't make them less crappy."

"No, it doesn't."

Her blue eyes held mine, an awareness passing between us. The urge to stand beside her was overwhelming me until she looked away.

"Ugh, emotions, right? So gross."

"Disgusting. Who needs them?"

"Exactly." She tapped one on the glass with her nail. "Someday, I'll get some pretty teacup just like this. Something to pass onto my children."

"You want to use one? I can wash the dust off one and make, um." I pictured my sparse pantry. Any tea I had was my mother's and likely expired. "I have coffee?"

She shook her head. "No. I wouldn't dare. Even if they are beautiful. Maybe some other time." Taking a seat on the stool, she grabbed hold of the bakery box and tried to pull it toward her, but I held tight.

"Is that oil change sticker on your windshield from the last time you took your car in?"

She wrinkled her nose. "Yeah, I keep topping it off, but I haven't had time to go into the shop and get hosed by the mechanics there. Normally, my dad would do it for me, but he hurt his knee at work a few years ago, and I don't want to ask him."

"You need to at least get your oil changed."

"Are you lecturing me on car maintenance right now? I've owned that beater for years. She's got plenty of good miles on her."

"Not if the engine blows up. I'll look at it."

"What? My oil? Why would you do that?"

Why indeed? Never in all my years of flings and short-term girlfriends had I offered to change their oil. Of course I knew how. It was one of the first things my father taught me.

"Do you want me to look or not?" I took a big bite of the cake and waited. Between the two of us, over half of it was gone.

As she crossed her arms, her boobs bulged over them.

I tried not to look but focused on her narrowed blue eyes.

"Do you know what you're doing?"

"I'm an engineer, Summer." I scoffed, my mouth still half full.

"And I've known enough mechanics to know that engineers are the ones they complain about the most."

Touché.

I swallowed and set my fork on the counter. "It's an oil change, not a transmission rebuild. Your car will be fine."

She nodded, waving in acceptance. "Sure, fine. I guess this means I owe you a second cake."

Crossing my arms, I stared her down. "Tell you what, I have a few work events in the coming week. I'll expect you to join me and play the part of my girlfriend."

"For how long?" She narrowed her eyes.

Before this, I wasn't sure of the calculation on how long I would have to date someone to ward off being set up again. But with her in front of me, I blurted the number I felt was right. I didn't need her to come with me any longer—not really, but I still wanted it.

"Until the end of summer. Nothing big, a few dinners and stuff. After that, you're single."

Her chin rested delicately on her hand as she surveyed me. "So, I'm supposed to be your girlfriend for the next nine weeks? The best time to have a fling with a hot fuck boy, and I'm supposed to give it up for you?"

At the mention of her finding some random guy to hook up with, my skin became too tight. Another man dancing with her, flirting, even kissing her. Someone else who got to pull her to his side and hold her close. Red heat licked my chest.

"Was that really your plan for the summer? Hooking up with assholes?"

"Not really your business how I spend my nights, is it? I won't be shamed for it. You think I can't tell exactly what kind of guy you'd be at a bar? I bet you haven't had a long-term girlfriend in years."

She was right, of course. And as much as it killed me to think of her with other men, it would never be my concern about who she spent her nights with. I had no rights to her.

"Almost a decade. And I'm not shaming you. I like a woman who knows what she wants. But that's not what this is about."

"Are you saying if we met at a bar, you wouldn't try to take me home?" She scoffed.

"No, of course I would. Look at you. But if you can put aside your rabid lust for me for a few dates, I'm sure we can work something out."

"Noted, Hot Rod."

"Just don't get any ideas or anything. I need to be clear right now. I don't do relationships or commitment or monogamy. Don't fall in love with me."

Summer rolled her eyes. "Are you always this dramatic? That won't be a problem, buddy."

I frowned.

She could have been a little more hesitant about agreeing to that. But would my ego survive her?

"Considering I just got free of my last asshole boyfriend, you won't have anything to worry about. I have my own rules." She pursed her full pink lips in consideration. "No funny business. Don't be a sleazeball and think that I owe you sex or something."

"Sunshine, you don't owe me an inch of your body."

But damn if I didn't want it all.

She stuck out a hand for me to shake.

With her palm against mine, a knowing spark traveled up my arm.

I fought the urge to kiss the back of her hand. Still holding onto her, I pulled her closer until we were both leaning against the counter. "First things first, though, let's get your car in better order."

She followed me out to the garage, where I instructed her to sit in a camping chair while I worked.

From my angle under the car, her legs looked damn near perfect.

Eleven

Summer

W ITH MY LEGS CROSSED in the canvas camping chair, I watched as Van slid under my car and began deftly changing my oil.

Admittedly, while I was raised by a blue-collar worker, most of my boyfriends had been business types. Cory had rows of crisp white button-downs and a special hanger for his ties. Casual to him was designer jeans instead of slacks. I doubted he owed a single pair of work pants, let alone steel-toed boots.

When I got with my first boyfriend, a perfectly nice guy who I ended up dumping for the asshole who left me at homecoming, my father told me I'd need one of two things in a man. Either one handy enough to fix things or someone who makes enough money to pay someone else to do it for me. While sexist and reductive to my gender, he wasn't wrong.

I had long held the belief that, since I wasn't about to climb beneath the undercarriage of my car, I'd need good money to have others do it for me. And there I was, watching this strong, handsome man fix it like it was his job.

Since the only people I had really watched work on cars were my father, uncle, and cousins, I hadn't realized how sexy it was. Seeing the skillful way he worked was heating me up, and I had visions of those fingers moving just as deftly across my skin.

I couldn't ogle him as he tinkered. That would be obscene and objectifying. I needed a distraction from the brawny man whose hands were on my underbody.

I pulled out my phone.

According to the notifications I was getting on Cory's email, people were responding to the fake ads. Now onto the next part of my plan.

I pulled up an AI-generating photo app.

While I wasn't a fan of using this sort of program typically, ethically, it felt better to have a made-up person for communication. Hair color, brown. Eye color, blue. Full lips and a smaller bust.

I popped all these into the generator and waited. Three down was the perfect fake girl. If Kodi and I could have been cousins, this girl would have been a half sister.

I downloaded several shots of her and created the account. It was an easy twenty bucks to buy fake bot followers. Between AI pictures, I included scenery photos, food, and generic quotes like the ones Autumn loved to send to us. Thirty minutes in, I had my catfish poised for Cory.

@Candy_is_Handy was born.

Van was finishing up with my car in my peripheral. He popped my hood, poured different fluids in various spots, commenting about how something or the other was low.

"Did you hear me?" He was standing over me, wiping his hands on a blue rag identical to the one he used on the day I busted in on him.

"Um . . ." I set my phone face down in the cupholder and gave him my most innocent smile. "Check my blinker fluid."

I may not like working on greasy cars, but I knew enough from being around people growing up to know the joke.

He scowled. "Hilarious. You need new wipers. Those are cracked."

"I can do that."

"And you probably need to get your tires rotated soon, too. There's more wear on the—"

"Hey, Hot Rod. I've got it. Chill." My attention was back on my phone screen.

A few random dudes followed Candy but no one I knew yet.

Grumbling, he threw the rag on top of his toolbox. "I'm going to check the shed. I might have a set in there."

Alone in the garage, I took advantage of the moment to scroll to Cory's account, liking random posts and commenting emojis under others. Since he'd have to make the first move, I'd wait for him to contact me.

A yelp screeched from the backyard.

Dropping my phone into the mesh cupholder, I rushed through the back door.

Van was sagging against the side of his shed, clutching his right foot. Sticking an inch or so out of the sole of his shoe was an old rusted nail.

"Oh God, what happened?"

"Fucking shed," he gritted out. He pinched the long nail head and pulled it out, then let out a string of curses as blood dripped from his shoes onto his hands.

I thought he would drop the nail, but he held it up to his eyes as if it were an errant child.

The sight of his blood was making me queasy, and I had to steady myself against the shed.

"We should get you to urgent care." I swallowed the vomit rising in my throat and kept my eyes on the sky.

If I were to have looked at his injury or even the nail for a moment longer, I could've gotten sick.

"It's fine. It's just a little poke."

His aloof words were downplayed as his balance wavered.

"Nope. Not fine. I'm taking you to the hospital." Before he could argue, I laced my arm around his waist and pulled him toward the house.

His shirt held the remnants of oil and grease, but an undercurrent of soap and lemon also lingered on his skin.

We walked slowly together. As we shuffled to my car, I turned away to avoid the temptation of his scent.

I bundled him into my passenger seat, having to reach between his legs to pull it all the way back for him.

At the wheel, I pulled out without checking behind me and almost T-boned an electric car with a coexist sticker.

The other driver laid on their horn as they swerved around me.

"You need me to drive?" he asked with a grimace.

"No. I'm fine." This time, I checked my blind spots before pulling out onto the road.

His knees were high behind the dashboard.

"You can drive faster, you know. The speed limit is thirty-five here."

A glance at the speedometer showed me it was going twenty-eight.

"Look, I'm a nervous driver, okay? So, be quiet, put pressure on that foot, and shush until we get there."

When we arrived at the urgent care, I helped him out of the car, much to his grumbling that he could do it himself. I led him to sit on a purple vinyl couch and then checked him in with his wallet, then brought back a clipboard the receptionist had given me.

After I asked him about the cursory information, he scowled at me, grabbing the clipboard. "My hands work just fine. I can write my own answers."

"Fine." I threw up my hands. "Works for me."

Minutes passed with the pen scratching paper and the *click-clack* of the receptionist typing on her keyboard.

I wished I had my knitting bag. My hands were itching to do something.

The image of that nail in his foot, the grayish pallor of his skin when he pulled it out. It was too much. Normally, a little blood didn't worry me. I was a woman, after all. But seeing Van hurt shook me.

He finished the paperwork, set the clipboard aside, leaned back against the fake leather couch, and closed his eyes.

His complexion looked wrong, too pale. Had he lost too much blood? The nail was big, but I thought the wound had stopped bleeding.

Van placed a hand over mine. "It's okay. You don't need to be nervous."

"I'm not nervous."

He squeezed my hand. "You're doing that thing with your thumb and nails."

I blinked at him.

I hadn't ever realized I was doing it, but he saw it. Never in my twenty-five years had someone pointed it out to me, but this man spends a few days with me and picks up on it?

"I'll be okay, Sunshine. Nothing to worry over."

Smoothing my hands in my lap, I gave him a placid smile. "Like I said, I'm not nervous."

Closing his eyes again, he said nothing, but the weight of his hand on mine was comforting.

As I savored the sensation, he slid his fingers over mine, flipping my hand over until we were palm to palm. He opened one eye and gave me a half smile. "I was pretty sure I was going to die of old age before I'd succumb to sepsis, but thanks for driving."

I huffed, trying to pull my hand away, but he held it tight. "When I'm calm, I am a perfectly adequate driver. I've never been in an accident or had a ticket in my life."

"Not even for impeding traffic?"

Scowling, I shook my head. "I got us here, didn't I?"

"Barely."

I opened my mouth to say something else, but a young woman in scrubs approached us.

"Donovan Logan?" she asked, checking her file.

"That's me." He stood, bearing all his weight on his left foot.

I grabbed the clipboard, rising to them and handing the medical assistant the paperwork.

Van took a shaky step forward, then stopped and glanced at me. "You coming?"

It wasn't quite an invitation, but somewhat knowing Van, I know he wouldn't want to ask me outright.

"Of course." After gathering my things, I walked behind him down the hall to the exam room.

Once there, he collapsed onto the table with a groan, and I sat in a small chair in the corner.

The medical assistant took his vitals, asked about the injury, and inspected the area. After taking notes, she assured him the nurse practitioner would be in shortly.

The door was barely shut before his gaze darted to mine.

"Do you think"—he furrowed his brow—"they're going to make me get a shot?"

"A shot?" I leaned back and crossed my arms. "Maybe? But after getting a nail through your foot, a shot seems like the least of your worries."

"I've never liked getting shots," he retorted, a pink flush climbing up his cheeks.

With narrowed eyes, I studied him. "Are you—no."

"I'm not." He asserted.

"I thought we agreed we wouldn't lie to each other." I bit back a laugh, swallowing hard as he lowered his head. "A lot of people don't like needles. It's very common."

"For children." The pink had turned into scarlet, tingeing his ears. "I'm thirty-two, Summer."

"Phobia knows no age. I'm terribly afraid of enclosed places—caves, small rooms. I had a guy take me on a date to a panic room once, and I was hyperventilating at the end."

My admission seemed to calm him.

"I've always felt this way. When I was little, my dad would hold me down to get my vaccines."

"Well, that might be why. Being restrained while getting poked would be traumatic for anyone. It's okay to be scared."

"I'm not scared. I just don't like them."

Instead of arguing, I stood and walked over. Stopping before him, I grabbed his hand and squeezed. "I'll be right here with you. You might need a shot because you could get tetanus, and you might even need stitches. But I won't go anywhere. If you want to blame it on me, you can. Tell them I'm the needy girl who needs support during your treatment."

"Thank you." A soft smile played on his lips. "I haven't had someone take care of me like this since my mom when I was sixteen."

"Are you comparing me to your mother right now?" I scoffed.

"Definitely not. Gah, how could you even suggest—" I gave him a withering stare, and he laughed. "No, I mean, I don't need anyone to look after me."

"Do you want me to go?"

"No. No. Stay."

His response was quick.

A knock came from the door, and a very pretty nurse with red hair walked in. Her scrubs were a turquoise, complementing her fair complexion.

"Hi, I'm Ana. I'll be working with Tomas today for your treatment and—oh. Hi, Van." A smile bloomed over her face. "I had a feeling that might be you."

"Ana!" His face relaxed. "I didn't know you worked here now."

The way he was smiling at this beautiful redhead put me on edge. Sure, she was gorgeous and had a kind smile and somehow looked cute in scrubs, but who was she?

With a zip of panic, I was jealous.

She set the file down and grabbed gloves from a drawer. "Didn't Xander mention it? Of course not. He thinks sharing stuff about us is boring. Yeah, I've been here for about a year now. Better hours than the hospital. After Maxine was born, it was hard finding care during the odd working hours. Xander is out the door at four in the morning, and if I had a night shift, it was impossible to find babysitters."

She turned to face me. "Sorry. Catching up. Ana Eberhardt. Van and I went to school together a lifetime ago."

"Summer Townsend."

She beamed at me, and I glanced at Van, but nothing in his look projected an ounce of attraction to this woman.

She mentioned a child and another man, but that could've been a brother or an ex or something.

After what I went through with Cory, I wasn't going to assume a man was unattached ever again.

Ana directed him to scoot back on the table to inspect his foot.

I thought he would want me to step back, but he grabbed my hand, keeping me level to his head.

After examining the area, she grabbed tools from a drawer and cleaned the wound, flushing water into the puncture.

Van didn't betray a look of pain but tightened his grip when Ana announced he would need a tetanus shot.

An older man walked in and consulted with Ana about their patient. He asked Van a few questions, approved Ana's job of cleaning the wound, and said he would give him two stitches.

I could feel the hitch in Van's breath.

By the time the nurse practitioner had brought out the tools, I faced him and as low as I could and directed him to look at me.

"Oh, I can't watch. Look at me and don't let me turn around, okay?" I declared loud enough for them to hear me. Placing another hand on top of his, I squeezed his palm, rubbing my thumb over the line of scars on his knuckles.

His gray eyes were hard, steel, and basalt, his jaw flexing as they stitched him up.

His gaze didn't leave mine, and his grip vibrated almost to the point of pain.

I wasn't going to let go. He had admitted his vulnerability, and I would not be taking it for granted.

By the time he got his tetanus booster, my hand was screaming, but I had gone this far with him. I couldn't back out.

"Alright, all done. That was a nasty one," the nurse practitioner announced. "I'm sending you home with a prescription of antibiotics and strict rest on that foot. Try to limit pressure on it for the next twenty-four hours, but after that, you should be okay." He looked at me. "Don't let him be a hero and rip his stitches out, or we'll be back here."

Once in the car, he was able to put the seat back enough for his knees to stop touching his chin.

I turned to him. "She's pretty."

"Who? Ana?" He furrowed his brow as he adjusted his legs.

"Yeah. Seems like you two have history."

He scoffed, running a hand over his face. "Because we went to school together? I've known her since we were little punks. She's married to one of my best friends. They have a kid together. I can assure you there is nothing between us. She is not my type."

"What, pretty? Sweet? Helpful?"

"Simple. Ana is as sweet as they come, loyal to fault. Would give the shirt off her back to strangers, see only the best in even the most terrible of people. And that is fine for a lot of men. It's great for Xander. They both deserve to be happy after the shit they went through. But I need something more in my women."

"So, you need someone mean, ugly, and traitorous."

"No. I like to be challenged. I like the chase. I want someone who calls me on my bullshit and doesn't get upset when I call them on theirs." He adjusted himself again, trying not to put pressure on his foot. "If I told Ana I didn't like a shirt she wore, she would offer to change it."

I snorted. "I'd tell you to fuck off."

"Exactly." He fixed his gaze on mine.

In the midday sun, his eyes were lighter, full-moon silver against mountain peaks. The space of the car was too small, the air thick and hot as I stared him down. I refused to look away first.

"Put the murder gaze away," I murmured.

"Killer eyes, disengage." He smirked as he looked away. "Why don't you get me home so I can put up my foot and watch some *West Wing*?"

I startled at the show name but said nothing. If I were to have admitted I watched that, he might invite me in to watch with him, and I'd accept—and then what? I'd start to like him? Want to kiss him? No. There couldn't be an attraction, not yet.

I had a vengeance plan for the summer, and he wasn't going to disrupt it with his sexy silver eyes and charming fear of needles.

When I dropped him off, I could barely park before he climbed out. Already in reverse, I waited for him to walk inside without me.

When he knocked on my window, I rolled it down, keeping my foot on the brake for a quick getaway.

"I'll text you about our next date."

Frowning, I pumped the brake harder to let out my excess energy.

I had agreed to this facade of dating. A few boring work events were the least I could do. He said he was an engineer, so most people he worked with would be, too. A bunch of nerdy folks who would drone on about specifications or geometry or something.

Engineering was a mystery to me. The upside was that the lame talk had to make him less attractive, or I was in big trouble.

"Okay. Yeah, of course. You name the time and place. As long as I don't have work."

He knocked on my doorframe twice before stepping back, a big grin stretching his face and that damn dimple on his left cheek peeking out.

Dimples were supposed to be for babies and plush dolls. Not for sexy men who knew how to fix my car and smelled like soapy lemon.

"See you soon, Sunshine."

I left him standing alone in the driveway, my hands shaky on the steering wheel. A few blocks down, I pulled over to the side of the road to catch my breath.

I couldn't be distracted by Van. Yes, he was hot, and I was more than a little obsessed with the way those muscular arms felt around me. His lips were ultra soft against mine, and he certainly knew what he was doing with his fingers when . . .

Nope. Focus. This summer was not about getting all heartsick over some guy.

It was about making Cory pay.

Grabbing my phone, I pulled up the fake account.

No new notifications yet for Candy. This had to work. I needed more concrete proof that he was a cheater if I was going to go to Cory's fiancée.

Swiping away Instagram, I navigated to my messages to shoot Van a text.

Tilting my chin up, I stared at the dirty ceiling of my car and wondered if I was making a mistake. Whatever Van wanted out of me might have been fake, but I couldn't help but admit this attraction was very real.

Van

SOMEONE WAS IN MY office.

My steps faltered as I crossed the threshold to find a woman from R & D sitting in my chair, studying my daily fun-fact calender, a pencil in hand.

"Hi, Savvy. Welcome to my desk," I said, setting my cup of coffee down.

She dropped the pencil and the calender. "Van! You scared me."

"At my own desk?"

Her face turned red, and she stood, my chair skittering back.

"Sorry, I was going to leave you a note and then I saw the calendar, and I have a Pomeranian. I had no idea two escaped the Titanic. You must like them, too, right . . ." Somehow, her pink cheeks got even redder. "Obviously, you do."

She moved around the desk, and I mirrored her movements until I was standing behind it, and she was in front.

"It's a basic fun-fact calender. My mom gets me one every year."

She had folded the page up, which had a little pencil smudge in the corner.

A flare of annoyance shot up, but I tamped it down.

Savvy was a nice enough woman, albeit a little enthusiastic.

"What can I hep you with?"

"I was wondering if you're coming to the bar tonight? A bunch of us are going for happy hour, and you haven't before, but I wanted to make sure you knew you were invited if you want to come."

I considered the offer. Aside from seeing Xander a few times and my brief run-in with Ana at urgent care, I hadn't spent much time outside of work with anyone. It would do me good to make acquaintances and build rapport with my coworkers.

"Sure, I'm in. Where at?"

My attention was half on my screen as I pulled up emails.

"Skol House at six?"

"Sounds good. I'll see you there."

It took me a minute to realize she was still standing in front of my desk.

"Was there something else?"

Her ears were pink alongside her cheeks.

"No, I'll see you there."

I pressed the bent corner of the paper, trying to smooth it down with my thumb but gave up after a minute. I would rip it off, anyway.

Skol House looked the same as it had when I snuck in at eighteen, with its dingy green floor tiles and chipped purple paint on the doors. However, they had since updated the neon signs from hard lemonades to hard seltzers. Vinyl posters of local sports teams had changed to a new roster, but the same black light menu hung behind the bar.

Savvy stood from her chair, waving to flag me down despite the bar being half full. "Van, over here."

On the other side of the empty chair was a thin man from research and development.

What was his name? We had been introduced a few times, but it was always in a group setting. Nathan? Nolan?

He was looking at the seat and back at Savvy with a pained expression she didn't notice.

"I saved you a seat. You can sit with me and Eldon." When I hesitated, her smile dropped a little. "Unless you have someone else coming? People said you brought someone to the parade party."

The gleam in her eye told me she wanted me to be single. Office romances were on my no-go list. If seeing the boss's granddaughter was a slight risk, dating someone you had to see every day was a huge mistake.

Savvy was a cute gal, with her short brown hair and green eyes, but I didn't feel enough attraction to commit career suicide over. Best to end any aspirations now.

Settling on a high stool across from the table, I leaned against the tabletop. "My girlfriend might join us. She works just down the road at the hotel."

I hadn't planned on inviting Summer, but I needed her to meet me.

In the days since I had last seen Summer, we had been talking more and more. At first, she would check up on my foot, telling me to rest it, followed by me reminding her to put on the wiper blades I had dropped off at her door. She sent me pictures of her car with a thumbs-up, and I sent her a picture of a teacup with pink roses.

It was innocent enough. Without having her in front of me, I could almost convince myself she wasn't as beautiful as I thought.

Then she tagged me in one of the pictures she took the night of the parade party, and I was back to fantasizing about her rose-scented skin near mine.

Focus. Keep it together. She could play her part, and I would keep my dick in my pants. I had thirty-two years on this earth without letting lust swallow reason. Not even Summer could shake my resolve. Right?

I excused myself to get a drink, bellying up at the bar.

While waiting, I shot a quick text to Summer, asking for her girlfriend services.

By the time my beer was set in front of me, she texted back a car emoji and a saluting face.

Everyone at the table was discussing the trivia competition when I returned. Savvy and some other woman, Gabriella, were talking about how well they had done at the last one.

Back in Seattle, I often went to trivia nights with my friends. It was nice to know I could start over here, too.

The conversation switched from defeat over the name of the small piece at the end of shoelaces to complaints about work, the ordinary pain-in-the-ass managers, and that one coworker who was always late.

"Whoa. Check her out," one of the guys at the table murmured, nudging the guy beside him.

I glanced up to see Summer walking in, her long blonde hair flowing over her tanned shoulders. She wore a low-cut light-pink dress over a white woven bra. The cotton hem swished around her upper thighs as she stopped in the doorway to scan the bar. When her blue eyes landed on mine, a wide smile stretched her face as she approached.

"Hey, Hot Rod." She leaned in and pressed a kiss to my cheek as if it were second nature.

I fought the instinct to pull her body to mine. To bask the roses and sunshine of her skin.

The spot where she kissed me seared with heat, and it took all I had not to connect her lips with mine. Her words from the other day playing in my head.

As much as I wanted to hold her, I couldn't put my hands all over her unless she wanted me to. What was the term she used—*sleazeball*? I had many terrible traits but to be sleazy toward a woman wouldn't be one.

As she pulled away, she frowned. "Oh, sorry. I left some—" She swiped her thumb across my cheek. "That lipstick is supposed to be smudge-proof, but you might have a pink mark on your skin for a while."

The last thing I was worried about was lipstick on my cheek.

"No worries."

"I'm marking my territory." She laughed, her clear-sky eyes on me.

It was the gaze of hot days on the water and the soothing feel of a sea-cooled wind.

"I'll allow it."

She grabbed my beer and took a sip before making a face. "Ugh. IPA. Disgusting."

Taking the beer back, I downed the rest of it, still watching her.

Her eyes darted to my throat before snapping back up to my face, her nose wrinkling.

"My cousin Oliver loves them. I don't know how you can drink that garbage. It tastes like an herbal-scented trash bag with a cigarette thrown in."

"Delicious." I smacked my lips dramatically.

She rolled her eyes, and I savored the sight of her face, beautiful, even when annoyed by me.

Turning to the group, I motioned. "Everyone, this is Summer. Summer, this is everyone."

When I went around the table and gave her each coworker's name, she did her best at shaking hands and repeating names back.

One of the guys, Eldon, looked starstruck, shaking her hand a few seconds longer than everyone else.

Afterward, I had her sit on the stool beside me. I wanted to place my hand on her knee but stopped myself. When the server came by, she ordered sparkling water with lemon, then whispered to me she didn't want another repeat of that first party.

"Summer." Savvy leaned forward, narrowing her eyes. "Nice dress. It's very"—she gave her a once-over—"bold."

Summer glanced over herself, her face blank, as if the comment wasn't rude. "Thank you. I knitted the bralette myself."

"You knit?" I asked, my brow raising.

"I contain multitudes."

"Apparently."

"Why are you so shocked? Lots of people know how to knit. It's not a bygone craft or something."

I coughed to hide my surprise. "No, I know. It's just that knitting is for grandmas and old people, not—"

She shot me a withering glare. "That kind of ageist thinking is exactly why I do it. Knitting is an art form. I've been a member of a local stitch and bitch group for the past few years."

I threw my hands up in mock surrender. "I concede. You can stitch and bitch as much as you want."

She smiled at me, then sipped her drink as feedback from a microphone shrieked.

A thin man in a terrible hunter-green fedora stood in the DJ booth. "Hello, beardos and weirdos. Welcome to Trivia Masters. I'm your host, Dr. Factoids. Get your teams together, and we'll be starting momentarily."

Summer's head snapped toward me with a gleam in her eyes. "Trivia! I fucking love trivia. I'm going to dominate."

"Is that so?" I raised a challenging brow.

Our team was in the lead with four points. We scored double on a question about the largest archipelago in the world but then lost when we couldn't define alektorophobia.

For the last hour and a half, I had successfully not pawed at Summer like some horny teen. Despite how cute she looked when she would furrow a brow as she struggled to answer a question. And the smile when she was correct? Words escaped me. The sunshine and confidence in it.

She blurted answers when she knew them and didn't hesitate to debate with the rest of the team, who she had just met. When she couldn't contribute, she sat back and let others take over.

For an entire one hundred and seven minutes, I kept my hands to myself.

The hardest moment was when she insisted we take a picture together, angling her body into mine. Her lush curves fit perfectly against me as she smiled at the camera. When she pulled away, I had to clench my hands into fists to stop them from lacing around her waist and pulling her off her stool and onto my lap.

My phone lit up with a notification that she had tagged me.

It was down to the final question. Only two points were separating our team, the CasaNopas, and The Little Lebowski Urban Achievers.

Eldon had said the L.L.U.A. won the last three months in a row and was getting smug.

On the mic, Dr. Factoid played a drumroll clip. "Aaaaaaand for the last question of the night. For a whopping eight points, according to IMDB, what is the highest-rated episode of political drama, *The West Wing*?"

The rest of the table glanced around with trepidation.

Some of the show's staff were likely born in the years after the show premiered.

"Two Cathedrals," Summer and I say in unison, then glance at each other.

"How—" I shook my head.

Nothing about this woman would surprise me, but it didn't include her knowledge of my fast-talking comfort show.

Since half of the table hadn't even heard of the show, Eldon wrote the answer down, reporting to the DJ.

We waited as Dr. Factoid announced our team as the winner of a twenty-five-dollar bar gift card.

Cheers and high-fives abounded as we celebrated our victory.

Our rival team shot us dirty looks, and one woman on the team hissed expletives at a man beside her with narrowed eyes.

Summer wrapped her arms around my waist.

With one arm over her shoulders, I squeezed her slightly.

Tingles shot up my arm, and I fought the urge to keep her tight against me. To claim her in front of this group.

I pulled away, a casual smile on my face.

I couldn't let my dick get me in trouble here.

A line formed between her brows as she pulled away, but she said nothing, high-fiving the team as if they had fought a hard battle for years.

Eldon leaned in close to me, a wide grin stretching his freckled, tanned cheeks. "You need to bring her every time. She's an absolute menace."

After slapping my back, he stepped away, giving double high-fives to Savvy, who had her arm around Summer's waist as they congratulated each other.

I could picture it all too well, Summer beside me at the bar, us dominating at trivia and winning each round with ease. Our knees knocking together, the feel of her fingers against mine as she steals the little pencil from me to write the answer.

It wasn't anything I ever wanted. Brief dates with women, sure. But to have someone around all the time?

"Yeah, I'll get her back here next time."

"She's a member of the team now. You must be serious about her."

Summer threw an arm over Savvy's shoulder and beamed at me.

The urge to cup my hand around her neck and bring her lips to mine was overwhelming. My mouth tingled from want.

"Yeah, of course," I said, barely registering the comment until after I agreed to it.

But there was a shift in how I was feeling about her. I could picture her joining me for these trivia nights, charming my coworkers, her hand holding mine under the table like some junior-high crush. But more than that, I could visualize what came after. What she would look like in the mornings, fresh-faced and still sleepy. How we would find each other in the night, our legs tangled and the air mingling.

The last time I had spent over thirty minutes with a woman after a night together was at least five years before, and that was more because she couldn't take my hints about needing to head out the door and parked herself on my couch with a box of Crunch Berries. That mistake both made me late for work and deprived me of all the red berries.

Somehow, I doubted Summer would be one to methodically remove fruit flavors from sugary cereal.

The group downed the rest of their drinks and covered their bar tabs. In ten minutes, half of them were out the door, leaving only a few of us.

Savvy was at the bar, ordering her last drink, and Eldon was watching her with lovesick eyes.

Was there a way to help him along?

Without the buffer of the group, Summer turned to me. "Okay, Hot Rod, what is up with you?"

As she waited for my answer, she fished the lemon out of her drink and sucked it into her mouth, ripping the fruit from the rind.

I stared at the empty yellow skin. "Did you just eat that lemon like an apple?"

"More like an orange, since it's a citrus." She shrugged. "I like lemons." Setting the rind down, she turned on her stool, her knees bumping mine. "Don't change the subject. I've been here for hours now, and you're acting . . . I don't know." She frowned. "Not boy-friendly."

"Not boy-friendly?"

"Yeah, side hugs, barely get a high five. I leaned in closer, the universal *put your arm around me* signal, and you ignored it."

"I was being respectful. You told me not to be a sleazeball. I didn't want to do anything that makes you uncomfortable."

"So, you went a thousand miles in the other direction?" She raised a brow, a smirk playing at the corner of her rose-tinted lips. "Don't you worry about me. I have no issue telling you to back off if I need it." Her gaze peered over my shoulder. "Speaking of, hold that thought."

Her chair screeched against the linoleum as she pushed it back.

Before I could ask her what was going on, she was at the bar, her gaze on Savvy, who was standing between two stools with a frown on her face.

A man with wrap-around sunglasses sitting backward on his balding head and a peeling sunburn on his forehead was leaning on the wooden surface. His eyes traced Savvy's body, and he gave her a lecherous grin.

"No, thanks," Savvy said, turning back to the bartender.

"Put it on my tab, Tim," the man said.

Savvy shook her head again. "That's really o—"

Summer grabbed the stool between them, pulled it out into the walkway, and slid beside Savvy, giving the man her back.

"Excuse you," the man slurred. "You bumped into me."

Summer glanced over her shoulder at him, her mouth pulled into a sneer and a single brow raised. "And yet you're still standing here."

On the table beside me, Summer's phone chimed and lit up.

I glanced down out of habit to see her screen filling up with notifications.

@corytheman now follows you
@corytheman commented: ☐☐☐fire emoji-peach emoji-sweaty emoji
@corytheman commented: "Beuatiful"
@corytheman commented: "prety in pink"

On and on, her screen didn't have time to rest as the notifications of this guy commenting and liking posts kept buzzing. Heart emojis and fire beside peaches. Then the message requests.

I had no say in who she talked to. Unfamiliar jealousy rose, a dark coil aching to take possession of her. I'm all wrong for Summer. Too stuck in my ways.

Long ago, I had promised myself I wouldn't hurt a woman the way my father hurt my mother. I had the obligations of my life and the promises I had made. There was no room for a woman.

I couldn't give her what she deserved, but damn if I didn't want to be the best one who tried.

Since the day of the parade, we followed each other on social media. She tagged me in a single photo in her story, not a real post. Afterward, she posted rarely but only flowers, pastries, and photo dumps of blurry selfies with her girlfriends. Ones with the rain-soaked streets of London and dimly lit pubs with pints of beer. A snapshot of curry sauce on fries and the view from a plane window. Nothing of her in pink, nothing that would elicit the horny comments.

As she stood at the bar, I pulled up my phone to see who this Corytheman guy was commenting all over her picture. I had to scroll back five months to find a single comment from him, *Blue without my blue.* No other mention of him. No tagged photos—and even more confusing: she wasn't following him, but he followed her. His own page was a nondescript one of beer signs and sports memes. Something wasn't adding up.

A few feet away, the man at the bar raised his voice at Summer, who was blocking his view of Savvy.

"I was talking to her." He motioned to Savvy with his beer glass, the drink spilling over his hand.

"And now you're not." Summer turned back at Savvy, who was still waiting on her bill, her eyes large and fearful.

"Anyway, like I was saying. This top really doesn't take too long to make if you—"

Most men would get the hint, but this man didn't seem to catch it. If anything, he looked even more determined to talk to Savvy.

"You interrupted my conversation with her."

Summer frowned. "No, I don't think I did."

"I see how it is. Cockblocker, are you? Why don't you run home to your cats so the rest of us can have some fun?"

At this insult, I stepped forward to give him a piece of my mind.

Summer put her hand on my chest. "I got this." Her smile dropped, and she cocked her head. "First of all. You aren't tall enough to make that joke."

People snickered behind their hands, and one woman cackled at the insult.

The man's brow knitted as he processed her words.

She stepped forward, causing him to lean back.

She was a small thing, couldn't be over five-five, yet the fierceness emanating from her made her seem seven feet tall.

All around us, others stopped talking and watched the scene with the drunkard and the warrior.

"And I can't block something you were never going to get. Anyone with eyes could see that you have hit on no less than five ladies at this bar. I've been watching you. No one wants that drunk pencil dick you have. So, quit being a creep and leave them alone.”

“You can’t talk to me like that,” he slurred.

“You must have some humiliation fetish, don’t you? She’s not interested. No one is. So, get lost.”

I sucked in a breath, tensing my fist in case he tried to place a hand on her.

She obviously wanted to handle the man herself. From that first day with her, Summer made it apparent she was a force. It was better to let her say her piece than have her turn it on me.

The guy slammed his empty pint glass on the bar top.

The bartender finally intervened, signaling a bigger guy at the door. “Okay, buddy, pack it up.” He handed the man his card and receipt. “We’ve had three complaints already. We’ve talked about this.”

The drunk man grabbed the receipt, glowering at everyone. “I’m going to the casino. At least they know how to treat a guest.”

The bar was unusually quiet until the door swung shut with a vibrating clang. Whispers and comments about drunk assholes buzzed around.

Summer rolled her eyes at the door. “Well, can’t say I’m surprised, but at least he’s out of here.”

I saddled up to her and placed a hand on her elbow. “Surprised about what?”

“That it took a man telling him to leave for him to listen. Did you hear the bartender? Three other women complained. I’m glad I spoke up.”

“That was a ballsy move. Could have been dangerous.”

She shook her head. “Well, someone had to. I could tell Savvy was uncomfortable.”

“He could have hurt you.”

She scoffed. “I’d like to see him try.” She left me to join Savvy, who was pulling on her coat.

I couldn't hear what was said, but Savvy gave Summer a hug before they pulled out their phones and exchanged information.

Eldon grabbed Savvy's purse off the table and motioned to the door.

The bartender placed another beer and something red in a pint glass down before me. I took our drinks, and we sat at the four-top.

The music was getting louder, and the late crowd was trickling in, replacing the happy-hour crew with the night drinkers.

"You and Savvy got along," I commented, jutting my chin at my coworker, who was laughing at something Eldon had said.

They walked out, his cheeks pink with the attention.

Good. Maybe he would get the courage to ask Savvy out.

Summer beamed. "I like her. She's smart and funny."

"And she likes you."

Summer faced me, her gaze narrowing. "Why wouldn't she?"

"Because I was getting the vibes that she was into me, and that's when I invited . . ."

Summer assessed me with a tilted head, a smirk playing on her lips. "Please, go on. Tell me how a woman should be devastated by missing out on you."

"Okay, fine. Point taken."

This woman was a total ego killer.

"I'm sure she thinks you're hot." She swallowed her cider, looking at me over the rim of her glass.

"You think I'm hot?" I teased. "You want this body so much you can't handle it."

"You have no idea what I could handle, Hot Rod."

Unbidden, the image of her beneath me, her body flush with want and her hands all over me as I thrust into her, flooded my mind. I shook away the thought.

"Despite what early aughts teen comedies might have taught you, most girls don't compete over men. I would wager that she won't be thinking about you at all now."

"I couldn't care less what that woman thinks of me. There's only one person I've been thinking about tonight." I leaned forward, still not wanting to touch her and cross that line.

But a little harmless flirting? That, I could do.

"Are you playing with me?" She quirked a brow and frowned.

"Trust me. There are many things I want to do to you, but I am one hundred percent serious about them."

She cast her eyes down.

I reveled in making her nervous until her shoulders shook.

Lifting her head, she pursed her lips, holding back a laugh. She let out a chuckle, covering her mouth with her hand. "Sorry. *One hundred percent serious.*" She imitated my voice. With a pat on my arm, she stepped back. "Keep it up, Hot Rod. Might work eventually." After emptying her glass, she set it back down. "I should probably head back to my place. I have to be at the hotel at seven tomorrow morning."

The rejection stung.

I wasn't so egotistical to have my come-ons work every time, but I had a good record.

Could this woman do a single thing the way I was used to?

She stood, her thin sweater looped around her bag's strap.

"Can I walk you to your car? In case there are meandering thugs with backward sunglasses who didn't end up at the casino."

She slipped the strap over her neck, letting it fall across her body. "I walked. I'll be okay."

"Let me walk you home, then."

She cocked her head. "Why? So you can stay three paces behind me and check out my ass?"

"I wasn't—that's not what's happening. Dammit. Are you always this quick to call a man out?" I grabbed a handful of the little chocolate mints by the door and popped one in my mouth.

She shrugged, her long gait already taking her out the door. "Yeah, kind of. Is it too much for your delicate feelings?"

"Obviously not." I scowled.

Instead of taking the sidewalk, she headed through the waterfront park and to the boardwalk spanning to the end of Freedom Bay.

Ahead of us was a group of teens throwing rocks into the muck of a low tide.

"I know I'm a handful, but you look like you've got two hands. Just say you don't have what it takes for me."

The quip stopped me as she walked away. It took me a few moments to catch up.

Summer

SOMEWHERE BETWEEN MY THIRD soda water and lemon and the question about which state invented curling, my knee bumped into Van's. He pulled away quickly, shifting to the other side.

When we were figuring out the tallest dog breed, I tried to lace my fingers with his while giving a high five. By the time the *West Wing* question gave our team the win, the message was clear.

For some reason, Van invited me to the bar to pretend to be his girlfriend but also acted like I was carrying some skin disease.

Even when I confronted him, his excuse of not wanting to be a "sleaze-ball"—a phrase I wouldn't use but nonetheless liked—didn't add up. He was hot and cold with the flirting and innuendos but would then back off. It made no sense.

Before he invited me out, I didn't see him in the days that followed, but when I came home from work three nights later, I noticed wiper blades resting against my front door with a note to put them on immediately.

As infuriating as it was to have him boss me around, there was a minuscule, barely-there rush of excitement in being cared for like that.

But that emotion was best kept under wraps.

After the Cory debacle, I would never get ahead of myself again.

A kind gesture was not loyalty. Flowers were not love. Hour-long Skype calls were not commitment. Oil changes could've meant a lot of things, but I wouldn't believe it was anything but a misplaced sense of chivalry.

Admittedly, my little sedan had been running better since his gesture, not that I'd admit that to Van.

The ebbing tide darkened the silt and barnacle rock shore of Freedom Bay. A whiff of seaweed and salt hung in the stagnant air.

I had nice eyes and a great ass. When I put in some effort, I could look pretty. We definitely had moments where I could tell he was, at least on a surface level, attracted to me. So, what was his damage tonight?

With only a few steps onto the boardwalk, I couldn't hold in my curiosity.

So, I tested him. I couldn't stop grinning as he stared at me.

Out of the corner of my eye, one of his coworkers sat on a bench at the park, a white ring of skunky, pungent weed smoke wisping around her head.

More than willing to use her being near us as an excuse to test him, I waved to her, and she waved back.

Looking annoyed with me, Van stepped closer to me, his T-shirt brushing my bare stomach. "What games are you playing with me?"

Raising my chin, I narrowed my eyes. "I don't know what you're talking about."

"Who's Cory? I saw the messages on your phone. Are you seeing someone else?"

Damn. I had been so distracted by the douchebag at the bar I hadn't thought to check my catfish account for news from Cory. My left foot somehow collided with my right and stumbled at the question.

Van snagged my arm to hold me upright.

His touch seared my bare skin, and I fought the urge to step on my tiptoes and pull his face down for a kiss.

"Huh?"

His thumb traced up my arm, pushing the strap of my dress back up on my shoulder, identical to the night of the party, when I almost flashed the street in my drunken stupor.

Shame flooded my cheeks, and I shook off his clutch and put on my innocent face. "Who?"

"Cory. When you were putting the fear of God in that asshole at the bar, some guy was blowing up your phone. All the same accounts. Cory something."

My shrug was a little overdramatic, but I couldn't compensate for it. "I'm not sure."

"The same account was all over you for several minutes."

I snorted, trying to take my phone, before he put a hand on my wrist.

"We had a deal. Nobody else. No fuck-boy summer. You're supposed to be mine. You need to act like it."

Crossing my arms, I glower at him.

Yeah, I had said that, but for him to act so mercurial in the bar to be jealous was laughable.

"But I'm not yours. This, us"—I motioned between our bodies—"is not real."

Challenge flickered in his eyes.

"Not real, huh?"

He wrapped a tendril of hair around his finger, then pursed his lips as he rubbed the strands with his thumb. "Not real, not mine."

"R-ight." I shuddered as he stepped toward me and wedged a foot between my own.

As I took a step back, he followed me until my butt hit the edge of the railing.

The fading twilight of the light reflected on the low tide of Freedom Bay, and the boardwalk was empty.

Tucking my hair behind my ear, he brushed the shell down to the edge of my jaw. "Not real. I don't know, your body is saying differently."

When he pressed his chest to mine, his heat warmed my thin sundress. His lips brushed my cheek until they met my ear.

My hands tight on the railing behind me, I tipped my head back, my eyes fluttering at the contact.

"That little hitch of your breath, the way your skin flushes tells a different story."

"It's all fake," I murmured, more to myself than him.

Not real, not real.

In my ear, he tsked. "You can't fake this." His hand settled on my hip, squeezing it. "Is the way you press against me fake? How about how perfectly you fit against me? You're telling me if I lifted your skirt right now, I wouldn't you find you drenched for me?"

"No."

My answer was shaky, the weakest response.

A small smile ticked up as his hands slid from my hip to the hem of my dress. There was time enough for me to bat his hand away, to sidestep, to stop the slow tease of his fingers as they traced up my inner thigh to reach my center, but I couldn't bring myself to do it.

"Look at me. This relationship might not be real, but we're not liars to each other, are we?"

I shook my head.

"Who made you this way?"

I let out a shaky exhale, my eyes darting away from his.

I wouldn't lie to him, but I wouldn't admit it either.

He lifted my face with a finger, tilting my face up to meet his gaze. "Answer me."

Those steely eyes on me, the *thud, thud, thud* of my heart in my ears drowning out the bird calls and waves lapping against the rocky shore.

With my lower lip pulled between my teeth, I bit back the answer. "No."

His other finger traced the seam of my underwear, edging under them. "I'm about to prove you wrong, aren't I?"

My silence is enough of an answer as his fingers found me. The hiss he let out as he parted my folds sparked inside me.

"You're fucking drenching my hand, Sunshine. I've barely touched you, and this cunt is begging for me, isn't it?" His eyes on mine, he brought his fingers up to his mouth and sucked them clean. "One taste isn't enough for me."

I couldn't give in and say the words—why would I when his hand was there, proving his point?

His tongue flickered around his finger, and I knew exactly what it would feel like against my clit.

"Fucking kiss me," I demanded.

His lips found mine, teeth clashing. With his hands on my waist, my feet were off the ground and my ass on the railing.

After hiking my dress up around my waist, he shoved his fingers inside me again.

This kiss was sun and melted chocolate. His lips score with my own, he traced his tongue along mine. Pulling me up to wrap my legs around his waist. With my grip tight on his shoulders, he didn't break the kiss. His arms were steel bands behind my back, both clinging me to him and holding me steady on the railing.

He slipped two fingers inside me, thrusting in and out, his thumb flicking over my clit with each motion. I gasped into his mouth, and he rewarded me by going harder.

End this now. It feels too good. End it . . .

I kissed him hard, my legs falling open wider. Between his kiss and his hands on me, I edged closer to climax.

It came on fast, a roaring in my ears as the coil inside me got tighter and tighter until it snapped, and I cried out. I raised a hand to stifle my cry. Sighing into my palm as the wave took me under. His mouth was on my throat, sucking and biting as I shattered. Sagging against him, I felt the railing vibrate under my ass.

No, that's not the railing. It's me. I'm shaking.

In a matter of minutes and with only his hand, Van gave me the best orgasm I had in years. Maybe ever.

"Let me take you home," he whispered against my neck.

Home. My life. My plans. I couldn't do this.

He didn't want serious. Van was clear on his expectations. While I had no issues with occasional flings, this utter lack of common sense the moment his lips touched mine was bad news. There was no room for sex when I was in the middle of my revenge. I could've gotten feelings mixed up and do something stupid, like fall for Van. I refused to be foolish over a man again.

Pulling back, I pushed his chest, sliding to my feet.

He let me go, his hand still on my waist.

A pulse *thud, thud, thudded* at my core, and all I wanted to do was pull him down on top of me and have him fill me up here on this splintered boardwalk.

I can't. I won't.

Stepping farther away, I moved the strap of my purse in front of me as a shield. "I need to finish this walk home alone." He opened his mouth, and I shook my head. "Please, Van."

A muscle in his jaw flexed. "No can do." When I tried to argue, he put up his hands in surrender. "You want to walk five paces in front of me so I can check out your ass, or you can walk beside me? I won't touch you. I won't talk to you if you don't want me to. But I'm seeing you home safe. What'll it be?"

Rolling my eyes, I turned from him. My skin still flush from my orgasm, I stalked away.

His footsteps pattered behind me.

As we got off the boardwalk and onto the concrete pathway through the trees, I slowed my pace until he was beside me.

Thousands of competing thoughts clouded my head as we walked. I was no stranger to fooling around. But there was an edge to Van's embrace that made me want more than either of us could give. While I was never the kind of girl who only did long-term monogamy, I also couldn't be content with no strings if that's how he'd be touching me.

In his embrace, I was wanton and messy and dirty for wanting more. But, also, I had never felt as powerful. He had met each dip of my kiss, going harder, giving me more when I needed it.

But this could never be real. And I couldn't get distracted by a beautiful man, even if he knew how to pull my hair just right.

I was determined to see Cory's demise through. Once I set my mind to something, I had to finish it.

Keeping some space with Van was the right call.

I took the wooden staircase up to the street level, Van a step behind me. True to his words, he didn't say a thing, his hands shoved in the pockets of his jeans.

I kept my hand tight on the strap of my bag as if it would protect me from the heat and wonderful musk of the man to my right.

Even without words, without his touch, he made me want things I couldn't have. Things that would only lead to humiliation. If he wasn't so good-looking or was stupid or didn't love the same show as me, maybe I could get over it. But this perfectly packaged man appears in my life, and I'm not supposed to want him?

"You never said who that Cory guy was."

Stopping beside the monument for fallen warriors of the Korean War, I glared up at him. "You probably don't know this, but women get unsolicited messages all the time. It's a fact of life. I can't be held responsible for every random man who asks me to be his sugar baby."

"That doesn't happen to all women."

His eyes were a grim steel.

"And you would know?" Annoyed, I glared at him and crossed my arms. "Every single friend of mine has gotten them. If you are a woman on social media, it's happened to you. The other day, my cousin Autumn posted a picture of her in dirty overalls and rain boots on the beach on a clean-up day and some guy commented, 'Nice tits.'"

"That's—"

"Besides, even if I had some guy I was talking to, you can't get jealous. You're not really my boyfriend, are you?" I raised a brow and dared him to contradict me.

A tiny spark of something flashed inside me, but I ignored it.

When his eyes slid away from mine, I nodded, and the spark died.

"If someone is bothering you, tell me, and I'll take care of it." He flexed his jaw as if he was preparing himself for some showdown between him and a shadowed army.

I frowned. "I can take care of myself. You don't need to swoop in with some misguided sense of justice, thinking you're saving me. I'm not some dainty princess. Why don't you worry a little more about yourself and less about the messages some basement dweller is sending me?"

The last thing I needed was for Van to get wind of my schemes. He could never understand what I was going through.

I patted him on the shoulder. "Thanks for the concern, though."

Before he could say much else, I trotted ahead of him.

"I'm sorry. My question came out wrong. All I ask is, tell me if there is someone else."

When he caught up with me, it was with a conciliatory tone.

"There's no one else, Van. Honestly, right now, *you* are too much."

His face broke into a wide grin.

"Sunshine, I bet I'd fit just right for you."

Ignoring the come-on, I picked up the pace.

He walked me up the stairs to my apartment, remembering which one was mine from that disaster of a first fake date.

As I unlocked the door, he leaned against the bumpy, spackled blue-gray wall.

"Are you going to invite me in?" He quirked a dark brow.

How I wanted to. The way he would hold my head by the nape, the sweet sting as his lips would find mine. The soft rustle of our clothes falling onto my hallway floor as we would make our way to the bedroom. His heavy weight as he would press me into the mattress, the suck of his mouth and the scrape of his teeth as they would travel down my body.

Wetness pooled between my thighs. It would be so easy—effortless, really.

"Ask me to come inside, Summer." His thumb traced the line of my jaw.

My eyes must have shown my thoughts because he leaned in closer, his sweet breath caressing my face.

"We can finish what we started." He curled his fingers tighter on the nape of my neck, his words a rough vow.

I wrapped my hand around his, squeezed it once, then pulled it off. "I can't. We can call that kiss an overzealous had-too-many-drinks thing."

"That was more than a kiss, and you only had one drink."

"I can't." I hoped my tone was firm enough. "As simple as that. I'm not some random girl you picked up for a good time. You have your reasons for needing me, and I have mine for saying no."

He took the rejection in stride. Most of the men I had experience with would have been pleading, trying to guilt trip me, or—worst of all—gotten angry.

"Next week, the weather is supposed to be good. I was going to take my buddy and his family out on the boat. Why don't you come with us?"

I narrowed my eyes. "A boat? What about your foot?"

He shrugged. "It's a few stitches. I'm sure I'll be fine."

"Is this some girlfriend thing? What do you want me to wait on you? Wear a little outfit?"

"This isn't about being my girlfriend. This is just fun. You wear whatever you want. Though"—he tilted his head as his gaze traveled down my body—"I can't say I wouldn't mind seeing you in a bikini."

As much as I wanted to falter under his piercing stare, I couldn't show a moment of wavering.

I smiled widely, winking. "I don't know if you could handle it."

He placed a hand over his heart and pretended to stumble back. "Oh, stop. You can't do that to an injured man."

"You'll be fine, Hot Rod." Shoving the keys back in my purse, I held onto the doorframe. "I don't think being alone is a good idea."

"We won't be alone. It's going to be me, Xander, Ana—you met her already—and their baby, Max. No funny business. Just water and sunshine."

Wrapping an arm around my chest, I considered him.

On one hand, it was a terrible idea to be alone with Van. On the other, I loved being on the water. Wren had gotten terrible seasickness, so as a group, we rarely made trips that involved water.

He bent down, and I thought he was going to try to kiss me again. But his mouth found my ear. His words hot and low. "I'm getting better at reading when your body language says yes."

He tugged my lobe with his teeth, scraping gently.

My knees felt weak, and my breath came out shaky. I had to will myself not to steady my hands on his wide shoulders.

When he pulled away, he wore a satisfied smirk I wanted to smack off his face but also kiss senseless.

To his back, I called out, "I didn't say yes."

He waved, already a flight down the stairwell. "Sure you did, Sunshine."

An hour later, I was resolute that my desire for Van was nothing more than a distraction.

I had a plan, which was solidified when my phone chimed again.

Sure enough, it was Cory.

As I changed into an all-black outfit, I responded.

Cory: Hey baeutiful

Candy: Heyyyy!1!

Cory: I love that picture of the mountains. Do you ski?

The picture in question had Candy on a mountain with a lake beneath. I had hesitated posting it, since the AI had screwed up the lettering on the jacket, but hoped it was too small for Cory to tell that it looked like a mixture between Russian, Greek, and hieroglyphics.

I was smearing the double entendre a bit thick. Hopefully, he would think with his dick and not get suspicious.

His response was quick, and it was easy to get him interested—after all, I knew his likes and dislikes to a T. As the conversation got more flirty, I screenshot every exchange, every wink, every *you're so hot* comment, and when he mentioned he was single and lied about where he worked.

He made it all too easy. His hubris would bring him down.

That made the next part of my plan all the easier to implement. Cory still was as big of a jerk as always. I wasn't special to him, and neither was his Kodi.

No, he deserved every bit of of his comeuppance.

The drive from my apartment to his neighborhood was mostly silent, punctuated by the occasional message from Cory.

He was falling for it so easily it was laughable. For a self-proclaimed smart man, you'd think he'd be suspicious when one of the bikini pictures of Candy featured four fingers on one hand and two thumbs on the other. I had thought it was only people my dad's age who fell for AI art, but apparently, twenty-nine-year-old cheaters did, too.

In Cory's neighborhood, staple gun in hand, I took great pleasure in the *thwack* of metal into the wooden pole.

Stepping back, I admired the craftsmanship Devin put into the flyer. Emblazoned across the top read:

Person of interest in the disappearance of Ranger!!!

Last seen at our home on Frigga Lane with this man!!

I placed a stock photo of a beagle beside a terrible Facebook picture of Cory. In smaller print below was a brief description.

Ranger is a five-year-old beagle. He was seen in our fenced yard on the afternoon of 6/2. This man was seen approaching our yard, and our dog has been missing ever since.

If you have any information about this disappearance or know the location of our beloved family pet, please call this number.

I included the Google number I had set up for the occasion.

Printed on bright yellow paper, the flyers would stand out on every telephone pole.

I started on the street I recalled had multiple new residents, five streets away from Cory's house. Far enough that most would see the flyer immediately before it was removed and close enough that they would see him in passing.

On my way home from the neighborhood, I stopped at the mail drop, sliding in the bright pink postcard addressed to Cory, confirming his follow-up treatment for chlamydia was on June seventeenth.

Content with my work well done, I made my way home to my knitting and vampire romance audiobook.

I was feeling bloodthirsty indeed.

Fourteen

Summer

Aʟʟ ᴡᴇᴇᴋ ʟᴏɴɢ, I was working twelve- to fourteen-hour shifts at the hotel. We had guest disputes, a server who quit midshift, and the ever-present *Why was I charged thirty dollars for a movie?*—because someone in your room ordered a porno.

After each day, I would collapse on the couch, exhausted and barely able to turn on *The West Wing*.

What I wasn't too tired to check on, was the unfolding drama of the mystery dog-napper. I didn't have to wait long for someone to post on the Ridgewood Community page after the flyer. People in the comments thanked the poster for alerting the public, while some thought it was unfair to accuse a man with no proof. Whether they were on his side, everyone seemed to think it was real.

I didn't need Cory to get in trouble. No Ranger existed to have been stolen, after all. But it seemed to amp up the fear of outsiders that most old-time Ridgewoodians had.

That nosy neighbor, Mrs. Partridge, had even commented, *My prayers to Ranger's family.*

I snorted when I read that.

Since it was only one of many, I enjoyed the discourse around it, the comment section soaring to over one hundred before an admin shut it off. All the busybodies in Ridgewood would talk about this, with the suspicious cars and the rumors of paid parking on Front Street.

It was my first day off in days, and I was frozen in front of my dresser, the weight of too many decisions heavy on me. Namely, what should one wear when going on the boat of a man they barely knew? Particularly when that man had broad shoulders and piercing gray eyes who insisted on changing your oil and walking you home from the bar?

After the trivia night, he would check in on me and updated me on his foot, while I sent him a picture of the blanket I was making.

It was all innocent. I could almost convince myself that the funny feeling between my legs when he leaned in close to me was all in my head. That the kiss we shared on that boardwalk was a little mistake, not to be repeated.

Still, I tried on all my suits while deciding which was best. Would I go with the neon green string bikini from a girl's trip to Puerto Plata or the sensible black one-piece I had reserved for water parks to avoid flashing everyone while going down the Cascade Scream Drop?

I pulled out a boring suit, a pale pink gingham print in a short tank style with a little ruffle along the bust and matching high-waisted bottoms.

I deliberated over wearing a dress or shorts and a T-shirt, then settled on the latter. Once I pulled the Ridgewood Marine Science Center tee I had commandeered from Autumn a few months before over my head, I got the chime of a text letting me know Van was in the lot, waiting for me, who had offered to drive so I wouldn't have to find parking at the marina.

I grabbed my bag, sunscreen, towel, and a small wallet and headed the three floors down.

Van was sitting in his green truck, with his arm sticking out the window. In the back was a small cooler and another bag with towels in it.

"Where's the boat?" I asked as I climbed in.

"Already in the water. I had Xander help me put it in an hour ago, so you don't have to wait on me."

"That was nice of you."

He chuckled. "To be honest, Ana told us that was the only way she'd come, so it was Xander's idea. He's going to grab her and the baby now."

We drove toward the edge of town to the marina. The air was unseasonably warm for the Pacific Northwest, forecasted to hit the mid-nineties by noon.

"Baby?"

He flicked on his turn signal in the left lane and glanced at me. "Yeah, I guess she's not technically a baby. She's like one or two or something. Max, super cute kid."

In theory, I liked babies but didn't have much experience with them. My cousins with kids lived too far away, and aside from one friend who had a kid at seventeen, no others had any yet.

The pressure to be good with this mystery child was heavy on me. What if I wasn't looking and it fell overboard? Was this some test?

Once we got to the marina, he strolled to the passenger side door to let me out, but I had already hopped down, bag in hand. The walk from the truck to the dock was subdued with the waves lapping at the boats and the distant barking of harbor seals who sunned themselves on a float.

As we reached the metal grate, Van's phone rang. He frowned at it, answering.

Whoever was on the other line, he spoke to quickly, assuring them it was fine, and he hoped everyone felt better. After disconnecting, he slid the phone back into his pocket.

"That was Xander. Max threw up. They can't make it."

The timing felt suspect.

I frowned at him. "Are you trying to get me alone on the water to murder me?"

He blinked in surprise. "What? No. If you don't want to go boating alone with me, you don't have to. I really did invite them. Xander helped me put the boat in. You can call him and ask. Or better yet, call Ana."

While I had been led astray by my instincts before, something told me he was being truthful.

I pursed my lips. "Alright, just know I already told Autumn and Devin what I'm doing today, so if I go missing, you're for sure getting fired."

"Noted." He quirked a smile at me, waving for me to go first down the ramp. "We won't waste a beautiful day like this, will we? The sun is shining. I have sandwiches and chips packed already. A few beers on the open seas."

"Technically, this is a fjord. Formed by glaciers."

I regretted my words immediately. I had no reason to be pedantic.

He raised a brow at the correction and smiled bigger. "A few beers on the open fjords and a lovely lady at the helm."

I shook my head, hiding my smile.

The boat was a cuddy cabin model. It was older, with fading blue paint on the sides, but clean.

Van grabbed the side, bringing it toward the dock. "Your ship awaits." He reached out to help me step onto it.

Swinging my leg over the side, I stepped on the white leather bench seat in the rear.

His thumb traced the back of my hand, and a sizzle traveled up my arm and down to my core. Barely on the boat, I knew this day was already testing my resolve to not dry hump Van.

Once on, I set my bag down and glanced around.

I had been on boats before. Wren's asshole ex had one he used to bring us on. He would speed around lakes, while a seasick Wren would struggle to keep down the contents in her stomach.

On the dock, Van untied the ropes and flung them into the boat before pushing off the dock and jumping in. Setting his stuff down, he gathered a small florescent item and lifted the bench seat to place it in there. "Don't need that anymore."

"You have a kid's life jacket on your boat when you don't have kids?" I paused. "You don't have any, right?"

He laughed. "No kids of my own, no. I knew I'd have to be outfitted if I had any chance of getting Ana and Xander on board. It's good to have anyway. You never know."

I nodded as if that made sense, but my mind continued whirring.

He handed me a green item. "Put this on."

I took it from him, holding it away from me. "I know how to swim."

He frowned. "Try it on and tighten the straps. I want to make sure it fits you before we go."

Rolling my eyes, I pulled it over my shoulders and tried fastening the buckle. After pulling the straps out, I tried again to no avail.

When he saw I was struggling, Van grabbed a different life vest and handed it to me. No comment on the size, no joke about how it didn't fit, just concentration as he helped it slide over my shoulders. "I take aquatic safety seriously. I was a lifeguard at the Ridgewood pool for five years." He gripped the bottom, sliding the zipper together. His fingers brushed the bare skin of my stomach, and an ache between my legs formed.

Once he was content, he tossed the life jackets into the empty cabin and directed me to sit in the pilot's chair.

We floated away slowly as he started the engine.

Soon, we were out of the no-wake zone and passing a float of harbor seals.

The sunshine warmed my cheeks as the boat picked up speed, the wind blowing my hair back.

Freedom Bay was glassy smooth as we made our way out of the narrow channel and into the wider sound.

I held on tight to the edge of my white leather pilot's chair as we cut through the water, the outline of the Olympic mountains soaring above us to the west.

Beside me, Van stood behind the steering wheel, salty gusts whipping his dark hair off his face. He glanced at me and smiled, and I unraveled.

In books, authors would describe a smile as devastating. I never understood that phrase. Never in all my years of dating, of the men and women I flirted with, did I ever suffer more than little butterflies from a smile. A smile could be charming, suave, or shy. But I clung to the belief that I was far too sensible to be caught up by a *smile*.

Until that day on the boat.

When Van smiled at me, his whole face lit up, his mouth crooked to the right. His gray eyes crinkled at the corners, and his cheeks stretched to show a dimple on his left side.

Fucking dimple.

The breath I let out was shaky, and I had to swallow to fight the rising urge to lick my lips.

I had seen him smile before, with his little smirks and friendly grins. But this?—Oh, this, what he gave me, sucked the air from my lungs.

There was no reason I could know this, but I did. That smile was for me and me alone. The whooshing of the wind died, and all I wanted—no, *needed*—was for Van to smile at me like that again. To assure me that I was the only one.

At some point, he cut the engine, letting us drift around in the tides. I moved to the back bench seat, stretching out. Without the sea spray and rushing air, the sunshine was balmy on my skin.

Abandoning my sandals, I wiggled my bare toes as I tipped my head back against the padded bench.

Van fished a beer out of the cooler and handed it to me. I popped the top and brought it to my mouth when Van reached behind his head and pulled his shirt off.

I knew he had a nice body, having felt enough of it pressed against me on the boardwalk. But nothing could have prepared me for the sight of him, sun-soaked and strong. A smattering of dark hair covered his chest, and his shoulders were broad and muscular. A faint pink scar about three inches long marred his right collarbone. His wasn't the body of someone who spent all their time at the gym, sculpted and lean. Instead, it was sturdy. The kind you could wrap your arms around, and it would keep you steady.

With the can almost at my lips, I froze.

He glimpsed me, his brow furrowed.

Huffing loudly, I chugged half the can and looked away. Somehow, I willed my cheeks not to flame red at being caught ogling him.

He had to know what he looked like, right? I wouldn't be the first woman to stare open-mouthed at his man.

Either he was polite enough not to call me on it, or he didn't notice my absolutely batshit response to his bare chest.

Turning the pilot's chair to face me, he stretched his feet out to rest alongside mine.

He had nice toes. I never thought I'd notice a man's toes, but I did.

He tipped his head back, his eyes closed, the sun bright on his face.

Well, if he can take his shirt off, so can I.

Tossing it to the side, I watched him open one eye and then another. A muscle ticked in his jaw as he looked me over.

"Fuck me." He murmured so low I knew he didn't mean for me to hear it. His tongue darted out to wet his lips, and he let out a big sigh.

I smirked, laying back on the bench. Content with torturing him the way he was with me, I closed my eyes.

Small waves splashed against the boat, creating a sense of serenity. Somewhere in the distance, a horn sounded, and birds called to one another. The ambiance lulled me, and my thoughts drifted away.

The rocking of the boat had my eyes snapping open, a dull buzz in my brain signaling I hadn't just rested my eyes but had fallen asleep. Weird.

Falling asleep in front of a man was never something I enjoyed doing. At Cory's, I couldn't fall asleep until he did, waiting until his breathing became snores before I'd allow my mind to rest.

But this was the second time Van had seen me sleeping. I couldn't think too hard about that.

I blinked the mid-afternoon film from my eyes and rolled over on my side to look at Van.

With a can of soda in one hand, he raised the other at a passing boat. Likely the reason ours teetered in the wake.

"How long was I out?" I asked, my voice scratchy with sleep.

"Fifteen minutes? Something like that."

I sat up, rubbing my face. "Sorry, I didn't mean to doze off. I guess the long hours finally got to me."

He shrugged, a small grin playing up his features. "I don't mind. You're cute when you're sleeping."

"As opposed to what?" I arched a brow, pulling myself up to sit.

He threw his head back and laughed at my haughty expression. "Oh, no. You're not trapping me like that. Don't act like you don't know you're beautiful."

Heat that had nothing to do with the high noon sun warmed my cheeks. It certainly wasn't the first time someone had said those words to me. But his absolute confidence in not only finding me beautiful but knowing that I, too, knew it was a shock.

It was with a sad realization I recalled that most men used compliments like this as a gateway to get what they wanted. As if they were the only ones who could see me that way.

But not Van. He not only appreciated how I looked, but he was glad I was secure in myself. It was a rare thing.

"Switching to soda?" I motioned to his hand.

"I have a buddy who got a BUI. Trying to be careful here."

The word sounded like "buoy."

"A what?" I laughed.

"B-U-I. Boating under the influence. BUI."

A brow raised, I assessed him. "That's responsible."

He shrugged. "Well, I'm an adult. Plus, I have precious cargo."

He winked at me, and a flutter flared between my legs. If I were reading it in my historical romances, I would have used "loins."

He handed me another drink.

As I took it, I noticed it was my favorite flavor of a small craft brand. This wasn't one you could buy at any store but would have to drive to the next town and get it from their taphouse.

"I bet you say that to all the girls." I took a sip of the huckleberry-flavored drink.

"Only the ones I can't stop thinking about." A grin crossed his lips, a playful glint in his eyes.

I gulped the cold drink, trying in vain to cool myself down from the heat of his gaze.

"Don't play with me, Van. I'm serious. I'm not some silly girl for you to jerk around."

"Who's playing?" He leaned forward. His feet planted on the floor of the boat, his elbows on his knees as he grew serious. "Seems to me you're the one in charge here. Walking onto my boat in those little shorts and that smart mouth that's begging to be kissed."

"I don't want to kiss you. What happened the other night was a—"

He shook his head at me, tsking. "No, we won't do that. No lying to me, okay?" He moved to the bench and leaned over me.

Moving my ankles from the bench, he placed them on the floor, my feet touching his upper thigh.

I should've told him to move away from me. This was perilous. I wouldn't want him this way, not now. But I couldn't bring myself to back down.

I tugged my shorts down over my legs and tossed them onto the pilot seat. My eyes bored into his as he watched me, the corner of his mouth pulled up in a small grin.

I shrugged. "Okay. No lying. Got it."

Leaning closer, he braced a hand on each side of me. My head fell back against the padded rest. Poised over me, his thick thighs wedged between my own, his breath hot on me.

Only my thin suit and his board shorts separated us.

My face inches from his, I stared into his determined eyes as he said, "I mean it. Promise me that, whatever happens, we won't lie to each other."

I couldn't think of words. His muscles flexed between my legs as he held himself over me.

"Now, if you don't want to tell me something, that's fine. Tell me it's none of my business, and that will be it. But don't lie."

"Same for you." My words were more solemn. "You don't tell me what I want to hear. Or whatever it would take to get into my pants."

He threw his head back, laughing, the long cords of his throat straining.

Against the blue and white of the sky, he looked like something out of an early aughts ad campaign for an All-American clothing brand.

"Sunshine, I wouldn't have to say a word to get into your pants."

Most women would giggle at that, bat their lashes, blush. But I squared my shoulders, a smirk playing at the corner of his lips.

The twinge between my legs manifested into a ticking bomb. I resisted the urge to close my legs. I wasn't about to give him that satisfaction.

"You think I'm that easy?"

An edge of challenge laced my tone.

"No, darling. I'm just that good."

The pulse quickened between my legs. Dear Lord, I could almost believe him. At the very least, he believed it of himself. Damn if that confidence wasn't sexy in a man. Especially in one who hadn't said anything about himself he couldn't prove later.

"So, do something about it."

His mouth found mine as he pressed me into the foam bench. Tracing the seam of my mouth, his tongue begged for entry.

My hands roamed over his backside, pulling him harder against me, his full, rigid length grinding into my center.

As his kiss deepened, his hips moved, rubbing the delicate place that needed him.

I moaned into his mouth, and he trailed kisses down my cheek, down my throat, and down the hollow of my collarbone.

"You're driving me crazy with this suit, you know that?" he whispered against my throat.

"It's nothing special," I breathed out, wrapping my legs around his waist.

"It's everything. The pastel, so innocent-looking on that body." He groaned and pushed harder against my core. "So fucking sweet. I want to peel it off and feast on you."

"If this is how you react to a boring old tank suit, what would you have done if I had worn my string bikini?"

His breath hitched as he stared down at my body.

"Dear God, I can't even handle that image right now."

He scraped the soft skin of my throat with his teeth, and I tightened my grip around his waist. His hands on my breasts, he pulled down the front of my suit. One popped free, and he took one into his mouth. With a light stroke of his tongue, the air cooled my damp skin bared to the summer sky. A nip of his teeth shot sparks from my aching breasts to my clit, and I whimpered.

"Oh my fucking God," I gasped out. Guiding his head with my hands in his hair, I held him steady as I brought my hips up to rub against his cock.

My bikini bottom was so thin he could've easily pushed it to the side and slid right into me.

Dragging his teeth over to my other breast, more aggressive, he scraped and sucked. "How long I've thought about you like this? How are you this perfect?"

I didn't have a moment to think about his words before he slid my bottoms off and put his mouth on my clit. His fingers delved between my folds, parting me. As his mouth worked on my clit, his fingers swirled around, hitting that spot on the front that always makes me shudder.

He had talented fingers.

"Your cunt tastes like sunshine." He groaned against my inner thigh. With his free hand, he dug them into my ass cheeks, bringing me deeper into him.

My hands were in his hair. Whether I had been pulling or pushing, I couldn't tell.

My climax built inside me, conjuring indiscernible murmurs. The familiar cacophony of waves, birds, and ferry horns became white noise to the sensations coursing through me.

Van's tongue swirled around my clit, sucking it in rhythm with his fingers, and I cried out. As I fell apart in his arms, he held me on the bench.

Senses floated back to me slowly. First, the kiss of wind on my exposed body, then the pressure of his face resting against me, still between my legs.

"Come home with me. Come home, and I'll take care of you all night."
His gray eyes melted me, heat still flooding through me. He pressed a kiss
to the delicate skin of my inner thigh.

It's a bad idea. Bad, terrible, treacherous, but I can't say no.

I nodded at him, and his smile turned triumphant, the promise of more
and the assurance of nothing. It's sin and sex, and while this choice would
make it hurt all the more when he stuck to his word, nothing could make
me refuse him.

He climbed over my naked form again, kissing me. With his hand in my
hair, he pressed the ridge of his hard cock against my clit.

"Do you need me to—" I motioned to the sizable issue in his shorts.

His smirk had me conflicted.

"No. Let me have something to look forward to."

As he climbed off me, air grazed my exposed flesh, a reminder of how
bare I was to the radiant sky.

As I dressed, he went back behind the wheel to start up the engine.

As the water behind us frothed like churned milk, less than a minute
later, he hit the throttle, and we headed back to the port.

We moved from the wide expanse of Puget Sound to the narrower
passages between land. On our left was the town of Illahee and to our right,
the posh island of Manzanita, home of millionaires, California transplants,
and—if rumors are to be believed—the summer homes of members of the
rock band Prevalent Notion.

Van motioned for me to join him at the front, letting go of the wheel.
His hand on my waist, he positioned me behind it.

"Have you ever driven a boat before?"

I shook my head.

As a child, my father and my uncle Victor would go out crabbing with
my older boy cousins, while Autumn and I got left behind. The urge to
drive a boat, even a little cuddy cabin like this one, never occurred to me.

But I had to admit it was a rush to grasp the wheel and cut through the water, the sizzling heat cooling in the rush of salty air over my face.

He rested his hands on my hips, pulling my ass into his still-hard cock. As we sliced through the blue-green waves, his mouth trailed to my ear, telling me all the dirty things he wanted to do to me back at his house.

He moved to the front of my unbuttoned shorts, playing with the seam of my bottoms. "Could you keep the boat straight while I touch you here?"

My grip tightened as he eased one finger inside me, then another. His thumb traced over my clit.

Still sensitive from the orgasm, I felt the tension coiling from the slightest touch.

Leaning back against him, I let my eyes drift shut.

His hard cock rubbed against my ass as his fingers moved in and out, taking me closer to another climax.

Across the waterway, another boat passed but was too far away, but the knowledge that other people were out on the water while Van was knuckle-deep inside me thrilled me.

If I had known how to cut the engine, I would have done so, turned on my feet, and sat him in that pilot's chair to ride him—condom or not.

I pulled his hand out of my suit and placed it on the steering wheel. Turning my body to face him, I made sure his arms were on each side of me.

I'm short enough. He could see over my head.

"Keep your hands on the steering wheel," I ordered.

"What are y—"

Sliding down his stomach, I moved down to his cock. I palmed it, gripping it under the thin fabric.

"I don't think—fuck."

When his hand fell from the wheel, I tutted at him. "Hand on the wheel, Hot Rod. I've got you."

Grabbing the front of his shorts, I pulled his cock free and kept my eyes on him as I spit into my hand.

The tendons in his arm tensed as he cursed under his breath.

I slid my hand up and down, gripping tight.

He tilted his head down to watch my motion.

I shook my head, pausing. "Eyes on the water. Keep us straight, and I'll keep going."

Tightening one hand, I used the other to cup his balls, my short nails running along the area behind them.

His arms were a barricade around me as I stroked him, faster and faster. Soon after, he cursed and came, the substance spurting over our stomachs.

Sticky on me, it dripped down my torso, and I brought a little up to my mouth, licking it off my finger.

With one hand, he slowed the boat, while still keeping us straight, his eyes molten on me.

"You're going to kill me," he whispered.

"But what a way to go, right?"

He let out a low, derisive chuckle. "I have never met someone so dangerous for me."

I smirked at him. "Good. I'd hate to be boring."

The familiar skyline of downtown Ridgewood approached as we came into Freedom Bay.

"The things I'm going to do to you tonight. You're going to wish you never tempted me."

"Is that a challenge?" I crooked a brow.

"It's a promise. And remember what I said. *We don't lie to each other.*"

In the small cupholder beside the seat, an odd chirping rang from his phone.

He dropped his playful expression and the hand that was holding me between the wheel and his body.

A message that read *I need you* flashed in my vision, but I couldn't see anything else on it.

A muscle ticked in his jaw, and his once molten gaze cooled.

"Change of plans." He tossed his phone back in the cupholder and turned the boat toward the marina.

Van

SERVICE ON THE BAY was too spotty for the repeated calls to get through, despite calling several times.

When we got back, I paid the exorbitant fee to dock my boat in a guest slip.

Summer followed me to the truck, and I helped her up into the cab, then dialed again to be sent to voicemail.

I need you.

I need you.

Cursing under my breath, I got behind the wheel, and we took off.

I pictured her lying on the floor, her wheelchair across the room. Bleeding from a head injury. Would she have called 9-1-1 if she was hurt? She could be so damn stubborn sometimes.

"So, what, you're ditching me for some random girl? Was my hand job not enough for you?" she asked, her arms folded over her chest.

"Your what?" I blinked at her. "What are you talking about?"

"Whoever that girl you have of your roster that just hit you up. I saw it. *I need you.* If you want to fuck around with some girl, just tell me. Saves me the embarrassment of fucking you when you have a dozen others lined up."

"You think—" I tried to process her odd jealousy. "That was my mom."

"Oh." The fight vanished. "Well—" Her cheeks flamed pink. "How was I supposed to know that?"

I snorted, turning the car to the right. "You could have asked."

"Oh yeah, like you'd tell me."

"Why wouldn't I?"

She blinked at me as if I were speaking another language. "I can come with if you want. That way you don't have to battle rush-hour traffic downtown to get me home."

"You want to meet my mom?" I raised a brow.

"I'm great with parents. Mothers love me. One of my exes? His mom still sends me a Christmas card every year."

The last girl I had brought around my mom was my prom date. A shy redhead who ended up leaving the dance with her girlfriends halfway through. I later found out she had an older boyfriend her parents didn't approve of.

"Alright." I turned toward the other side of town.

I let myself in the door, prepared for a bloodbath of her sprawled on the floor and howling in pain.

Instead, I found her on her back patio watering her favorite red geranium.

"Mom."

She glanced up at me, setting the water can by her side, and her face broke into a wide smile, her gray eyes so similar to my own, wrinkling at the corners. "Donovan, what are you doing here?"

Waving my phone around, I scoffed. "You texted me *I need you.* I came as soon as I saw it."

Mom furrowed her brow, turning in her chair. "I said I need you to pick up more of those mint chocolate balls next time you go to the store. I ate them all last night while binge-watching that show with the underwear model chef."

Ignoring her lusty comments about men half her age, I retorted, "No, you said I need you. I called you four times, trying to get through."

Once inside, she grabbed her phone off a side table and scrolled through it. "I'll be damned." She glanced up and grinned. "Well. You're here now. How about you introduce me to this lovely lady who's hovering around you, looking confused?"

Behind me, Summer tapped her nails against each other on one hand but fisted her hands once before stepping forward and thrusting the other out.

"Hi, I'm Summer. Nice to meet you—" She glanced at me, probably confused by what name my mom went by.

My mom took her hand in hers, covering it with both hands. "Glyndon Logan. Call me Glyn."

Summer's smile got wider.

"Glyn. It's so great to meet you. Van has told me so many things about you."

Mom glanced over at me, a mischievous glint on her face. "Has he? Well, come have a seat while he makes us some coffee, and tell me everything you've heard."

As Summer settled into the floral print couch, she angled her legs to face my mom, who parked herself beside the couch.

Bouncing on the balls of my feet, I watched as Summer asked my mom about the show she was watching the night before.

A few minutes later, Mom glanced at me and frowned. "Where's our coffee, Donovan?"

My cheeks heated, and Summer bit her lip to force back a smile.

"Right away."

Once in the kitchen, I grumbled to myself as I rummaged her cabinets.

Everything had to be low for my mom to access independently, so I had to stoop.

Through the small cutaway between the kitchen and living room, I listened as Summer was telling her about her job at the hotel. Mom described the last time we went to a restaurant and how difficult it was for her to maneuver around the tightly packed tables with her chair. Summer nodded and laughed when Mom mentioned she had bumped a chair and caused a meatball to roll across the floor because the server wouldn't help her through a tight spot.

"Serves them right." Summer agreed. "If I were you, I would have flattened the meatball into the carpet with my wheel."

"Don't think I wasn't tempted."

Holding two mugs of coffee, I came out of the kitchen and set them down for the ladies.

I sat beside Summer on the couch, my arm alongside the back, fingers dangling above her shoulder.

Mom sipped from the mug, grimaced, then set the drink down. "Sweetie, you know I love you, but you really need to learn how to make a decent cup of coffee. This is like sex in a canoe."

Beside me, Summer blinked as if trying to make sense of that comment.

I groaned, then whispered, "Fucking too close to water."

"Damn straight," Mom barked before taking another sip and setting it down on the side table. "It'll do for now, though. Now, tell me how you two met." She narrowed her eyes, assessing me. "Let me guess, it was about six weeks ago? Am I right?"

Summer sucked in a breath between her teeth and glanced at me in surprise. "Did you—"

"No, I didn't say a thing." Somehow, my mother was as shrewd as ever. I shook my head. "Mom."

"I am, aren't I?" She clapped her hands together in triumph. "I knew a little something was going on. A mother knows these things. Tell me, tell me. This place gets so boring."

With a raised brow, I shot Summer a glance. "Go ahead. I'd love to hear you tell the story."

Pulling her lower lip between her teeth, she seemed to be considering how much truth she wanted to tell and tapped her nails together before fisting her hands. "I ended up in the neighborhood, for reasons that aren't important." She shot me a warning glare. "And it started raining, so I sought refuge in Van's—oops—I guess it's *your* house. Only the door was unlocked, so I kind of let myself in. Van found me in the hallway as I waited for my ride. I'm lucky he didn't call the cops on me."

"I'm still considering it."

Strictly speaking, Summer told the truth about our first meeting, but there was something more. She said it wasn't important why she was in the neighborhood, but no way was that the case. I didn't need to know her life story if she didn't want to tell it. But a part of me, at the very least, wanted to know that whatever I got from her was true.

I saw her that day, and the more I got to know her, the more I could tell she had been through something upsetting. I was no detective, but every day spent with her, it was getting easier to put the pieces together in a muddy narrative.

Mom raised a brow at the story but didn't question Summer.

Summer's phone rang, and she excused herself onto the back patio.

The sliding door hadn't been shut for more than a second before my mom said, "You really like this girl."

Leaning back against the couch, I scowled at her. "It's not serious."

"Not serious. You brought her here, didn't you?"

"Because I thought you had an emergency. It wasn't intentional."

Mom hummed in disagreement. "Don't act like you aren't crazy about that girl. I see the way you look at her. Reminds me of my younger years."

"Sorry if I don't trust your judgment, since the last person you dated was Rick," I retorted, then cursed myself for the comment. Scrubbing my face with my hand, I rested my elbows on my knees.

"You're not your father, Donovan. Rick was—*is*—a complicated man. I knew that when I married him."

"And yet you stayed. After everything he did."

Mom pointed at me, her tone sharp. "You don't get to judge me for my choices. Your father is not evil, just weak. He couldn't handle my sickness, so he pulled away. It happens."

I snorted. "Right. Just like how he fell into his assistant's vagina."

Mom quirked a smirk at that comment. "He's not perfect. But no one is. But I made mistakes, too."

"Don't make excuses for him."

"I'm not. I knew who I married. Did you know that tart he's been dating wants to marry him?"

I blinked at this news, trying not to let it hurt.

Until she said the words, I hadn't recognized the little spot inside me that wished my parents would've stuck together.

"But he won't do it. Not while his insurance is covering my care. We might not love each other anymore, but your father is not the monster you're making him out to be. It's not black and white. He may have missed the faithful part of the vows, but he's supporting me in his own way."

"I'm not forgiving him. In my opinion, he abandoned you."

Mom shrugged. "And you came home to me. I've made my peace with your father. Lord knows I would never want to be married again, washing another man's dirty socks? No, thank you. But this way, at least, I'm provided for. You don't have to forgive him. That's between you two. But don't hold on to that anger on my behalf. I'm happy here." She hesitated, a teasing grin spreading. "Though, if you wanted to make me truly happy, you'd find someone like that cute Summer to settle down with. I need some grandkids already."

"That's not likely." I glanced at Summer, who was still on the phone, laughing and waving dramatically.

Since eighteen, I hadn't allowed myself to think about settling down. From the first date to hookups, I was clear I wouldn't get serious with them. It was easier than having mixed-up feelings later and disappointing what would often be a great woman. I had told Summer the same thing. And yet. And yet—

Why did this pull toward her feel different? In the safety of my mom's presence, I could admit I was thinking about Summer far more than I should've been. When I read an interesting fact on the back of the cereal box, my first thought was *I bet Summer already knows that.* When I watched our favorite show, I had to pause and wonder what Summer thought when Sam left the White House to move back to California. The roses in my yard bloomed wide, the same shade of pink as her lips after I kissed her.

She was invading my days. As for the nights. After that time on the boat, I would be thinking about her.

"It better be. You're too old to be playing these games, Van. Time to grow up." Her tone softened. "It's okay to be vulnerable with someone."

"I know that."

My tone was sharper than I meant, but Mom didn't react.

Hesitating, I opened my mouth, then closed it. "But what if—" I swallowed hard.

"You know you're nothing like your father, right?"

Blinking, I studied her face.

How could she see me clearly?

"Your father was always a little selfish, with money, with his time, in bed."

"Mom!" I gagged at the thought.

"But you have never been like that. You used to be so sweet, offering to make me toast every morning, burning it half the time. I saw you with your girlfriends in high school. Remember how you got that job at the grocery store just so you had enough to take that girl out on dates? Then, after you found out about your father's infidelity, it was as if something broke in you. I'd ask you about girls, and you never had someone. At first, I thought it was just the college years. No big deal. But then you're twenty-five, then twenty-eight. Now, here you are, thirty-two."

"I know how old I am," I grumbled.

"Love isn't a task. It's not something you take apart to find out how it works. You can do every step exactly right, and something can still go wrong. People get sick." She motioned to herself. "People fall out of love. And it cannot be explained. There is no step-by-step guide on how to protect yourself."

"What if the person you're protecting isn't you?" I asked, my voice low.

She smiled. "If you care enough to spare them heartache, then I'd say you're halfway there already."

On the other side of the sliding glass door, Summer pulled the phone away from her ear and shoved it in the back pocket of her tiny shorts. Her full lips were taut in a devious smile, and a desperation to know what made her so happy lanced me.

I wanted to know her more. I wanted more. Full stop.

An hour later and two more canoe-sex coffees, I said goodbye to Mom. Kneeling, I wrapped my arms around her shoulders.

Mouth to my ear, Mom whispered, "I like that one. Let me know if you need any advice."

I whispered back, "I don't need your advice about women, Mom."

She barked out a laugh, shaking her head. As she pulled away, she cupped my cheeks in her hands the same way she did when I was little. "We'll see about that."

I pressed a kiss to her cheek before standing.

Mom motioned to Summer. "You, too, sweetie. Don't think you're leaving without a hug."

A hesitancy clouded Summer's eyes as she bent down to wrap her arms around Mom.

Still in her embrace, my mom muttered, "You have him bring you by again, okay? Even though I tell him he doesn't have to, he insists on bringing me groceries once a week, so I make him dinner. You should come."

As Summer pulled herself up, she grasped Mom's hands, her head tilted. "I'd be honored."

Once back at the truck, I paused, keys in my hand. "She likes you."

Summer glanced up at me, the lip balm stick an inch from her lips. "I told you she would. Why are you surprised?"

Why was I?

Hesitating, I wrinkled my forehead. "I don't bring women around to meet my mom. Sometimes, people are weird about it. I've seen people shout at her like her hearing is gone, not her mobility."

"Those people are assholes."

Snorting, I turned the key in the ignition. The truck rumbled to a loud start. "Yeah, they are. Still—"

The years I had spent away from my mom weighed on me. She never mentioned how bad she had gotten during my absence, and if I hadn't received the call from the hospital, I wasn't sure she would have told me. Shame flooded my face. How could I admit I had abandoned my mom for years to live my life in Seattle?

"MS is a gradual disease. Sometimes, It can get better for a bit, but to be honest, I've never known a time where she wasn't somewhat affected by it. When I was younger, it was her being tired and in pain after a long day. She had to use a cane for a while, then a walker. But then she'd get better. She'd be on a treatment plan that worked well, and she would be walking around. And then it would relapse. The wheelchair has only been for about the last year. I wish I was there before but—"

Summer took my hand. Lacing her fingers with my own, she brought them up to her mouth and pressed a kiss to my knuckles. "You're obviously here now. And, to be honest, she seems to be doing well where she is now. From what I saw, she is what my dad likes to call *a tough broad.*"

Her sky eyes bored into mine, a smirk on her face.

I squeezed her hand, her warm palm fitting perfectly with mine.

"Come home with me."

A small smile appeared on her face, almost hesitant. She nodded, and a tight feeling I hadn't realized had been coiling in my chest released.

With my free hand, I shifted into drive and continued one-handed, never letting go.

Summer

V AN DROPPED ME OFF at home, saying he needed to get his boat out of the water.

In truth, I appreciated the time to freshen up. As cute as my swimsuit was, I didn't feel like wearing it all night.

I packed a small bag of clothes and toiletries, then hesitated.

Was this for a few hours or to spend the night? Was it presumptuous to pack an overnight bag for the first time? Would there be a second?

Oh Lord, we were going to have sex. It had been a long four months since having done that. If his skills on the boat were any indication, I was in trouble. In more ways than one.

Already, Van was creeping into my daily thoughts. While knitting, I wondered if he would like a blanket next.

On impulse, I snagged all the banana-flavored taffies out of the front desk candy dish and shoved them in my purse. While looking up new china, I came across teacup sets, just like the ones at his house. *The West Wing* used to be my own little escape, and I sat there, wondering what he thought were CJ's best moments.

I was becoming too attached to this man. Every day, I tried to keep up with the demands of my scheme on Cory. But more and more of my thoughts were drifting toward Van.

It might have been desire. I could deal with that. I had to. It was that or creating distance with him and the idea of not seeing Van, of never texting him a random trivia question.

No, I was strong. I could do this. I could have both.

With my bag packed and set on my kitchen counter, I pulled out my phone to look through the messages Imogen had sent me.

The fuzzy pictures couldn't do the event justice, and I wished I could have seen the chaos in real time.

It was all too easy to have the package of butterflies delivered to Cory and Kodi's home for their engagement party. The event popped up on my feed, unbidden.

Who was I not to take that opportunity?

Purchased with a Visa gift card, I had it delivered an hour after the party kicked off. Following their initial visit to the hotel, I was happy to say they did not pick the Ridgewood Inn for their wedding but had hired Imogen as their day-of coordinator.

She shared with me that they had invited her to the engagement party to get a feel for "how the theme should look on the big day."

No one would suspect me of malice. After all, who would be deathly afraid of butterflies to the point of running and crying into their house in front of all their friends and family?

When Imogen called me to tell me about it, I had to contain the urge to ask her a million little questions. Luckily, she was an open book, telling me all about what everyone was saying, including the bride's older brother, who had called Cory a pussy.

I knew it was a dark, petty thing inside me that was happy Cory was embarrassed like that, but I couldn't bring myself to stop.

He was still messaging Candy regularly, asking for nudes and sending several unsolicited pictures of his hard-on under gym shorts and a video of him jerking off.

Anytime I felt guilty, I would look at yet another obnoxious message, and all remorse would disappear.

He deserved it all and more for what he put me through.

A few days before, I went to the police station and spoke to a detective about him showing my naked photos to others, but the cop was no help, asking me, *Why did you send them if you didn't want people to see them?* Who also told me I needed to talk to Cory and ask him to delete them. As if I was about to put myself through that again. The police force in Ridgewood needed sensitivity training, and I needed to handle it in my own way.

Much more effective.

As I pulled into the driveway, I noticed Van's truck was moved to the gravel drive on the side of the house, giving me the single lane of cement. It wasn't the slight difference in distance but allowing me the spot closest to the door tugged at something inside me.

Assessing my overnight bag on the passenger seat, I decided to grab it later if necessary, but I wouldn't play my hand until I was sure of what Van wanted.

The sun was setting on the manicured street as I approached the white door, with its stained glass of lilies. I was on the second step when Van opened it and came out to greet me.

I couldn't get a "Hi" out before I was in his arms.

This kiss was slow, sensual, deep. One hand was in my hair, the other around my waist. We walked backward into the foyer, where my purse fell. My back hit the wall as he pressed his body into mine, his muscles hard under my hands. Fire raced over my skin, and I wanted more, more, more.

When he pulled away, his eyes, his silver eyes, were glazed over. "Where's your bag?"

"It's in the car."

He left me in the hallway and returned with my bag in one hand. When he came back in, he kicked the door shut behind him.

Taking my hand, he led me into the dining room, where a spread of food was on the table.

"What's this?"

"Dinner. I figured you hadn't eaten. Have you eaten?"

I shook my head. "But you don't need to go through all this trouble."

Red tinged his cheeks.

"It's really no trouble. I grabbed a few things from the grocery store on my way home. Didn't even cook."

A chilled bottle of my favorite wine sat in the middle of the table. I recognized it as my favorite brand, named after a famous neo-noir crime film. Did he know it was my favorite? Or did he just guess? It's hard to tell.

"Wow, you thought of everything, didn't you?"

He smirked. "I just want you to feel comfortable."

This should've just been sex. But he was making it so difficult to separate that from the growing warmth for him. From my wanton pulse.

I grabbed a cube of cheese off the tray and popped it into my mouth, glancing around.

The room looked the same as the first day. Same pink wallpaper, same teacups. But it felt different. Like a place I could settle into.

I held up the cake in the bakery box. "Is that okay?"

He moaned. "Of course it's okay. I could eat that every day." He took the box from me and set up the cake on the table beside our spread.

He motioned to the chair, where I took a seat, then bustled around me, handing me a plate and encouraging me to get food. "I don't know if I'm that hungry."

He smirked at me. "You'll need your strength for what I'm about to do to you."

I stuffed a big green grape in my mouth.

Afterward, he asked me about my work, my friends, my cousin, and my dad. We talked and talked until the cheddar cubes sweated to a glossy sheen. Conversation flowed between us as I snacked. I couldn't remember a time when I had opened up so readily.

What we discussed wasn't deep or meaningful. But he would lean forward as I told a story, cringed at my second-hand embarrassment of watching Wren barf on her asshole ex, and laughed at the right moments, like when I told him Autumn had tried to take a squirrel home when she was five. I mentioned my fear of enclosed spaces after going on a tour of caverns in Montana, and he mentioned watching his mom give herself injections.

He fed me more than I should've eaten, but a rising nervousness rolled in my stomach.

As I pushed my plate away, he rose, holding out his hand. "Come on, let's finish the wine in the backyard."

He led me through the French doors with one hand while holding the half empty bottle of wine in the other.

I sat in a yellow Adirondack chair as he took my empty wine glass and refilled it without me asking.

As he plopped down opposite me, I sipped the wine.

The backyard was small but fully fenced, with a lush azalea bush blooming ruby red against evergreen.

"This is my favorite wine," I commented, setting the glass on the wide arm.

"I know." He took his own sip, looking at me over the rim of the glass. "You posted a picture of the bottle on your Instagram a year ago. *Favorite wine with my favorite gals* and tagged your friends in it."

Blinking, I processed this information.

It wasn't a secret, but who goes back a year on someone else's social media? Not that I didn't try with him, but he had practically nothing to go off.

"That's stalker behavior if I've ever heard it." I took another drink, a smirk playing on my lips.

Not taking the bait, he shrugged. "It's working, right?"

"Is this how you got all your girlfriends?"

He shook his head. "I don't do girlfriends, Summer. I told you that."

I quirked an eyebrow. "Really. So, I'm just supposed to believe that I'm that special?"

"Am I to believe you don't know you are?"

That was a compliment I wrapped in irritation.

He used *know*, not *think*. Unlike the men who would sneer, *You think you're so hot, don't you*, it was an objective fact. Once again, he had a belief in me that no one ever had. He thought I was worthy and, more than that, knew that I knew. It isn't the false modesty that most men expected, a humility that we stuff our achievements under. It was him wanting me to shine.

I couldn't respond. What could I have said?

He shook his head. "You can believe whatever you want. I'm telling you the truth. I haven't had a girlfriend in over a decade."

My hand stilled on the glass halfway between the arm of the chair and my mouth before I set it on the table with a *clink*. "What do you mean you haven't had a girlfriend in a decade?"

He raised an eyebrow. "Exactly what I said. I told you I don't have girlfriends or serious relationships."

I frowned. "So, then, what is this?"

He furrowed a brow and looked at me. "This is new to me."

"Well, I do boyfriends, and I have to tell you, it's been a long time since someone wined me and dined me like this. Most guys don't even try anymore. Of course, I seemed to be in the habit of falling for douchebags, so there we go." I snorted, shaking my head. "You know, maybe I need to find some nice guy and settle for him."

"You don't want a nice guy," Van scoffed. "The damage you would do to a nice guy."

"Okay, asshole." Leaning back in my chair, I glared at him. "Way to make me feel shitty."

"Nothing I'm saying is news, Summer. You aren't nice. Nice is telling people what they want to hear. It's apologizing when it's not your fault. What you are is kind. I hear the way you talk about your friends. You're loyal. You defend them. You deserve someone who knows the difference." He ran a hand over his hair, making the front poof up. "I won't be a nice guy for you. But I'll tell you the truth. I'll call you out when you need and expect you to do the same. And I will always put you first. You deserve someone who will do right by you."

"Oh."

The word settled on my lips, a prickle expanding across my skin at his words.

They weren't soft reverence, far from the flowery language of my favorite novels nor the swelling music over the third act in a movie. A harshness had crept into them, a razor edge I recognized in myself.

With Cory, with all my previous lovers, it was words and little else. This was recognition, a mirror of who I am and what I should've expected of others.

What was I supposed to do with that?

Autumn used to tell me, *To be seen is to be loved*. But I'd never been seen like this before. Maybe most women would've been happy, but that kind of recognition? I wasn't sure I liked it. If he saw me, truly saw me, he wouldn't stick around. He wouldn't want me.

Van leaned forward in his chair, fingers on his chin. "Do you wanna talk about your ex?"

I shook my head. "No, I don't wanna talk about them. I don't wanna think about them."

He didn't react to the harsh words.

"Okay, then." He nodded and smiled. Reaching forward, he grabbed my hand, pulling me toward him. "Come over here."

I resisted, my mind still whirling from his confession that stung my ego and formed a fissure in my chest, which seeped emotions manifested from a bad idea. Emotions like wanting him to care for me, wanting to trust in him.

He pulled my hand harder, and I slid over to him. When I was close enough, he wrapped his arms around my waist and scooted me onto his lap. One arm on my back, the other cupping my chin to face him. "You are fiercely beautiful."

"Do you mean that?"

"Truly."

Truly. Such a simple word. Not a declaration but a fidelity just the same.

"This is getting tricky. I'm not supposed to want more from you," I admitted. "It was never meant to be real for either of us."

"Why are you complicating this, Summer?"

I huffed out a laugh.

Why was I? I wanted to sleep with him. Judging by the immense ridge digging into my left butt cheek, he wanted the same. That nagging voice in the back of my mind faded as he drew a circle on my exposed knee with his fingers. Then a heart, then a star, then a spiral, then the long stem of a flower, moving under my dress.

"Can we just be? For tonight, no labels."

"But—" Why was I doing this to myself? "This was fake."

"How I want you haven't been fake since the day I picked you up from your hotel lobby for the parade. Nothing about how I feel is fake. Nothing about the compulsion to kiss you senseless is fake. So, don't use that as an excuse to push me away."

"But—you don't want—"

I'm silenced by his mouth on mine, his hands in my hair holding me as his fingers traced from my knee up to the apex of my thighs.

The kiss was demanding, filling my senses with heat and a beat of want. Every dip, every caress drew me into him. I was free-falling into us.

"I need you. Truly, I do." Peppering kisses down my neck, he trailed his fingers between my thighs, easing my lace thong to the side. "Tell me you want this."

"I do."

He stood, with me still in his arms.

Twisting my legs around his waist, I heard the wine bottle clink as it landed on the ground, and he stumbled up the stairs, carrying me.

His touch scorched my bare skin, with his lips on my neck, my jaw, my mouth. After he tossed me onto a soft bed, I barely had time to take a breath before he was on top of me, his muscular thighs between my open legs. As he kissed me, his hands pulled my dress above my breasts and threw it on the floor beside his shirt.

"Since that first day, I've imagined you here. On my bed. I've pictured a thousand different ways I could have you."

"And now?" My words were shallow as he cupped one breast, flicking his thumb over my pebbled nipple. "But even after all those daydreams, I could never get you right in my mind."

"Am I better?" I writhed beneath him as he pinched my nipple, rolling it, sparking the sensation straight to my clit.

"You always are." His mouth captured one breast, sucking and biting me.

"I can't afford to want you. You're taking over all of me." Tracing along my waist with his tongue, he offered a whisper of a touch, sending flames down to my center. "I should have known touching you would be like a sickness I could never recover from. You're infecting everything in my life. I can't sleep, can't eat without thoughts of you. You're invading the very fiber of me."

My underwear was tossed to the other side of the bed, and I was bared to him. He cupped my mound, slipping a finger past my clit and parting my folds. "I can't be alone in these thoughts. Tell me you need me, too."

The fissure was widening. This wasn't a plea for sex but for its absolution. I couldn't say the words. If I would have started, I could've said more, losing everything holding me together.

I whimpered and gasped as he teased me. Before long, I was crying out, my pussy clenching around his scout's honor fingers.

His words were hot on my ear as he wrung out the last of my climax.

With his clothes gone, he was between my thighs, his hard cock against my inner thigh.

"As much as I like your moans, I'm going to love hearing you scream for me."

I gave him a wicked grin. "Truly."

With that word, he sank into me, filling me up in a single swift motion.

I screamed at the intrusion, my nails digging into his back.

I was being taken. There was no other word for it. The harder he thrust into me, the more I was giving away.

"You're so fucking tight for me, baby. Do you feel that?"

I nodded, the words falling into gasps.

"See how good you're taking me? See how I fit you?"

All I could do was hold on tight as he drove into me. My second orgasm was fast approaching as he hammered me, his fingers digging into my hips. At one point, my legs were brought up, my feet on his shoulders as he thrust deeper, hitting parts I didn't know I had.

My moans turned into cries, which then became his name.

"That's right. Who's fucking you? Who's making you come? Let all my neighbors know who's making you feel this way."

Over and over, I screamed for him, needing more and getting it, his stinging grip and slapping balls against my ass.

As the wave crested, it was with the scream Van promised he'd get from me. Van's cry mimicked mine as he came after me, every muscle in his body taut.

When he collapsed on me, I laced my fingers in his damp hair, pulling him closer until our bodies were flush.

"I'm too heavy," he murmured into the side of my neck.

"I can handle it."

He lifted his head and slid off me, his hand splayed over my bare stomach. "I know you can. That's what I like about you."

I raked his scalp with my nails, and his eyes drifted closed. His breathing evened out the calm wheeze and soft whoosh of sleep.

In the waxing moonlight, he seemed younger.

With a single finger, I traced the length of his nose, his scruffy jawline, the line of his straight brow. It was a strong face. An honest one.

Of course, I thought the same about Cory, and how wrong was I?

This was all too real. Van had never been anything more than straight with me about what he wanted. Once again, it was my own impulsivity that led me here in his bedroom.

But I didn't need to stay. To fall asleep beside him would only blur the lines he had so carefully set between us.

As quietly as possible, I climbed out of the king-size bed and grabbed my dress off the floor. Glancing around, I couldn't find my underwear, but I wasn't going to turn on a light to track that down.

My eyes caught on a pile of clean boxer briefs on top of his dresser. Those would do.

I pulled them on, and with one last glance at his sleeping form, I slipped out the door.

The next morning, I sat in a coffee shop. My conversations with Van had been scant, and I could tell he was getting frustrated with me not responding as much.

But I had to protect myself. If he knew how all I wanted was to call him or the way I had stopped at the bakery and stared at the cake we shared, wanting desperately to go back to that moment, he would be there beside me, expecting me to trust him with my heart, and that wasn't worth the risk.

My preoccupation with him was taking over, and I couldn't have that. It wasn't fair to Van, who had given me nothing more than kindness and amazing orgasms. My heart couldn't take another disappointment.

I had thirty minutes before I was expected at the hotel, but I left my apartment early to use the public Wi-Fi for the last of my plans.

Strictly speaking, it wasn't legal to get into Cory's emails the way I had, but it was also extremely hard to prove in a court of law. I wasn't altering anything besides a few forwards of incriminating info here and there. But every time I'd log in, I was pushing it.

Vowing that it would be my last time, I sipped my iced caramel Americano.

A few days before, I had compiled a zip drive of all the messages Cory sent Candy. Finding Kodi's email was surprisingly easy.

She posted regularly on her website, where she sold custom tumblers with kitschy phrases on them like *She's a little sass and a bunch of badass* and *Might be coffee, might be vodka.*

I sent a quick email, enquiring about her creating something for me, and she responded within twenty minutes.

Sending the zip drive through my fake email was far too easy. I hoped she wasn't too devastated, but knowing the truth before the wedding was better because, according to Imogen, she hadn't put down money for deposits yet.

Promising myself I'd only check his email one last time, I logged on to find a whole long conversation between him and another person describing how they had been fudging the numbers for a job, adding on a fake employee to pay themselves twice.

I forwarded the emails to my fake account and then deleted them from the sent folder, set on providing this info to the labor and industries, the IRS anonymous tip line, and the state patrol.

If what I saw was embezzling, he was sure to receive more than his share of punishment.

Maybe then I could move on. Maybe.

Van

FOR THE PAST DECADE, I had slept alone. Sure, there was the odd one-night stand who overstayed her welcome and a few friends-with-benefits situations that ended terribly, as they almost always do. But I was used to my space while sleeping, the full reign of my bed, and complete control of the blankets.

But the moment I woke, I knew she was missing. You would have thought waking up beside someone would feel wrong, but it was waking alone that left me bereft.

A quick glance around the room showed me she took her dress but left her underwear. Whether that was for me to find or if she couldn't find them while she absconded, I couldn't say.

She had only been in my life for the season. I had lived thirty-two years without her, but I missed her.

I brought the pillow she was on to my face and breathed it in. Breathing in the faint scent of roses and sunshine that was so innately her.

I dropped the pillow. What was I doing sniffing pillows? What kind of man was she making me? We had sex one time. One. And she was ripping down all my wards.

I didn't fuck for keeps until she came around. And I sure as hell never fucked without a condom.

While I meant what I said to her the night before, nothing about us felt fake anymore.

I tried reaching out, but my messages were returned with short answers. She wasn't avoiding me completely but also wasn't engaging. Minutes ticked by and then hours, and I was getting little more than a one-word response.

So, this is what it feels like to have a woman ignore you.

It was an unfamiliar sensation. Ordinarily, if a woman showed no interest in me, I would accept that as it was. No need to play games when plenty of other women were out there.

But that was before Summer. Before our night together. She had me pillow-sniffing, sappy poem-appreciating. Sucker.

And to top it off, Summer wasn't playing hard to pique my interest. She wasn't the sort. That night at the party, she was forthright—bold, even. There were no games to be played. Somehow, her genuine disinterest only made my thoughts of her more rabid.

Running my hand down my face, I got up, grateful that I had to work. Maybe the distraction would be good for me.

At the stoplight, the song changed. A familiar tune. Summer and Savvy were singing along to it at one point during the trivia night. The song was one I had probably heard a hundred times before, but all I could think about was the way her hair brushed her shoulder as she leaned forward to write an answer, her smile curving up a little more on the right side. The way her two bottom front teeth were slightly crooked. How her hand fit into mine and the way her body felt beneath me.

I was well and truly fucked over this woman.

A horn blared behind me, and I startled, glancing up to see that I had missed the green light. The guy behind me flipped me off, but I ignored him.

To my right was Garden of Eden Nursery.

I still had thirty minutes before I was expected at work.

My mom had mentioned her geranium died. Realizing she could use a replacement, I decided to take a quick peek at what they had to get my mind back to what mattered.

Only it wasn't my mom I was thinking about fifteen minutes later as I hefted a large potted bush up to the register. Really, how could I have refused when I passed the pink blooms, with their rich scent? Perfect buds matched the same shade as Summer's cheeks as she came the night before. Ignoring the hefty price tag, I bought it along with my mom's plant before I could decide if it was a bad idea.

My morning went slowly, planning meetings, checking on the progress of projects, and having to fix a new employee's mistake. By lunch, I had told myself that my obsessive thoughts all morning were nothing more than a postcoital hangover.

Not that I never had that before.

But then I glanced at the fun-fact calendar, which read, *A snail can sleep for three years.*

I desperately needed to see her.

The hotel was only a ten-minute drive from work. I could pop over and say hi, couldn't I?

She had told me she would get so wrapped up in work that, sometimes, she'd forget to eat until five p.m. and would become ravenous.

I couldn't have that.

Ignoring the little voice in my head telling me it was crossing a line to see her at work, I made my way downtown. Parking, as always, was a pain, with the bright summer sunshine bringing out all the tourists to the historic waterfront.

As I got out of the car, I glanced back at the rosebush in the back of my truck. Women like flowers, don't they? I snapped a bud off the bush and tucked the stem into my pocket.

On the walk from my thirty-minute parking spot to the hotel, I stopped in one of the many coffee shops lining the front street and grabbed a chicken avocado sandwich and a lemon sparkling water.

A young woman with dark hair was behind the front desk of the hotel, circling a few things on a map for the middle-aged couple before her.

Standing back with Summer's lunch in hand, I wondered if this was the wrong move.

I could tell her I wanted to do this because that's what a fake boyfriend would do, but I'd be lying.

The older couple left, and the young women turned to face me. "Hello. Welcome to The Ridgewood Inn. Checking in?"

"Uh, no." I set the lunch on the high counter. "Is Summer here?"

A smirk replaced the woman's customer-service smile. "She is. Can I tell her who's asking?"

"Van. I brought her lunch, I'm her—"

What?

The woman smirked. "I'll call her. She's in with our event coordinator, Imogen, right now."

The woman picked up the phone, her voice sing-songy. "Summer, there is someone out here who needs to see you."

She nodded before lowering her voice. "Just someone. You better hurry." She hung up and flashed me a winning smile. "She'll be out in a minute. I'm Lucia, by the way. Summer's talked about me, I'm sure."

With an unfamiliar nervousness rising in me, I twitched a smile and nodded.

What was Summer doing to me that I would be nervous? Summer must have mentioned me for her coworkers to act so sly.

The click of heels on the marble floor sounded and then there she was. Her light hair was swept up in a tight twist at the base of her neck. A crisp white button-down was tucked into a tight black skirt. Glasses sat on top of her head.

Summer was beautiful in her little sundresses, ripped jean shorts, and oversized T-shirts. And, of course, gorgeous in nothing but the moonlight through my window. But nothing could have prepared me for professional Summer, buttoned down and prim.

She was a wet dream come true.

When she caught sight of me, she stopped in her tracks, her eyes large.

"Van, what—" She glanced from me to Lucia behind the desk, then back again.

I jostled the to-go box in my grip. "I wanted to make sure you got lunch."

"That's very—um . . ."

I could tell I had surprised her. What was she thinking I would do after she left me in the middle of the night? Was the night before not a sign that something had shifted between us? I told her how I felt, yet she still left me—well, maybe my words weren't enough. I'd have to show her.

"Why don't you show me your office while you eat? I'm sure Lucia could spare you for ten minutes."

"Thirty," Lucia called out behind the desk.

Summer seemed to snap out of her stupor, glaring at Lucia, then turning her attention to me. "Ten. I have to call our maintenance man. A guest is complaining about the faucet in—"

"Room 207. I'll call him now."

"Aren't you efficient?" she grumbled as she keyed in the code on the doorknob and ushered me in.

Her office was a small cube, with little decoration.

She blushed. "I haven't had the time to decorate. Been opening a hotel and then running it, you know."

"Well, here, you can put this on your desk." I handed her the bloom, which she took delicately, rolling the thorny stem between her fingers.

"You got me a flower?"

I wasn't going to admit yet that I had, in fact, bought the whole plant with her in mind.

"I saw it and thought of you."

A softness caressed her face before disappearing.

"Thank you."

"I didn't know you wore glasses." I motioned to her head.

She touched her hair and laughed. "Oh, these are blue light glasses. They reduce eyestrain." She took them off, tossing them on top of her desk. After pulling the sandwich from its eco container, she took a big bite and hummed in appreciation before saying, "I didn't even know how hungry I was until I started eating."

"You need to keep up your strength."

She took another healthy bite and narrowed her eyes.

Leaning forward, I placed a hand on her knee. "If you close the door, I bet I could get you off in five minutes." I wiggled my brows.

She frowned and swallowed before setting the sandwich back in the container. "Absolutely not. This is my place of work, Van. I'm not going to have sex with you here."

"Who said sex? I bet I could slip my fingers up that tight little skirt of yours and find you ready. Tell me I'm lying, Sunshine."

I smirked as she crossed her legs and glowered at me. Reaching forward, I grabbed a little piece of bacon that had fallen out of her sandwich and popped it in my mouth. "Are you saying the orgasms I give you aren't worth it?"

She pulled her bottom lip between her teeth, and her glare softened.

I could tell she was imagining the night before.

Expression hardening, she blinked. "It's not happening here. First of all, you wouldn't like me if I were the kind of girl who would shirk her responsibilities like that. And second, no orgasm, no matter how earth-shattering, is worth my professional reputation."

I considered her and nodded. "Yeah, you're right."

"So, if you don't want to fool around, tell me why you've been avoiding me?" I asked as she chewed.

Her cheeks full, she paused, her jaw frozen in place.

Her big blue eyes reminded me of an old-time cartoon, and I could hear the *tink*, *tink*, *tink* with every blink.

Swallowing, she took a big swig of her water, then delicately placed it on her desk. "Um. I haven't been."

"What did I tell you about lying?" I cocked my head and waited.

She set the rest of the sandwich back in its cardboard container and closed the top slowly. Wiping her hands on the little recyclable napkin, she pursed her lips. "What do you want me to say, Van? I'm not sure what you expected me to do the next morning. Spend the night? Make you eggs and bacon in the morning, like some nice little girlfriend? You never asked me to stay."

"And you never said you were leaving. I woke up alone."

"How is that different from every morning before it?"

I opened my mouth, then closed it, processing her words.

She had a wall up inside her. Anyone could see that. Giving her sweet declarations would only cause her to shut down further. There were so many things I wanted to say but to do so would give away a part of me best kept guarded. So, I said the only things I could.

"I wanted you there. *Want* you there."

She shook her head at me, her lips pressed in a thin line. "You said that you needed a fake girlfriend. I did that for a bit, and it was fine, I guess. But now—this is all getting confusing, and the last thing I need right now is some man in my life, confusing me."

"I'm not trying to confuse you. I want—"

What did I want? I wanted her in bed at night, to talk to her every day. When she was gone, I missed her. I was willing to give her more than offered others. Couldn't she see that?

"Listen, I don't know what you think is going on here, but you don't need to bring me flowers and sandwiches. I'm not sure why you're trying so hard with me." She eyed me skeptically. "Should I not be?"

"In my experience with men, they only act this way to get what they want."

I tilted my head to the side. "And what is it you think I want? We already slept together. If I just wanted sex, I had that last night."

She threw up her hands. "We can't get emotions involved and only want—"

"Who said I don't want emotions?"

Her eyes flashed dangerously, and she scoffed, pointing at me incredulously. "You! You told me, *I don't do girlfriends.* I'm taking you at your word. If you want to have fun together, sure, we can do that. Just don't make me think there's more when you aren't capable of that. Don't bring me food and fucking *roses* and come to my work looking handsome and smelling good when you aren't capable of more."

Sitting back in my chair, I crossed my arms. "I said I don't do girlfriends because, up until a month ago, I didn't. I never said I wasn't capable of them. It may have been a while since I was in a serious relationship, but that doesn't mean the mechanics of it have changed."

When she wiped a hand over her face, a tendril of hair fell from her twist, skimming her cheek.

My fingers itched to tuck it behind her ear. To pull her face to me. To kiss away whatever this frustration was in her.

"What am I supposed to do with that speech, Van?"

Sadness laced her voice.

"Whatever you want. I can't force you into anything. We both know that. You are the most stubborn person I've ever met."

She cupped her face in her hands, and I thought she was covering tears, but her eyes were clear. Conflicted, but clear. No, Summer wasn't the sort of woman to cry over me—or any man.

"But you also deserve someone who will go to any length for you."

"Is that an offer?" she asked with a snort.

"Maybe? Is it so hard to believe that I would?"

"Yeah, men like you don't."

"Why do you think you know what kind of man I am when you refuse to get to know me? Huh? You told me once, when someone shows you who they are, believe them. Is there anything I have ever done to show you I'm not completely serious about you?"

"Well, no, but—"

I raised a brow, silencing her. "We aren't liars, are we? I told you yesterday on the boat. I won't lie to you, and I expect the same from you. So, when I tell you that you make me feel things I know are dangerous, believe me."

"Dangerous for who?" she murmured, her eyes flickering to mine.

"Anyone in my way, to get what I want."

"And what do you want, Van?"

Her words were softer, lower.

She rested a hand on my chest as she leaned forward.

"I want to own you. I want to spend hours, days, weeks savoring the taste of you on my tongue and the heat of your skin as you move beneath me. But more than your body, I want all of you. To possess every little thought in your head, pull them apart, and break them down until there is no you or me, just us."

"Van, I"—she hesitated, closing her eyes as if summoning courage—"I don't need to tell you I have a hard time trusting people."

I nodded, a tenuous hope growing.

If I were to have stopped her, she may not have had the courage to keep going.

"You can trust me. Truly."

The deepest sorrow lined her eyes when she opened them.

"Truly?"

"Come to dinner with me."

She quirked a brow. "A work dinner?"

"No, a date. An actual date, just you and me. No one else. Tonight, seven."

Conflict passed over her face as she bit her lip.

"I don't know . . ."

"Or tomorrow—if that works better."

"You're determined, aren't you?"

I flashed her a smile. "When it comes to getting what I want, you're damn right I am."

"Okay."

Standing, I reached forward, helping her to her feet.

"Can I—" I tensed my jaw, oscillating between asking and leaving without a word.

It had been hours since I had last seen her. Too long to not feel her skin under my fingers, to not smell the roses and sun of her hair. As a man deserted, I would take this refuge in her.

I swallowed. "I'm going to kiss you now."

"Van, I'm at work."

I stepped closer, taking the evasive strand of hair and curling it around my finger as I cupped her chin. Her eyes widened as I leaned in closer. "I'm going to kiss you because I can't stand one more moment without your lips on mine."

My name was her agreement and then her lips were against mine, the soft curve of her body in that white button-down and black skirt pressing against me. My tongue traced the seam of her lips, and I allowed my hand to wander down to her ass, grabbing a handful and pulling her to me.

It wasn't a long kiss, but it was the promise of more later.

As I pulled away, I tucked that lock of hair back behind her ear. "Tonight or tomorrow?"

Her cheeks pink, she blinked at me as lust filled her eyes. "Tonight."

As I left her small office with a spring in my step, I sent Lucia a jaunty wave.

Eighteen

Summer

T HE BOATHOUSE WAS A local favorite in a local town. Situated on a large pier, the waterside tables boasted floor-to-ceiling windows overlooking the narrows of the Salish Sea and the hourly appearance of the Seattle ferry. Seafood restaurants were common, but The Boathouse was one of the nicest in the county.

On sunny days, people would leave their boat at the private dock and come up the metal grated walkway to dine on Pacific salmon, Dungeness crab, and oysters from Hood Canal.

Work ran late when a guest kept me for twenty minutes to talk about the time she saw JFK Jr. at the local Italian restaurant in 1991. I had to rush home to change.

The quick effort must have been good enough because, when Van showed up at my door twenty minutes later, he stepped back and let out a low curse and a big grin.

Cut in a sweetheart neckline, the dress had a fitted waist that flared out just above my knees. The blue patterned fabric reminded me of something from the old-time movies Autumn loved to watch. The dress code was almost always casual, so I had little opportunity to break out my finer things. It was a running joke in our group that, sometimes, it was hard to tell who was homeless or who was trendy. It was the birthplace of grunge, after all, and with the cloud covers and nine months of rain, wearing a rain jacket over a hoodie and a mustard-colored beanie was the norm. Dressing up was putting on your nice performance fleece vest.

Seeing the look in Van's eyes made me glad I erred on being overdressed.

On the drive there, he grabbed my hand, our fingers entwined. When I asked to change the music, he told me to turn on whatever I wanted. He asked me questions about my favorite colors, foods, and memories. We talked of my dad again, about London, about childhood pets, and about sports I had tried and failed at.

When I told a long rambling story about the hotel, he laughed at the hijinks of when a housekeeper found a snake and how the guest had tried to hide it from us by placing it inside a nightstand. At the restaurant, he made me wait in the truck until he could get the door for me. I never had someone do that for me.

As he helped me down from his truck, he brought the back of my hand to his lips and kissed my knuckles.

For a moment, I felt just like Beatrice with Viscount Rodolphe in my romance book.

He slipped the hostess a tip, asking for a waterfront table.

I thought that was only for the movies.

Seated across from each other, he insisted I pick the wine, letting me know I had better taste than he ever did.

Halfway through the first glass of a local Sauvignon Blanc, I envisioned future dates we could have. I was never a big dreamer—that was for Autumn and Devin. They could build worlds in their minds, create scenarios, and picture futures. Never me. I wasn't going to sit there and let my imagination take me to such lengths as marriage and babies—but more dates like this? That, I could handle.

We ordered our food, and when it came, we realized we didn't need to get three appetizers and two full meals.

Van took it in good spirits, offering to send all the leftover crab cakes home with me for my dad, knowing they were his favorite from an offhand remark I made.

We were halfway done with our meal when the door clanged open on the other side of the restaurant and a group walked in, then sat at the bar.

I stiffened, my lips tightening into a narrow line.

No, no, no. This could not be happening. I was having such a wonderful night.

I should've looked away from them. It was obvious I was blatantly staring, but I couldn't tear my eyes away from the man who had violated my trust and violated my wonderful date.

Tentatively, Van set his left hand on my arm.

Instinctively, I flinched away to fold my hands together.

"You okay?" he asked, following my line of sight to the group.

The three men and two women looked completely normal, but one was the devil incarnate.

Returning my gaze to Van's, I blinked, hoping I could conceal my heightened panic.

I tapped my nails together and smoothed them over the hem of my dress, confident that my smile didn't quite match my eyes. "Totally."

The cool wine was suddenly too sweet on my tongue as I gulped down the rest of my glass.

"I have to, um—be right back."

Luckily the chair didn't shriek an embarrassing screech as I pushed off from the table and rose.

In my heels, I hobbled to the bathroom.

While I wouldn't risk my makeup enough to splash water on my face, I could at least hyperventilate in the privacy of a stall before figuring out my next step.

Plopping down on the toilet seat, I studied my toes peeking out of my nude wedges. They were in desperate need of a pedicure. Maybe I could talk Autumn into going to the nail salon with me, even if they use nonorganic materials.

What were the chances that Cory would show up at the same bar as me and Van?

Was he going to confront me?

Did I have too much wine?

Someone walked into the bathroom, and under the stall door, I saw small feet in gold strappy sandals trot to the sink.

Well, now I'm not coming out until she goes into the other stall.

That was basic bathroom etiquette.

I counted to ten, then thirty. She was still there, not moving an inch.

Time was up. I couldn't sit on this toilet all night. Van was waiting for me.

I pulled the door open, and Kodi looked at me.

Holding a tube of bright red lip gloss, she had only done her bottom lip.

She paused, setting the tube down. "Hey, I know you."

Gulping, I joined her at the sink.

It was that or retreat into my toilet fortress.

The water was cool on my hands, and I watched as my fingers laced under the stream, the foam from the soap washing away.

"I'm not sure—"

"No, I never forget a face. You work at that hotel my fiancé and I were looking at. We were there a month ago. We thought it might be cute, but you guys were too small. Cory said *nothing but the best for me*, and, of course, my parents want to invite, like, two hundred people."

I gave her a weak smile. "Weddings can be like that."

"I was looking at the garden reserve, but it's impossible to get an email back from there."

"Oh, call and ask to speak to Pam. She's the coordinator. She's very old school and doesn't believe in email. Or texts. But she'll call you back if you leave a message. And if you're looking to cut costs, I know their Friday and Sunday weddings are a fraction of the price."

I wasn't sure what came over me, likely the years of customer service.

Clasping her hands together, Kodi jumped, her chunky heels whacking the floor. "Thank you! That is so helpful. You don't even know."

Before I knew what was happening, her arms were around me, pinning mine to my sides, as she encased me in her lingerie store scent.

"Don't mention it." I pulled an arm free to pat her half-heartedly on the back.

She beamed at me as she pulled away. "I'm so glad because this wedding is getting expensive. I have my job with Dr. Christian and, of course, my custom tumblers—"

"I love tumblers. I need to order one for my cousin's wife. She's expecting in a few months."

This was my in. I wasn't sure if she read the proof I had sent a few days before.

Some women will stand by their partners. But if I could direct her to them, maybe she would leave him.

"Give me the name, and I'll order one tonight."

She showed me her online shop, and I looked it up on my phone, then showed her that I found it.

When she got to the door, she held it open for me to step out before her.

I didn't want to like her, but I did. For the first time since planning this scheme, I felt guilty. Kodi didn't deserve to be caught up in that.

I hesitated.

Should I tell her?

Blurting out that her fiancé was a lying, cheating asshole in the middle of a high-end seafood restaurant wasn't the best idea. But she deserved to know. No, she'd check her email that very night. I was sure of it.

"Nice chatting with you," she called out, waving at me.

As she reached Cory, his eyes shot straight at me, and his jaw tensed.

I couldn't do much to dodge him. Might as well have gotten a little dig in.

"It was great talking with you, too. Remember what I told you, okay? Good luck with everything. You're going to need it." I gave her an exaggerated wink.

Red blotches formed on Cory's throat and crept up to his ears.

He leaned over, whispering something at Kodi, then got up and stalked toward me.

As he passed, he hissed, "Get the fuck in here, Summer."

Kodi was facing away from us, talking to someone at their table.

Rolling my eyes, I followed him into an alcove. My arms crossed, I glowered at him. "What?"

"Why are you talking to my fiancée?"

Keeping my face impassive, I flicked my eyes between Cory and Kodi. I laid a hand on my chest and let out a shocked huff of air. "What? I can't make new friends? Isn't that what you asked me for at the hotel? You wanted me to be friendly, right?"

"Don't talk to her."

"Why not? Are you afraid of what I might say, Cory? Scared to see what she might do if she knew the real you?"

"You don't know a fucking thing about me."

I snorted. "You'd be surprised what I know."

"Stop being such a bitch and leave me alone."

"Oh, name calling—I'm wounded, really. You're so mature." I stuck out my bottom lip, feigning pity.

The brightening color on his neck was hilarious.

"At least I have someone. There's no hope for a crazy, raging cunt like you."

"Oh, trust me, there are plenty of people who would love this. What did you call me, a raging cunt? For the right person, I can be very nice. Some might even say I'm as sweet as *Candy*."

I allowed the word to hang between us, quirking a brow, watching the realization dawn on him.

His face turned from pink to red to puce. "You—You—You . . . What have you been doing to me?"

"I have no clue what you're talking about?"

"Yes, you do. The emails and phone calls, my neighbors won't talk to me anymore. Some kids egged my house the other day and called me a dog abuser."

"Oh, dear. That sounds serious. You should get in front of that before it does lasting damage to your reputation. This is a small town, you know." I raised a brow in mock sympathy.

"My Facebook got hacked. It took me weeks to get back into it." His words were spewing out of him. His hand shot out, grabbing onto my elbow and twisting it hard. "Has it been you all along?"

I tried to yank his hand off me, but his grip was too tight, nerve pain shooting up my fingers. "Let me go," I hissed.

Cory dug his nails into my arm, little half-moons of red along my bare skin. "Admit it. You're the one who's been fucking with me."

I twisted and pulled, but he, stronger than I expected him to be, wouldn't let me go.

"I'm not telling you anything. But whatever you have going on, I'm glad. Sounds like what you deserve. Now, let me go."

We struggled for a moment, and I was about to yell when a voice said, "She said let her go."

Van stood in front of us with my purse in one hand. His jaw was tight as he stared at where Cory was gripping my arm.

"Stay out of this—"

"I told you to get your hands off her." Van wrenched Cory's hand off my elbow in a move so quick I couldn't understand.

Cory was left kneeling, clutching his wrist to his chest. "What the fuck, man. This isn't your business."

"Not my business? What kind of man puts his hands on a woman? Even if I were a stranger, you'd still be on the floor." Van hissed, towering over Cory with a malicious glint in his eyes. "But I'm not a stranger. So, I'll say this once and only once. You will never again touch what is mine. Do you understand? You lay a finger on her, and I'll break it and every other bone in your body."

Redness crept up Cory's neck as he huffed and contorted his face. "Whatever. She's not worth it." His hand still on his chest, he got up and walked to the group.

"Did you break his wrist?" I asked.

"He'll live." He narrowed his glare on Cory's back. He glanced at me, and for the first time, I saw his unbridled might.

Never was there a moment I didn't think he was strong, but to have that power turned against you was a sight.

I took an instinctive step back.

Van took my upper arm, gripping enough to steer me but not to hurt.

I followed, tripping in my heels.

His jaw was a hard line as he stared straight ahead. We made our way down a dirt path that led to a waterfront park.

A few feet away from the rocky shore, he stopped at a tree, bracketing me with his arms. The abrasive bark dug into my back as I stared up at him, half scared, half entranced.

"Care to explain why another man had his hands on you like that?"

"It's none of your business." I stepped forward to get away, but his arms were too strong on each side of me.

"Don't push me, Summer. I'm an inch away from going back in there and committing a felony."

"You wouldn't." I gasped. "It's not worth it."

His jaw setting, he glared down at me. "Being with you is pushing me to my limits. At this point, I'm torn between beating that man within an inch of his life or fucking you against this tree so that you know who you belong to."

Indignation and desire warred in me.

"I don't belong to you. Of all the pigheaded, fucked-up things to say."

He stepped closer, his hard body pressing me against the rough bark.

Goose bumps traveled up my arms, and I realized we were alone.

With one hand, he coiled it around my throat. His thumb traced my lower lip. "Your body says different. I never wanted to possess someone before, but you bring out the worst in me."

His anger rolled off him in waves.

"I want—" He gritted his teeth, huffing loudly.

"Then, fucking do it."

The kiss we shared at his house was tender passion, but this was raw, a sharper edge to each flick of his tongue.

Somehow, he unzipped my dress, and it was falling over my shoulders, my breasts bared to the night. His teeth scraped the side of my neck as he bent down as the tree bark rubbed my bare skin, but I didn't care. He hoisted me up, and my legs wrapped around his waist.

After fumbling with the front of his pants and shifting my underwear to the side, he thrust into me in one long stroke.

I cried out, taking him to the hilt. My head flung back and hit the tree with a *thunk* before he stepped back two paces and held me up, still pumping with nothing but himself to set the rhythm.

For each beat, his forearms flexed, his raw strength taking over. This primal heat between us spurred us to go faster, come together, harder.

Anger for what happened only minutes before gave me strength, and I funneled it into riding him.

This was punishing, his thrusts in a frenzy as he pounded into me over and over again.

Raking his back, I hooked my ankles together to keep me upright as he squeezed my ass, pushing me up and down his cock.

My gasps and cries were too loud for the public place, but I couldn't stop myself. As my climax built, I sank my teeth into his shoulder, muffling my cry into the fabric of his shirt. My muscles tensed, and I shuddered in his arms, the light behind my eyes blinding and white hot.

His sounds, guttural and animal-like, even, deepened as his whole body tensed. He took one hand off my ass but left him inside me as he leaned against the tree, our foreheads touching.

His kiss was reverent.

"You're fucking me up, Sunshine. I'm not supposed to feel this way."

His words were a whisper, so soft and tinged with emotion.

"I know," I murmured.

I did. It wasn't supposed to be this explosive, to hold this much longing. But it did.

Pulling back, he looked down at me. "What are we going to do?"

I pulled free from him, standing on shaky legs.

I knew what I wanted. To fall into him, to allow him to cover me with his body, and to stay in the safety of his arms for the rest of my days. I wanted to trust that he could feel the same.

But the only person I could trust was myself.

Time and time again, the world has proven that. It didn't matter if I was falling for this man. It wasn't enough.

Before he could stop me, I made my way onto the path. "Go home."

I hadn't realized until I made the trek back how close we were to both the restaurant and the parking lot, where there would, likely, be people.

With his long legs, he was able to catch up with me in a matter of seconds.

"So, you gonna tell me who that was?"

"No one. An asshole. It's fine." I rubbed my elbow, easing away from the spot where Cory had tugged me.

Van inspected the red print on my arm, a muscle ticking in his jaw.

Anger rolled under his skin, and I could see the effort it took for him to keep it in check as his finger brushed the four red crescent marks.

His touch was light, feather-soft, and cool on the swollen wounds.

"It's obviously not. Who was he, Summer?"

Pulling my arm from his grip, I gave him a shaky smile. "No one. I swear, he's not imp—"

"Don't you finish that lie." His features hardened as he glared at the restaurant door as if considering going back and finishing what he started.

"Trust me, you don't want to get involved in my mess."

If he were to find out about Cory, what would he say?

I loved the way Van saw me. The strength and confidence I had when I was in his presence.

He couldn't find out about how foolish I had been. The stupid girl who sent naked pictures to a man I didn't really know.

Van would never respect that woman. I couldn't even respect her.

"You're wrong about that." Huffing out an enormous sigh, he placed a hand on my lower back and led me across the parking lot. "I like your mess. I like everything about you."

The late summer wind was picking up off the salt water, cooling my skin. The waxing crescent moon hung low in the sky, scattering shadows along our path as we made our way to his truck.

He paused at the passenger's side, his hand on the handle. "I'm gonna take a wild guess that was the ex."

"It didn't end well." I shrugged.

My arm stung, but I fought the urge to rub the sore spot.

Our romp in the woods had created new scratches, and I was pretty sure a sliver of a pine cone had gotten stuck in my hair.

"And that's all you'll say?"

"And that's all I'll say."

"Summer, why you got to be so . . ."

I waited for him to pull out the words so many men used on me. *Stubborn, difficult, bitchy. Crazy.*

Reaching under his arm, I pulled the passenger side door open myself, then climbed in and slammed it shut in his face.

I didn't owe him an explanation. There were no promises made between us. Van didn't want labels. I didn't want to trust my shame to him.

He glared at me through the window before walking around the truck and hopping in.

Once the engine started, I turned to him. "You told me you didn't want me to lie, but that doesn't mean you get to know everything about me."

"I know."

His voice was low and dangerous, as if rage had been simmering underneath it.

We drove in silence for a long time.

"Do you still have feelings for him?"

"No. Definitely not."

"So, why talk to him? Why would you give him the time of day if he was so terrible?"

"Are you saying I deserved to be hurt like that?"

He huffed loudly. "For fuck's sake, Summer. Of course not. No woman deserves to be grabbed like that. I wanted to punch those veneers out of his face. But I don't understand why you couldn't ignore him. It makes no sense."

"No sense to you. It does to me. He deserves to be knocked down. He's a piece of shit, and he needs to be as miserable as I was."

I realized that, once the words left my mouth, I had said too much. Gave it all away.

I waited for his outrage, his disgust over my venom, but there was none. "Did you love him?"

"No. This isn't about being in love with him. Which I wasn't. I believed him when he said I was the only one, and he made me look silly. I can't trust anything now, and it's his fault. Men complain all the time about crazy women. 'Look at that crazy bitch, so obsessed.' Who made them that way? Who drove them to the edge and took off the brakes?"

"Then, let him go, Sunshine. You think I can't tell that something about that guy is holding you back? Leave him behind. You'll be happier if you do."

"Don't tell me what I need to be happier. Who is supposed to make me happier? You? Mr. No Commitment? Who needs labels, low stakes, different gal every weekend?"

"It's not—" He scrubbed a hand over his face. "I haven't been with anyone since you and I—"

I raised a brow. "Am I supposed to believe that?"

"Believe what you want. You always do, right? You'll jump to conclusions and won't ask questions like, 'Van do you want me to spend the night?' 'Van, were you able to eat while we were apart?' 'Van, would you absolutely beat my ex-boyfriend to a bloody pulp if he looked at me the wrong way?'"

His tangent took the air from my frustration.

"When I went to London, he sent me this bouquet of bright blue tulips. He said they looked like my eyes." I let out a low laugh. "At the time, I thought it was so romantic. But then I looked it up, to see what type they were, and you know what I found? Blue tulips aren't even real. They're genetically modified to look like that. Dyed. It's fake, just like everything I thought about him."

I glanced over at Van, who was listening intently. "I was the other woman. He was seeing us both, and I had no idea until I came home to his engagement announcement. The day I broke into your house, I was confronting him. We argued, and I started walking home." His brow furrowed. "After throwing an expensive bottle of champagne at his head."

One brow raised, his mouth took on a downturned smile of approval.

"Did it hit him?"

"No, of course not. I wouldn't be talking to you if it did. I'd probably be in jail."

"Shame. His face is begging to be rearranged."

A lesser woman might have disapproved, but I reveled in it. That gave me the courage to relax.

"No arguments there."

We passed Ridgewood's downtown exit, moving farther north.

"You're not taking me home?"

He scoffed at me, taking my hand. "Of course not. You're staying over. And no leaving in the middle of the night like some cartoon villain."

Nineteen

Van

TRUE TO HER WORD, she stayed. We showered together, where I had to scrub sap out of her hair, and I made it worth her while afterward by bending her over the rim of the tub and taking her.

As we collapsed into bed, she tucked her head between my arm and my chest and ran her fingers over its sparse hair, coiling them around her nails.

"I wish it could be like this forever."

Forever. Such a terrifying concept. Never in all the years of women, sex, and short-term girlfriends did that word come into play.

I waited for the familiar dismay to grip me, the icy warning that it was time to unlace my arm from her shoulder and send her on her way. Rolling the word around in my head, *forever, forever*, playing for keeps.

Did I want that with Summer?

Instead of fear, a warm sensation seeped over my skin, a small glow that started in my chest and radiated out into my fingers.

I pulled Summer closer.

Is this what it felt like to fall for someone? A new anxiety crept in. Would she feel the same way?

With that on my mind, I drifted off.

I woke with her still in my arms. After pressing a kiss to her forehead, I slipped out of bed.

As I made my way downstairs, I hummed to myself.

The night before confirmed a lot of theories I had about Summer and why she was so closed off. As I knew, she was hurt by him, and it would take a while to earn her trust enough to be let in. My actions would have to do the talking.

With that, I busied myself, making breakfast.

My normal routine of sweet cereal wouldn't be enough. I had to break out the big guns of bacon and eggs and toast. She mentioned the night before that, while she wasn't supposed to go into the hotel, she needed to stop by later to check on new furniture set to arrive. That meant I only had a few hours with her before she'd have to leave me again. But we'd make a plan for dinner afterward.

No noise rustled from upstairs, so I tidied up for when she would wake. I even cut a rose from the bush and set it in a small vase I had found under the sink.

In the living room, an alarm pinged from her charging phone.

As I picked it up to silence it, her screen opened. I was surprised to find she didn't have a code. On the screen was a list half checked off.

GOAT AD

GYM PICTURES

BUTTERFLY ATTACK

STI notice

Lost dog

Cheating proof

Fraud

As the items on the list went on, they got worse. I could never understand what went on in a woman's mind, and this bizarre list was one I
would file away under Summer being Summer.

With a garbage bag in hand, I stepped out onto the porch. The door
hadn't even closed behind me when I stopped in my tracks to see a familiar
old truck pulling in.

Our eyes met, and it was too late for me to turn tail and go back inside.
Inside, where a beautiful Summer was sleeping naked in my bed. Inside,
where I could hope to be a better man for her.

Instead, I stood on the front porch, waiting for my father to descend
from his ridiculously lifted truck.

The years had not been good to him. His once-shiny dark hair, laced
with stringy gray strands, was in desperate need of a trim. His brown eyes,
once so mischievous and clear, were rimmed red with puffy bags.

He groaned loudly as his feet hit the pavement. "Donovan. Long time
no see."

His statement rolled out as if we were old friends, as if my last words to
him ten years before weren't a vow to never see him again.

"Bruce."

I affected a flat tone.

He ambled up the walkway, his hands in his pockets.

He was thinner, sporting a new bicep tattoo of an anchor with *Refuse
to sink* in block letters.

"How you been, son?"

Gripping the bag tight, I considered how much of a mess it would be to
dump the trash over his head.

It was a juvenile thought, but if you can't feel juvenile about your shitty parent, when can you?

"Fine."

He rocked back on his heels. "You gonna invite me in? It's my house, after all."

"No. It's Mom's. Passed down to her by her father. Her name was on the deed. I've been paying for the upkeep for over a year now."

"And who paid it for years before that?" he asked with a smirk.

"Was that before or after you were fucking your nineteen-year-old assistant?"

He chuckled. "Oh, come now. We're past all that, aren't we? I get why you were miffed at the time. You were a kid, and I'm sure it was confusing for you, but you're a man now. You get how the world works."

"So, maturing to you is having free rein to cheat on your chronically ill spouse?"

He flapped a hand at my argument. "Glyn is over all that. Seems happy enough—"

"No thanks to you."

He frowned that same thin line from when I would ask him for help with my homework as a child. The only thing he ever taught me willingly was car maintenance.

"Look. Was I perfect? Of course not. No one is. But me and your mom, it's complicated. But that doesn't mean you and I can't patch up this squabble."

"I have nothing to say to you." Pushing past him to the garbage can on the side of the house, I lifted the lid and tossed in the bag with more force than necessary.

"Van, come on. Don't be like this. I came over here to see if we could tal—oh, hello there."

Slamming the lid with a deafening clang, I glanced over to the porch.

Summer was standing there, arms wrapped around herself, wearing my old University of Washington shirt.

In any other circumstance, I'd be ecstatic at the sight. But her long tanned legs on display and her hair a glorious mess were more than I could handle in front of my father.

"Bruce Logan, Donovan's father."

Summer took his hand, hesitation flickering on her face. "Summer."

He turned to face me, Summer's hand still in his. "Well, she is a looker, ain't she? Nice work, son."

Before he could step closer, I rush to her side, pulling her hand free from his and stepping between them. "Go inside, Summer."

"But—"

An irritated expression crossed her face, and I could tell she rankled at being ordered around.

"Please," I hissed out between my teeth.

Scowling at me, she turned on her heel, muttering, "Fuck you very much."

Alone on the porch, I crossed my arms. From my spot two steps up from him, I towered above.

"Nice work, champ. Seem like you take after me in more ways than one. Of course, we always knew how to attract the pretty ones, don't we?"

"I'm nothing like you."

He chuckled at me. "Of course you are. You're a Logan, after all. Ladies love us. That one, though—phew. I bet she's fun to have around."

My feet and hands were moving faster than I could think. One moment, I was standing on the porch and the next, my father was slammed against the side of the house, his shirt in my fist as I spewed, "Don't you say another fucking word about her, or I will bust your teeth in."

"Alright, alright." He put his hands up in surrender. "No more talking about your pretty little girlfriend."

Smoothing out his shirt, he shook his head. "That's no way to treat your old man. Can't say I'm not impressed with how strong you are, though. You work out?"

This entire exchange was getting too ridiculous.

Sinking onto the front step, I cradled my head in my left hand. "Can you tell me why you're here so you can leave?"

He rocked back on his heels again as if I hadn't just threatened him with bodily harm. "Tracy has been on me about patching things up before the baby comes."

My hand dropped from my face, and I stared at him, dumbstruck. "The what? I sure as shit hope I heard you wrong. My fifty-eight-year-old father didn't get someone pregnant."

"Strong swimmers." He grinned at me. "She's four months along. It's a boy."

"Un-fucking-believable." I shook my head. "You can't seriously be telling me this."

"Well, I thought you'd want to know you're going to be a big brother."

"Big brother? Big br—I'm thirty-two years old. The time for younger siblings passed twenty-five years ago. You can't think that I'd have anything to do with you, whatever floozy you found, and the spawn you created."

"Don't you disparage Tracy like that."

"No, you don't. Get off my lawn. Stay away from Mom, away from Summer, and away from me."

"I thought you could be a man about this, but I guess not." He sniffed as if I was the out-of-line one. "You know where to find me when you want to be a part of this family."

Glaring until his taillights were pinpricks in the distance, I stood in my driveway, my arms crossed.

I stomped inside the house and slammed the front door, rattling the stained glass window.

Summer was seated at the bar, sipping coffee from the teacup I had so diligently washed fifteen minutes before.

"What was that about?" she asked, nibbling on a corner of toast.

"Nothing."

"Doesn't look like nothing."

"You don't want to talk about your shitty ex, and I don't want to talk about my shitty dad," I snapped. "Just taking a play out of your book, right?"

Her eyes flashed dangerously, and she dropped the toast on the plate and leaned back on her stool, scoffing. "Whoa. You want to try that again?"

Clenching my fists, I shook my head at her. "Drop it, Summer. I don't want to fucking talk to you about it."

Summer set her teacup down softly, her jaw set and lips a thin line. "Cool. I'm leaving."

"What—no, don't. I—"

"No, I am. You obviously don't want me here, and watching your little tantrum was too much."

"But you'll come to trivia again, right?"

She sighed. "I don't know. We'll see."

"How are you getting home? I drove you here."

Clicking her tongue at me derisively, she shrugged. "I'll walk. I don't know."

"You're not walking. I'll take you home."

Her eyes narrowed, but she nodded. "Fine. But I don't want to hear a word out of you on the way home." With that, she grabbed her little bag by the door and walked out.

The drive was silent. When I tried to say something, she would put her hand up and say no.

My offer to walk her up to her apartment was met with a door slamming in my face.

Watching her make the three-story trek up the stairs, I scrubbed my face, the day-old scruff abrasive on my palm.

I screwed up. The words left my mouth, but I was too pissed off at my father to say the right things.

I vowed to patch this up later.

Summer

I FUMED ALL DAY over what happened. It wasn't his unwillingness to talk to me about his dad. It was how I was wrong.

Sure, for twenty minutes after he dropped me off, I was annoyed with him for being short with me. But once I cooled down, I realized he was right. I did the same thing to him the night before. Verbatim. We took turns with our little tantrums, but we both had them for various reasons.

Once again, it was proof that I didn't need this kind of complication in my life. Seeing Cory had set something off in me.

I liked the way Van was protective of me, but at the end of the day, he wouldn't understand my choices. And if he ever found out, he wouldn't accept it. Who would?

I was being silly, but my pride couldn't admit it.

I would make amends with Van soon.

After seeing how upset Cory was, I knew I made the right choice in sending the proof of his cheating alongside the embezzlement evidence. It had only been a few days since I had sent it in, but maybe justice would be served quickly.

In a few hours, I was expected at my dad's for dinner.

At the grocery store, I swung by the coffee shop inside, grabbing their biggest iced pink energy drink spritzer.

Waiting on the side for his drink, Nico Evjen hovered around the counter.

Taking my place beside him, I bumped him with my shoulder.

He was surprised but gave me a wide smile. We chatted for a few minutes as he got his tall dark drip—a boring choice, but whatever—and I got my drink.

He scrunched up his nose, grimacing. "Those things are full of chemicals."

"So is everything else in the world." I took a big long drink from the straw and moaned. "Mmmm, tastes so good."

He snorted, then grew serious. "I was actually hoping to bump into you."

"Oh, no, last time you said that, I spiraled all night and ended up barfing up neon red shots."

He furrowed his brow, shaking his head. "I've been hearing complaints from that Cory guy. Turns out someone out there is making his life miserable. I guess some gal he was chatting with online messaged his fiancée with proof of him cheating, and she moved out this morning. His phone is going off all the time from people asking for cows and landscaping. And something about lost keys. He said someone posted that he kidnapped a dog, even. So, now, none of his neighbors will talk to him."

I stuck out my bottom lip in false sympathy. "Sucks to be him. Karma is a bitch, isn't she?"

Nico tapped the rim of his coffee lid. "I would hope if a single person was behind all this, they covered their tracks well. Maybe used a VPN and a different email address, stuff like that."

"I don't know what you mean, but I'm sure they did."

Nico clapped me on the shoulder in a reassuring, brotherly way. "Glad to hear it. I got to head back to work. Tell everyone hi."

"You could tell them yourself if you come to trivia tonight at the Skol House. I'm dragging Autumn out with me."

Unlike Wren, Devin, and me, Autumn never let go of her crush on him, and while he wasn't the guy for me, maybe I could set him up with my sweet cousin.

Something passed over his face, and his eyes softened. "Man, I haven't seen Autumn in almost a decade. She was just a kid. I wish I could, but I have to get going. We'll have to all get together some other time."

"Enjoy your lame coffee."

Walking away, he waved at me.

Well, that was better news than I was expecting. Karma was working fast for me.

After placing my twenty-four-ounce bright pink drink in my cart's cupholder, I steered it to the produce section with a spring in my step.

The front door was unlocked. No matter how many times I had reminded him to lock the dead bolt, my father refused.

Walking into the small rambler where I was raised, the house was eerily quiet.

I called around before ominous clanging rang from the garage.

Flinging the door open, I found the man standing on the concrete floor in his coveralls, a greasy rag in his hand. Pungent oil wafting in the air caused my stomach to turn, and a twinge of pain jolted in my head.

"Dad, what the fuck. You're not supposed to be getting up and down on that knee." I motioned to his body and pointed at the car lifted on a jack, a silver pan underneath it.

"I'm fine."

"The doctor said you have a torn meniscus."

He flicked his wrist at me. "That pansy? I can manage just fine."

"Until you blow your knee out and can't walk." Crossing my arms, I glared at him. "What's so important that you need to climb under that old car?"

"It needed an oil change."

"An oil change? Dad! I would pay for someone else to do that."

"Pay for some pimply nineteen-year-old to change my oil? I'd rather die. Now, bring your car around. I know it's due soon."

"It's not."

He flung the rag onto his tidy workbench.

Growing up, our house wasn't always kept in the most organized condition, but his massive toolbox was always pristine, with its wrenches, screwdrivers, and ratchets lined up.

"Summer Louise Townsend, I taught you better than that. At least tell me you took it to a reputable shop and not some hack job place that doesn't know the difference between motor oil and transmission fluid."

"I didn't take it to a shop. A friend did it." I waved in front of me, suddenly feeling overheated.

Dad narrowed his eyes. "What friend? Not that bitch-boy you were seeing a while back—yes, I know all about him. Autumn told her mom, and Lorelle told Victor, who told me."

"This family is the worst bunch of gossips I've ever seen," I grumbled, fanning myself. "No, it's a new friend."

"Is that all you're gonna tell your old man?"

"Yeah, sure is." I pointed at the car. "Finish up. I expect a gourmet dinner tonight."

By the time Dad placed the tater tot casserole in front of me, my stomach clenched.

I hadn't eaten much all day, and the comfort food of my childhood was a welcoming balm. Never offering the healthiest option, with green options rarely making an appearance, my dad tried his best while raising me. He could do a passable French braid and took me to all my activities. He had a few items he could cook—well, aside from the manly art of grilling, of course. But he was proud of keeping me fed.

A few bites in, I put my fork down and studied him across the small round pine table. "When's the last time you heard from Cheryl?"

I wasn't sure when I had stopped calling her mom, but it was a young enough age. On the rare occasions, she'd appear in my life and didn't seem to be bothered by it. Or was smart enough that she had little room to ask for an honorific after deserting me and Dad.

Dad leaned back in his chair, his fork still in one hand. "Been, oh, I don't know, 'bout seven years now."

"And you never thought about dating again?"

He shrugged, shoveling a bite into his mouth. "Not really. You know, it gets lonely, but who's out there for an old fogey like me."

"Lots of people, Dad."

He raised a brow, looking at my phone, nodding. "Hmm. Well, I don't know 'bout that."

His words were dismissive, but I saw a spark of interest in his eyes.

"You can't let your regrets about her stop you from moving on."

"I'll never regret Cheryl. She gave me you. I wasn't going to have kids. You were a surprise, for sure. At my old age, I thought there was no way. I loved her, something fierce, but I never could trust her. She wasn't good for you. For a while there, I thought a girl needs a mother, but by the time she left, it was good riddance. You had your Aunt Lorelle and Autumn, and we got on okay, didn't we?"

"We did." I patted his hand.

He was never much for physical affection, so he allowed it for a moment before pulling his hand away.

"Where's all this coming from? You've never asked me about me and your mother."

"Just curious, I guess." I took another bite of the casserole, even though my stomach was hurting more, my fork slick between my clammy fingers.

"Nah, I don't think so. It's this friend giving you ideas, huh? What's his name."

"Van, but it's not like that, Dad."

With a dismissive look, he grumbled in disagreement. "You might fool those other schmucks, but I got your number."

This conversation was making my head pound. Hard.

Pinching my lips together, I rubbed a hand over my face. "Can we talk about this later?"

Dad frowned, worry creasing his weather-worn face. "Pumpkin, I don't like the look of you. Why don't you go lay down in your old room?"

Picturing my old room made my stomach roll harder. The Tiffany-blue walls I had decided were so chic and the posters of artsy movies I never understood were once thought to seem sophisticated.

"I'm fine, just—"

My stomach heaved, and I barely made it to the bathroom before puking.

Dad followed me down the short hall and brushed my hair back from my face.

"Gross," I mumbled. "Sorry, Dad."

"Pumpkin, I've had you spew *on me*."

Resting my forehead on the cold seat, I groaned. "I must have eaten something bad."

"Couldn't be my casserole. I made it the same way . . ."

"No, I'm sure it was something else."

"You sure you don't need to stay here tonight? I can run to the store and get you that alphabet chicken soup you like."

The one I last had when I was eight.

"No, I'm okay, Dad. It's only a few minutes back to my place. I'm sure if I lay down for twenty, I'll feel better."

With my stomach empty, I was able to make the trek from the bathroom to the car and up the three flights of stairs to my apartment.

I set my bag on my counter and got myself a glass of water. I sent a quick message to Dad that I was alive and safe in my apartment.

All day, I felt a little dizzy and sweaty, my throat burning. I swallowed water down and then refilled it and swallowed all that as well.

My head began to pound, and I rested it against my hand. On my phone was the last text from Van.

> Van: Trivia, special theme tonight. 80's movies. See you there?

> Van: I'm sorry I was a dick. Truly.

I started a reply but stopped.

Guilt piling on top of my pounding head, I was in no condition to go to the bar.

I'd take a nap and see how I felt.

Collapsing on my bed, my hand missed the bedside table, making my phone fall on the floor, where it would remain for the next twenty-two hours.

Van

I T HAD BEEN THREE days since I heard from Summer.

This time, she didn't respond to my texts and calls at all. I had sent messages, sent food to the hotel for her lunches, and stopped by there to be told she was out. I had even texted Devin to check on her, who responded that Summer was fine but offered no more information.

Time had run out alongside my patience.

She didn't want to have this thing with me anymore, then she could tell me to my face.

I had to knock over a minute before she opened the door.

With a sudden step back, I took in the sickly, wild-haired woman before me.

"Why are you knocking so loud?" she asked with a craggy voice.

"I—" Clearing my throat, I reassessed why I came over. "I hadn't heard from you and—"

"Because I've been sick," she croaked.

"You're not—" I motioned in front of my stomach.

She recoiled. "No, gross. Ugh, not gross but not now. Ack—" She ran a hand over her sallow face, then shook it out as if something were crawling on them. "No. I'm not pregnant. It's some nasty flu or something."

It's not as if I wanted her to be pregnant. We were—well, we weren't in a place to have a baby, that was for sure.

But instead of a hearty relief, there was a spark of disappointment. The idea didn't scare me the way it should have. A flash of grey-eyed, light-haired children. Summer with a bundle in her arms. I liked it.

"That's good."

She groaned, running a hand over her mouth. Eyes bulging, she bolted to the bathroom.

I followed and leaned against the doorframe.

Once done, she propped her face on her chin and turned slightly toward me, her eyes closed. "I don't want you to see me like this."

I laughed. "Are you forgetting our romantic first date? I've already seen you barf, Summer."

She groaned again, pulling herself up to stand. At the sink, she swished water and spat it out. "And once was enough. I can handle this myself. You don't need to stay with me."

"I know I don't. I want to."

She stumbled past me, making her way into the bedroom, where she collapsed on her messy bed and kicked the blanket over her feet. "Ugh, why are you so nice?" She grumbled. "Where is the fuck boy I was promised? Huh?"

"Is that really what you want?"

The sickness was bringing out a vulnerability in her she wouldn't normally allow.

"Yeah, because if you're an asshole, I won't start feeling things that are terrible for me. I can fuck a guy, and it's fine. But to . . . like . . . him, ugh. Trouble, trouble."

I wasn't going to press her on that, not while she was half asleep, but I would revisit it later.

"Go to sleep, Sunshine."

She wrinkled her nose at me and snorted a whimper. "Fine."

Her breathing slowed and body stilled.

Content that she was finally back to sleep, I pushed myself up to stand.

I was no more than two steps into the hallway when she called out, "Are you leaving?"

"No, I was going to get you a fresh glass of water."

"Okay." Her voice softened as she closed her eyes. "Can you stay?"

"There is nowhere else I want to be." I tucked sweaty hair away from her face.

There was no response, just a gentle snore.

Two hours later, I returned, grocery bags in hand. I kicked my door closed and headed for the stairs when a door opened and a pretty woman with blue eyes and auburn hair poked her head out.

"Hey. Van, right?"

Stopping, I furrowed my brow. "Yeah?"

Her door left wide open, she approached me. "I'm Autumn. We haven't met yet, but I've heard all about you."

"Autumn." I grinned back at her. She had a sweet disposition and looked exactly how Summer described. "The cousin."

"The same." She motioned to the bag in my hands. "Do you need help? I know Summer is sick."

I thought about declining but decided talking with Autumn might give more insight into Summer.

Handing her the lighter of the two bags, I motioned for her to go ahead of me.

Once we were back in Summer's apartment, Autumn set the bag on the counter, unloaded it, opened the fridge, and arranged the items. Crouched in front of the open vegetable drawer, she glanced over at me. "It's nice of you to take care of her. She doesn't normally allow that."

Taking out the box of crackers, I opened one side to slide a sleeve out. "It wasn't without some choice words. She was irritated when I showed up."

"That's Summer. Always there to fight for you—but can she show weakness? Of course not."

I snorted.

"I'm glad she had you. She won't say it, but I can tell you're good for her. Especially after that asshole."

"Cory, right?" I asked, my interest piqued.

"I don't like putting negativity out into the world, but if I saw him—*ooooohhhhh*." She balled up her fists and narrowed her eyes. "After the shit he put her through, the cheating and then—" She glanced at me.

"He's a piece of shit. Absolutely."

I was allowing Autumn to think I knew more. I felt slimy doing it, but there was no way Summer would open up to me, and if I had to learn the truth through a little deception, so be it.

She relaxed. "I know she told him to delete the pictures—and the fact that he not only didn't but also showed people makes me so mad."

A bolder formed in my throat as I added up Autumn's tale. This was so much worse than a cheater. My jaw was hard steel, and I struggled to swallow the rage filling my chest.

Leaning forward, I placed both hands on the edge of the counter and squeezed, my knuckle white from the force.

"You knew, right? Oh, God. I always do this. I open my mouth, and I don't mean to spill secrets, but I can't help it. The words come out, and—"

Autumn's rising panic distracted my anger enough that I could relax my fist.

"It's okay. We'll be alright." Clearing my throat, I got up, slapping my upper thighs. "I'll be back in a minute with the rest of the stuff."

I hadn't left anything in my truck, but I needed an excuse to get out before I would break something.

At the edge of the parking lot, my fingers digging into my thighs, I bent over.

Deep breaths, in and out, I tried to temper the fever, but my hands were shaking while my blood boiled. I prided myself on keeping my emotions in check. I was a large man, and to rage would make me fearsome. But nothing was holding back the ferocity inside.

Stalking to a nearby tree, I couldn't think about the ramifications, couldn't control the need to strike out. My fist went flying against the trunk, and the branches shook. My knuckles split against the rough pine bark. Blood sprayed the pavement as I struck again. The bark gave way, splintering to the side.

Still, my anger wasn't ebbing.

How could someone do that to Summer? Was this the same man who she was arguing with a week before? That scrawny, chino-wearing asshole, with that stupid smirk as he watched her leave. If I could have gone back in time, I would have pummeled him into the white carpet of that boathouse restaurant.

The soft clack of vegan sandals on the pavement sounded behind me, and I glanced back.

Autumn was standing there, her eyes flickering from the mangled tree to my bleeding hand.

"Come on." She waved at me. "Let's get you cleaned up."

My anger wavered as I followed her into her ground-level studio. Cupping my bleeding hand, I tried and failed at not dripping blood all over her floor.

She instructed me to sit on a patchy vinyl stool at the breakfast bar. "I can't believe I spilled Summer's business like that. She's going to be so pissed at me."

"I can't imagine Summer being mad at you."

Autumn raised a brow. "I like you, but I don't think you have any idea what my cousin is capable of."

"I would never underestimate her."

Autumn snorted, dabbing at my hand with a wet paper towel.

"I wish I could find that guy and kick the shit out of him." I shook my head. "What's his last name? Tell me so I can take care of him."

Autumn cocked her head, wearing a playful smile. "You don't need to do that."

"I don't understand."

"Summer has her own way of dealing with people. Do I approve of her methods? Of course not. But let's just say Cory is paying the price for hurting Summer."

"What does that mean? Did she punch him in the face? What?"

Autumn frowned at me as she dabbed antibiotic ointment on my stinging knuckles. "So violent. I guess it makes sense why Summer likes you so much." She straightened, screwing the lid back on the tube and nodding at my mangled skin. "That's as good as it's going to get."

Frustration bubbled up inside me again, but Autumn seemed to ignore it.

"When I was fourteen, there was this girl in my art class, Amy-Rae. She was always making rude comments to me. Critiquing my shading and such. Nothing too bad, but still a mean girl, right?"

I nodded, not sure where this was going.

"Then, one day, in class, I'm finishing up my final project, this big watercolor painting of seas anemones. I'm putting the little touches on it when I'm called to the office. I get up there, and they give me a note that is supposed to be from my Aunt Tina. Only thing is, I don't have an Aunt Tina. When I return to the class, the water jar is tipped over my painting, ruining it completely. The only girl around is Amy-Rae. She said she had accidentally bumped it, but there was no way. The moment Summer sees me crying after class, she demands to know what happened." Autumn paused, letting out a big sigh. "Do you want to guess what happened the next day?"

I nodded, apprehensive.

"Amy-Rae showed up to school, and her eyebrows were gone. She had to pencil them on for months afterward. Missed our freshman formal at the end of the year because she was so embarrassed."

Autumn cleaned up the first aid supplies, sliding them under her kitchen counter. "I don't know how she did it, and honestly, I don't want to know. To this day, Summer calls it nothing more than karma from the universe. But I know better."

"So, you're saying she's going to remove Cory's eyebrows."

Autumn shook her head. "Summer had a knack for finding weak spots. Amy-Rae was vain, so what happens to her? She gets her beauty taken. I don't always like it. I try to talk her out of it sometimes, but that's Summer. You want to punch him in the face? Summer will go nuclear on him."

Hesitating, I thought back to the list on Summer's phone. "Did any of this nuclear option involve butterflies and an ad about goats?"

The smile gracing Autumn's face told me everything I needed to know.

Ten minutes later, I thanked Autumn for cleaning me up and for talking to me.

As I left her studio, I wished I had more clarity on who Summer was, but the new information only confused me more.

Letting myself back into Summer's apartment, I peeked into her bedroom to find she had turned over in her sleep.

On her stomach, she was breathing deeply, her tangled blonde hair over her face.

Was this the face of a woman who would remove a girl's eyebrows? Others might have been appalled by the story, but all I could feel was a sense of understanding.

Summer was protective of herself and, more importantly, protective of those few people she loved.

Wouldn't I do the same for a friend? For my own family?

My urge to beat this Cory guy to a pulp was born out of the same desperation as Summer had.

Flopping down into the chair she had at her vanity, I studied Summer's sleeping form.

What exactly was this nuclear option Autumn seemed so sure Summer had been acting out? What had she already done to him, and what troubles lay in wait? And why did it make me want her all the more?

Watching her dream, I was struck with her beauty. Being loved by Summer was a hard battle, and it was one I intended to be the victor of.

Hours later, she woke up, still bleary-eyed, but her skin took on little pink spots.

After a quick shower, she came out into the living room, where I was watching a season four episode of *The West Wing*.

She settled on the other side of the couch, pulling her knees up to her chest. "You stayed."

"You asked me to."

She blinked at me, chewing her bottom lip as if embarrassed to admit she would do such a thing. "I did, didn't I?"

"Are you really that surprised?" Leaning forward, I placed the back of my hand on her forehead.

Her fever seemed to have broken.

"Still surprising. Especially after kicking me out of your house the other day."

I ran a hand through my hair. "That was dumb of me. My dad showed up, and I—" Huffing loudly, I shook my head. "My dad was a shitty husband to my mom—you know that. Seeing him again after being with you . . ."

Summer frowned but let me keep talking.

"I've spent a decade telling myself that the worst thing I could do was to become my father."

Summer shook her head, scoffing. "It's obvious to anyone you're not your father, Van."

"I know it's irrational. To have some trust in me and to see that trust shattered. I didn't want you to see him. To see what he does to me."

Her eyes took on a softer look, and she reached forward, squeezing my hand. "You don't need to explain. To be honest, I'm not sure I wouldn't have the same reaction if my mother showed up on my doorstep one day. Being abandoned by a parent makes you second-guess who you are as a person."

A coil of nerves released inside me. Until she said those words, I hadn't known how much I needed to be seen by another.

I brushed the wild hair out of her face, cupping her cheek. "When I didn't hear from you, I thought I blew it."

"You didn't. I knew I overreacted pretty soon after you dropped me off. I was going to tell you at trivia but then I got sick and could barely move for a few days."

Her admission was enough for me. "The idea of losing you because I wasn't honest with you about how I was feeling? These three days have been hell."

"What are you saying?"

Her voice was tentative, and there was a nervous flicker about her eyes.

"I'm falling for you, Summer. I think I have been since I found you dripping rain on my rug."

She blinked at me, shock clouding her features, then disbelief. "That's not true. Don't lie to me, Van."

"I'm not. I spent three days away from you. Going half crazy over the idea of losing what we had. Loving you the way I do and losing out on you because I was too scared to take that chance? That would be the end of me."

She shook her head. Her tangled hair swayed around her face. "You told me, 'Don't fall in love with me.' You said that, and I believed it."

Surprise colored my tone as I stared back at her. "Are you saying you don't feel the same? Do you really think that what's been happening between us is normal? That another man could make you feel the way I do."

She bit her lower lips, grimacing. "It doesn't matter, Van. You told me not to fall for you. You said this was casual. Don't make me want more. So, don't make a fool out of me," she warned. "Don't tell me you're serious when you aren't. I mean it. All I have is my pride, and if you take that away—"

"If anyone is going to be a fool, it's me. I think about you night and day. At work, I can barely concentrate because I remember the way you smiled at me. At stop lights, I forget to drive forward because a song you like comes on. I bought a rose bush for my house because they remind me of you."

"You did?" her voice soft and unbelieving.

A smile forming, I nodded. "The guy at the nursery called them pomponella roses. They'll bloom pale pink, the same shade as your cheeks when you blush." Cupping her face in my hand, I ran my thumb over her cheekbone. "I'm the fool, Summer. Can't you see that?"

"No, no, no," she mumbled, her voice rising.

"Tell me you don't love me back. Say it." My gaze brokered no arguments. There were only two ways out of this. One of us would be left broken.

"You can't love me," she whispered. "You don't know me enough to. If you knew—if you—"

"I know exactly who you are."

Panic was rising in her voice. "This was supposed to be sex. Sex and sunshine and fun over a single summer. I'm sorry I was the person around when you changed your man-whore ways. I'm not a girl you can love, Van. We both know that. You'll find some other nice girl, and you can fall in love with her."

"Don't tell me what I want. And for the record, you are nice. You're loyal to your friends. You defend people in need."

"You don't know a thing about me. If you knew what I've done just in the past three months, you'd go running to the hills."

"What? The stupid pranks on your ex? The butterflies and the keys and the fake doctor's office notices? You think I don't know about those?"

She blinked at me, stammering, "How—what . . ."

"I saw the keys in your car that day you came over to apologize. You left your list out. Quite detailed, too. I've been adding it up. This whole time, I knew there was more to your story."

"There's more. It's not just that."

"And you think I would care? Look, I know about the pictures. Autumn let it slip a few hours ago. If all this man got was a few sleepless nights, it was less than he deserved."

"Shouldn't I be ashamed I sent them?"

"Shouldn't he? You weren't the one who shared them without consent."

This response took the fight out of her argument, and her voice was sad—scared, even.

"What about if this doesn't work out? Aren't you scared of what I would do to you? Don't you think I'm some crazy ex?"

"Why are you making yourself the villain in this story, Sum? You're not. You were wronged. You deserve justice. If I had known from the beginning, I would have helped you. I would have done anything you asked of me. That's how much you mean to me."

"You can't mean that."

"Tell me you don't love me. Say it, and I'll leave."

She opened her mouth, her voice cracking. "I-I . . ."

I waited for her to return my words. To fall into my arms and say she felt the same way.

I knew she did. She had to.

Instead, tears formed at the corner of her eyes. I had seen so many versions of Summer over the season but never had I seen her cry.

Judging by the angry way she brushed them away with flicks of her fingers, she didn't cry often.

"This is all so sudden. You weren't supposed to love me. Cory, he broke my pride. But you, if I let myself love you back and if this goes wrong, it will break my soul. I know it."

"It won't—"

"It can. I can't risk it. You have to know that. I'm being held together by the thinnest strings. I know I seem tough, but I'm not."

Confessing my feelings on the heels of her getting over her illness was a mistake. I would get nowhere with her.

"I pushed you to admit it before you're ready, but I'm not going any-where. So, when you're ready to love me back, I'll be here."

"You're making me feel worse."

I shook my head. "No, you're making yourself feel that way."

"I need time, something. I don't know how to process this."

"Fine. Take your time. Wallow or scheme or do whatever it takes, just know I'm waiting on the other end."

It felt more like a threat than a love declaration, but everything with Summer was a battle.

Standing over her, I bent down and pressed a kiss to her forehead. "Truly."

The next morning at work, I checked my notifications for the hundredth time. No response from Summer. With my phone in my hand, I studied our parade picture from all those weeks ago. The sunlight haloing our faces. The way her blue eyes were bright and warm. Those full lips that, only an hour later, would be under mine as we kissed beside the azaleas.

I missed her to the point of absolute distraction. That morning, I had almost walked out the door without shoes, and I was pretty sure I forgot to lock up behind me. Hopefully, no one would break in and steal my twelve-year-old television.

Breaking in. Once again, everything reminded me of Summer, my little thief. My roses and sunshine. I told her I'd give her time, but I should have been more specific. I would give her exactly forty-eight hours before going back. Turns out, when it came to Summer, I was not a patient man.

"Donovan, do you have that report of the—" Mr. Haruki stood in the doorway, a file in his hand. Frowning, he looked from my phone to my face. "Girl problems?"

I set my phone down, my face heating. "Sorry."

He waved my comment away and sat in the cushioned chair opposite me. "What's going on?"

"Mr. Haruki—"

"Dennis."

"Dennis. You don't want to hear about my relationship issues."

Mr. Haruki studied me over his wire-rimmed spectacles. "She did a number on you, didn't she?"

This was an inappropriate conversation to be having with my boss, but he was here, and I felt so raw.

Burying my head in my hands, I nodded. "I told her I loved her, but she doesn't feel the same."

On the blue upholstered chair across from me, he leaned back, his right leg bent and his ankle resting on his left knee. "I had a feeling this would happen. That's why I told you to be careful with her at the party."

Dropping my hands, I stared at him with a furrowed brow. "I thought you were to be careful not to hurt her. Like, if I screwed up the relationship, I'd be in trouble."

Mr. Haruki laughed. "Oh, that's rich. No, no. Summer has always been the toughest girl. Devin told me once that a boy in their English class called her homely. Summer found the boy, stole his backpack, and threw it into the creek before pushing the boy in after it. He never bothered Devin again. They were ten. I love Summer like another granddaughter, I do. But if she thinks someone is doing the wrong thing, she doesn't think, just acts. It never bothered me because she was so fiercely protective of Devin. And, to be frank, Dev has struggled with assertiveness over the years. But to be on Summer's bad side"—Mr. Haruki whistled, shaking his head—"I wouldn't want to be that guy."

I thought back to the day I met her. She was frantic, her clothes soaked with rain, and a wild look on her face. Then I remembered her words the night I asked her to come to the party. Something about a cheating ex. The way she stood up to the man at the bar for Savvy. But also her defensiveness. The defiance in her eyes when she told me something she didn't think I wanted to hear. And the surprise in her eyes when I would choose her. When I'd be honest.

She was hurt and wasn't the type to believe words. So, why did I think a simple *I love you* would make her fall into my arms with gratitude?

"A woman like that, it won't be easy, but to know her in a way no one else could? If you're the right guy, you'll find a way."

After he left me alone in my office, I sulked in his words.

I wanted to be that man. I could be. If only I could find a way to show her.

Twenty-Two

Summer

I T HAD BEEN TWENTY-SEVEN hours since Van told me he was falling for me, and I was no closer to knowing what to do.

This whole thing had been built on a lie. How could he think their relationship could be any different with a few declarations? Never had I wanted to throw away all sense and dive into love with him. But they were only words. Hollow. It didn't matter how much I wanted him. That I felt the same way. What we had was built upon deception. How could I ever trust my choices again?

Work was unbearably slow. Ordinarily, summer is the busiest season, and I would rush around, placating guests, ordering more stock, and calling employees to fill in. But a late summer storm had rolled into the bay, and the rain and low temperatures had driven away our impromptu guests.

Front Street was dead, with only the stray person passing our windows with a coffee in hand, rushing back to their car.

The weather reflected my mood all too well. I worked in a lull, catching up on the most monotonous paperwork I kept putting to the side. Between the inventory costs for the breakfast buffet and figuring out switching mouthwash brands, I checked my phone for the millionth time.

True to his word, Van hadn't reached out. He was giving me time.

I missed him. I asked for space, asked for time, and only one day later was I cursing myself for both.

A few days before, I would have loved hearing those words from Van.

But seeing Cory had triggered something in me. As much as I hated his words, they still rang in my ears.

Van was so good, so utterly perfect. Telling myself that it was better not to be hurt by him was a punishment of my own making. Months before, I allowed Cory to make me look foolish, and once again, I let him mess with me.

As much as I hated *the best revenge is a life well lived* phrase—wouldn't that be exactly what he deserved? And, more importantly, wasn't that what I deserved? What Van deserved.

Sinking into my chair, I grabbed my phone and scrolled through my contacts.

I had a few with whom I felt comfortable talking about my conundrum and even fewer who I knew could give me advice.

I couldn't reach out to Devin, who seemed to get bored with the men she dated before the check arrived. And as positive and helpful as Autumn could be, her dating experience couldn't fill a postcard.

Wren picked up on the second ring. Wren shushed a shrill bark of what I could only assume was the small wiry-haired dog she had brought to the brewery.

After pleasantries, Wren paused in the middle of her story about her boyfriend, Adrian, who had been trying—but failing—to teach her how to fish in the river behind their home.

"What is going on with you? You didn't laugh once at my story of falling into the river." She lowered her voice. "Something I do more often than I'd like to admit."

"Van said he loves me."

"The guy you were dating to get back at Cory?"

"That's not—he's not." I blew out air through my nose. "Things changed between us recently, and I—" I paused, a hundred different questions running through my mind. "After what happened with your ex, how were you able to trust someone again?"

Wren huffed out a large breath. "Adrian and Buck couldn't be less similar. That helps. For me, it was feeling more like myself with Adrian over a single weekend than I ever did with Buck over our years-long relationship. I liked myself more. And Adrian liked me—loves me. As that person. All the things I felt I had to hide or diminish to be the right kind of girlfriend. I don't need to do that with Adrian. Plus, the sex is better than anything."

"Okay, okay. Enough about your orgasms," I grumbled.

"You're not me, though, Sum. I can't tell you how to feel, but I will say that the right man for you is the one who can handle all of you, embracing every part of what makes you so special."

"But if it doesn't work out—"

"But if it does—" Wren paused, gathering her words, like she'd always done. "Summer, you build up this armor around yourself, as if being vulnerable would make you less than. But it's not true. You deserve someone who loves you exactly as you are. Truly."

Truly.

Truly.

Never had Van seemed the type to give falsehoods. If he said he was falling for me, he was.

Truly, truly, truly.

The words ricocheted around my head.

Not only was he a man of his word but a man of his actions. Never had had he done something contrary to his words.

Truly.

"I got to go. I'll call you—"

"Talk to you in a few weeks." She laughed.

I stopped at the store, buying two dozen banana-flavored taffy sticks and a ribbon.

Whoever said men can't receive bouquets?

I tied them together, admiring my work.

It might have been silly, but I knew Van would appreciate the thought, an apology of sorts. I decided against going home to change.

No, I wanted to meet him in his space. To go back to where this all began and start anew.

Romancing someone was a new feeling for me. Sure, I had been taken out, had flowers and wooing, and all the stuff. But to declare yourself to someone? To apologize for being too stubborn to see the beautiful affection blooming between us until it was almost too late? To win him back? Those were new.

Arriving earlier than him before he could get off work, I hesitated in the driveway, almost talking myself out of going in.

But I could do this. I could be brave. I could take this risk.

The door was, unsurprisingly, unlocked. He really needed to be more careful about that. For the second time this summer, I let myself in the front door.

The hallway looked the same as that day in the middle of June.

From under the kitchen sink, I pulled out a milk glass vase and arranged the banana taffy bouquet in it before placing it on his counter.

Outside, boots stomped on the porch, and keys jingled.

Maybe I was wrong. He must have seen my text and left early.

"Van?" I called out, my spirits lifting as he marched down the hall.

Framed by the open door, Cory stood on the landing, staring at me.

Summer

DARK SHADOWS COLORED THE bags under his bloodshot eyes, and his normally gelled hair was sticking up in a mess on one side.

"What—" I glanced at the open door and swallowed hard. "What are you doing here?"

"You think you're the only one who can be a detective?" He cocked his head, his red-rimmed eyes narrowing. "How do you think, Summer? I followed you. I saw you leave work and figured we could have this conversation at your place. But, no. You came here to, what, whore yourself out to whatever man will take you?"

"Fuck you," I spat. "You don't know anything about me or Van."

"Oh, I know plenty. After your little stunt at The Boathouse, I started doing some digging. It took me a little while to connect everything. Do the math. My free time, my reputation in my neighborhood, that was an annoyance. My friends making fun of me because of the embarrassing pictures I somehow posted. Frustrating. I had to change my number because of all the calls I was getting. Whatever. But then my fiancée tells me she has proof I'm cheating on her."

"You were cheating on her."

"She didn't need to know that? Why couldn't you let it go? Why did you have to ruin my life?"

"Your life isn't ruined. Take some responsibility for your actions. There was nothing I did to you that you didn't have coming."

"You're a heinous bitch."

I shrugged. "I prefer *tempestuous*."

"They fired me this morning. I moved here for that job. Security had to escort me off base. They're opening a case against me."

I raised a brow, not even trying to school my features. "How would they know if you didn't tell them, Summer? Why couldn't you leave me alone?"

Losing my temper was the wrong call, but I couldn't contain it.

"Why should I? You made your choices. You think you can go around hurting people, and no one would want to fight back? Was I supposed to lie down and take your deception? The invasion of showing off pictures of my body and not fight back?"

"Yes." He screamed. "It's not my fault you were a slut who sent me those photos. It's not my fault you fucked me without asking me if I had a girlfriend. And it's not my fault you wanted a relationship out of me."

"All I want from you is for you to get out of my boyfriend's home."

He stepped toward me, then another, his pace languid as if he were a large cat stalking his prey. "No. I've got you, and you're going to pay for what you did to me."

"This is Van's house. He's going to be here any minute now."

I hated using another man to get him to back off, but the closer Cory got to me, the more obvious his gaze was too frantic to hear reason, his body too tense.

"No, I don't think he will."

"He will. He gets off work at five, and I asked him to meet me here."

Cory tsked at me. "No. He's still at work. I put a location tag on his car." Cory brought out his phone, checked the screen, and turned it to face me. "See, still fifteen minutes away. His car hasn't moved in five hours."

He advanced closer to me, and my shoulder hit the shelf of Glyndon's teacups, rattling them against their saucers.

"I'll have plenty of time with you."

"What do you want from me, Cory? An apology? I'm sorry you were found out."

"It's too late for an apology, and we both know that wasn't one." He shuffled his foot between mine and yanked a chunk of my hair, jerking my face to his.

"I want to know what makes you think you have to right to fuck me over like this? Huh? A little fucking nobody. Barely graduated high school, still works in service, has done nothing with her life. Who the fuck do you think you are."

My scalp screamed, and despite trying to keep myself together, I couldn't stifle my reflexive tears.

"That's right. Cry for me. Let me see those alligator tears. Not feeling strong now, are you?"

Panic rushed through me as he wrapped a hand around my throat and pressed down on my trachea.

"No, you're not tough at all. Just a dumb bitch trying to take away what I'm owed." His vise grip made my vision swim.

Scrambling against his chest, I pushed, scratched, punched for him to let me go, but my fight brought out a new strength in him. I clawed at his arms, but my nails couldn't dig hard enough to get him to relent.

A vicious glint formed in his eyes as he squeezed, and my ears began to ring.

Is this terrible man's face the last thing I will see? It can't be.

I had Van. We were going to be together, and all of that was fading away as quickly as my sight as Cory crushed farther in.

I said a quick vow to whoever was listening, *Please let me fight my way out. Please give me another chance. One more day with Van. One more.*

I love him. I love him. I love him, and I need to find my way back to him.

Blood pulsed under my skin as I flailed around, looking for something—anything—to hit him with.

A teacup.

Holding it by the handle, I slammed it against his face where the china shattered, cutting his cheek open.

His grip loosened enough for me to drag a single breath of air in before he forced his weight on me again.

Black edged my vision.

Grasping what was left of the handle, I jammed the jagged edge into his face.

I couldn't see where I was hitting, but I did it again and again.

At the sound of tearing flesh, something gave way, and hot, sticky blood poured down my hand.

He let go of me, and as I breathed in big jagged gasps of air, I stumbled to get to the front door. To get to the street, find a neighbor, something—anything but be in that house with him.

I took three steps down the hall as my sight returned, and I was almost to the door when I'm wrenched back by my hair.

As I kicked out behind me, my bare feet brushed off him a few times before I could make contact.

I opened my mouth to shout, but the sound was strained by my neck being pulled taut as he yanked my head back again, the act burning my throat.

As I fell onto my stomach, his heavy body landed on top of me.

Why didn't I pay attention to action movies?

I bucked and flailed under him as he took my head in his hand and bashed my face into the floor. Blood poured as my nose cracked.

He screamed obscenities, calling me names, as he pulled my head back again.

A painting plummeted to the floor, shattering glass all over, and as he brought my head down, a piece sliced my neck.

The searing hot pain of being sliced paired with my weakening screams.

I used my remaining energy to roll to the side, kicking him in what I hoped was the groin. My foot made contact with something, but I didn't look back to see what it was.

Scrambling to my knees, I crawled onto the front porch. Blood poured out of my nose and onto my white button-down as I dragged my body as fast as I could.

Cory grasped at my ankle, trying to snag it again, but I kicked at him, not caring what I hit.

Finally on my feet, I ran down the path.

A big truck turned onto the street, and I waved to get it to stop.

To my right, Cory stumbled to his car. He reversed onto the road and knocked me to my knees.

I wondered if he was going to run me over, but he sped away.

The truck parked in the middle of the road, and Van climbed down.

My body collapsed, the concrete digging into my flesh.

I'm alive, I'm alive, I'm alive, and no pain has ever felt so good.

Van

WHEN I WAS FIFTEEN, young and foolhardy, I drove off a cliff on a four-wheeler. My friend Kenneth invited me up to his family's vacation home in the Cascades for a mid-winter trip. After all the adults went to bed, Kenneth and I snuck out the back door under hanging icicles and pushed the four-wheelers down the powdered road until we were out of earshot of the cabin.

Fueled with little more than pilfered beer and teenage recklessness, we headed up into the snowy logging roads.

The turn I took was too sharp, and while Kenneth was able to stop in time, I flew forward, the four-wheeler catching air, and there was nothing beneath me. For a moment, only the crisp night sky and adrenaline coursed through me.

Then the panic set in.

I couldn't see how far I would fall before I hit the cliff's snow-covered rocks. The four-wheeler landed first, heavier than me, the crunch of metal and gears cutting through the hushed night.

Landing only a second later, with a dull crack, my body cut through the month's worth of snow and a crack against a rock. The fresh blood cooled instantly on my head as I lay there on the cliffside, broken.

Seconds ticked by with nothing but the breaking branches under the four-wheeler and my rasping breaths, and I wondered if this was the end of me.

A bone-chilling fear invaded every pore, and I knew I would never be as afraid as that moment.

I was wrong.

The fear of falling off that cliff, of the accident that gave me seven stitches and a permanent scar on my head, of the cold snow, and of the heat of my bruising would never compare to the moment I turned onto my road to see a battered Summer. To see the blue sedan reverse out of my driveway, to see the bumper strike her, and to see the only woman I could ever love fall; bloody and broken onto the road.

My engine still running, I kneeled at her side, the hard concrete cutting through my work pants and digging into my knees.

Her face was so bloody I couldn't tell where she was injured. As she wheezed between the rivulets of blood, distinct purple marks on her throat snagged my attention.

"Can you move? Can I move you?"

Nodding, she opened her mouth, but only a rasp of air came out.

One arm around her back and the other under her legs, I carried her to the small grassy section of my lawn.

Safely out of the road, I inspected her body. The blood was shiny on her face, and bruises were forming over her skin. Her nails were broken, full of blood and dirt. A gash on her neck poured over her shirt.

I put pressure on her wound with my hand. "Who?"

There was only one man who would do this to her.

My jaw tense, I pulled my phone out with my free hand and called 911.

Summer grabbed my hand, squeezing it as I gave the instructions for the police and the EMT to arrive as soon as possible.

With the operator in my ear, I held tight to Summer and watched as she passed out, her blood soaking into the grass.

You would think that, after years of being in and out of hospitals, I would be used to antiseptic and rubber permeating the halls. But nothing could prepare me for the drawn-out hours of waiting rooms.

As I followed the paramedics, who refused to let me ride with her, I called Devin, who called Summer's father.

When he arrived at the hospital a few minutes after me, I recognized those same blue eyes and waved him over.

I introduced myself and told him what happened as best I could.

After an awkward fifteen minutes of silence, he turned to me. "So, you're the one who changed her oil, are you?"

Furrowing my brow, I thought back. "Yeah, I did."

He made an indistinguishable sound in the back of his throat as he assessed me. "I won't tell you not to break my pumpkin's heart because, if you did, I would be the least of your worries."

I swallowed hard.

"But I'd stay behind her with my tire iron."

"Noted, Mr. Townsend."

His gaze didn't falter as he looked me up and down, his eyes snagging on my hands and the blood over my shirt.

He leaned in closer, asking me, "What are we going to do about this piece of shit who hurt her?"

"I haven't planned that part out yet, but I have a few ideas."

In the moments after I saw Summer, my only thoughts were on getting her safe and healthy again.

But Cory had to pay.

While they had loaded Summer into the ambulance, I had given an officer Cory's name and the make and model of the car and let him know I couldn't give him a full statement until I knew Summer was stable.

The doctor approached us, her brows pulled together and mouth downturned, darting her gaze between me and Summer's father. "She's being brought into surgery now. There was some internal bleeding we need to repair, and she has damage to her trachea. The glass that cut her wasn't deep, and luckily, it missed the artery by a few millimeters, but she still lost quite a bit of blood. Unfortunately, we are low on her blood type, so we're waiting on a delivery from a blood bank in Seattle now."

Seattle. That could've been an hour or more, depending on traffic and the ferry system. I needed Summer to be well sooner than that.

Standing to my full height, I stared Dr. Pearce down. "What's her blood type?"

"B positive," Peter said, shaking his head. "From her mother, I wish I could give mine, but I'm AB positive. I can't."

"I'm O negative. Take my blood."

The doctor frowned. "This is highly irregular."

"But can I?"

"Yes, but—" Her eyes shot down to the chart, then back at me as she bit her lip.

"Then, do it. Run any test you need to first, but take my blood."

She shook her head in disbelief. "Alright. Let me get you set up with someone."

I followed her, the weight of Summer's father's gaze on my back.

It was a waiting game. The bandage on the inside of my arm tugged my skin every time I shifted in my seat. But, for the first time, I welcomed the feeling. I did something that could help Summer. The doctors and fate were in control of the rest, but I had done something.

After an hour, Peter grumbled to himself, got up, and left me.

Five minutes later, he returned with an old work T-shirt. "Might have some grease stains on it, but it's clean."

I took the shirt, thanked him, and changed in the bathroom. It was too wide and short for me but better than the bloody button-down I had been wearing for the past two hours, which I tossed in a biohazard trash can.

A detective in a suit approached me, carrying a tablet with a small keyboard. He acknowledged us with a curt nod, his bushy blonde mustache not moving. "Mr. Logan, I'm Detective Rhodes." He turned to Peter. "Peter. Good to see you, even under these circumstances."

Peter stood, putting his hand out to shake the officer's. "Calvin, any news?"

"Normally, we'd send a patrol officer over to have this conversation, but I wanted to talk to you in person." Detective Rhodes motioned to the chairs beside us. "About forty-five minutes ago, a man went into the emergency department in Rosedale."

I furrowed my brow.

Rosedale was almost an hour away from Ridgewood, on the southern tip of our peninsula and in the neighboring county.

If he had driven across the bridge, he would have made it to the Seattle side, where he might have disappeared in the larger population.

"He had substantial damage to his left eye, scratches all over his face, arms, and neck, with severe bruising on other parts of his body. His injuries are consistent with a physical fight, likely caused by someone smaller than him fighting him off. He was also covered in more blood than his injuries could cause. The staff there notified the sheriff's office, who was able to track me down." His gaze swung to me. "I would need a positive ID from Summer, but it would appear that Cory Thompson will soon be behind bars."

Conflicting emotions warred in me. I was proud of Summer for causing enough damage to make him need hospitalization, but I was also angry I couldn't get my hands on him first.

Beside me, Peter cracked his beefy knuckles, likely with the same thoughts. "Rosedale, huh?"

Detective Rhodes widened his eyes, frowning with a head shake. "Peter, he's being observed by an officer of the Pierce County sheriff's office. He's not going anywhere. We can hold him on Mr. Logan's account of the car matching the one seen driving away and his injuries for now."

"You sure that sheriff can't take a little break and give me five minutes?" Peter asked.

"No. He won't. Let justice take over. For now, focus on Summer." The officer put his thick hand out, and Peter shook it, then offered it to me. "You did a good job getting her here, son. If it wasn't for you being there, she might not have made it."

I couldn't take the compliment. If I had been home earlier, she wouldn't have been hurt in the first place. But Detective Rhodes was not the person to have that conversation with.

"Thank you, Detective."

When he left, Peter and I were alone again, in the quiet of the ever-approaching night.

I clasped my hands together and waited for the woman I loved to stabilize.

Summer

EVERYTHING HURT. I HAD said that phrase countless times. After a long hike with Autumn, the day after I got the bottomless mimosas with the girls for my twenty-third birthday, after catching the flu.

But never had my body hurt more than waking up in that hospital bed.

The bright lights burned my eyes as I tried to open them, blurry shapes clearing into human forms into the face I held in my mind as I bled out.

I opened my mouth to say his name, but no sound came out. My throat burned, and I placed a hand on it to feel the bandage where I was slashed and likely deeply bruised.

Van saw my motion and got me water from a large clear plastic cup with a bendy straw. The water was lukewarm but helped soothe it.

"How do you feel?" he asked, taking my hand.

"Like an asshole cut off my air supply and beat my ass," I croaked, the words scorching my throat. Planting a hand beside me, I tried to shift in the bed, but my aching muscles wouldn't allow it. Flopping back on the bed, I knew I had to conserve my energy and words. "Cory?"

A darkness flashed over his face.

"Arrested in Rosedale yesterday. Came into the ER blind in one eye. They're holding him for vehicular assault for hitting you with his car, since I saw that. Once you're able to talk to the police, they'll be able to add attempted murder to his charge."

Attempted murder.

I could have died.

"You fought like hell. I'm proud of you, Sunshine."

Shame filled me.

If I hadn't provoked Cory the way I did, if I had let things go, he never would've followed me that day. Heat filled my face, and I realized I was clenching my fists.

"It was my fault," I croaked.

A shadow fell over his face.

"No. It's his."

I opened my mouth, but the thunderous expression on Van's face stopped me.

"Don't you dare take this on, Summer. He was a weak man, bent on hurting you. But he'll never do that again. Am I pissed that you were in that position? Of course. But nothing you did to him, no matter how inconvenient, means that you deserved to be hurt."

The doctor came in, a clipboard in her hands. She approached the empty side of the bed, looking over my vitals and comparing them to whatever was on her chart. "You are looking much better, Summer." She beamed at me, her tanned skin bright against the white of her jacket.

She didn't seem to be that much older than me, and I was struck with how impressive it must have been to be that successful under thirty.

I shifted and forgot the silly idea.

She poked and prodded, then declared that I was well enough to get up and walk. "Careful not to pull out your stitches. We don't want your boyfriend having to donate his blood all over again, do we?"

With that warning, she left me alone with Van.

I glanced over at him, his cheeks flushing pink at the comment. "You donated blood?"

He shrugged, and in that moment of humility, I knew I would never love a man the way I loved him.

"But you're afraid of needles."

He swallowed hard. "Seeing the woman I love almost die in front of me has changed my idea of fear."

Tears stung my eyes, and I didn't wipe them away this time.

Concern creased his face.

"Are you in pain?" He took a step away from me, dropping my hand to head to the door. "I'll ask Dr. Pearce to give you more medicine."

"No," I cried out, tears dripping down my chin. "I mean, yes, everything is sore and aching, and I'm sure once the drugs wear off, I'll be howling, but I'm not crying over that. You love me."

Worry transformed into incredulity, then into joy.

"I told you I do."

"I'm sorry I didn't believe you."

My words were scratchy, each syllable rough as it came out.

He took my hand again, his expression soft. "Don't worry about that. You don't need to explain."

"I do—" I coughed, then swallowed.

The pain medication was taking the edge off, but talking was difficult. I had likely stretched my voice to its limit by my thirty-odd words.

"No, you don't." He drew up a chair beside me, his hand gripping mine. "We have forever to talk this out. For you to call me on my bullshit and for me to call you on yours. Right now, all I need from you is for you to get better. To heal. And you won't heal if you're working yourself up and talking and—"

I slapped a hand over his mouth, cutting him off and raising my brows. "Let me say this and then I'll rest."

He frowned but waved begrudgingly for me to go on.

"I love you."

There were flowery words I wanted to use, soliloquies on his gray eyes, and there was the way he made me feel safe. That there would be hard days ahead. I had been living in reality after all. But as long as I had Van beside me, I would be alright. All my anger and doubt couldn't exist in a world where he loved me.

He bent down, pressing a tender kiss to my mouth, his nose missing my broken one. His last word a vow against my lips.

"Truly."

Epilogue

Summer

September 22nd, The Autumnal Equinox

I T HAD BEEN A long four weeks of recuperation after my release. Labor Day cookouts and boating trips were replaced by a quiet affair in Van's backyard. My nose was still tender, but the bruising had healed from two black eyes and a purple nose to an unsightly chartreuse.

The criminal justice system ran slow, and Cory was out on bail until his hearing. I was able to get a protection order in place, keeping him away from me. Still, Van insisted I shouldn't be alone.

It was too soon to move in together, but with his home being far bigger than my little apartment and much more comfortable, I ended up staying there most nights.

When Autumn suggested we all get together for the equinox, her idea was to perform what she called a release ritual. She wanted to do a four-mile sunset hike up to the top of a nearby peak.

I vetoed that idea, and instead, we met at a beach, where we wrote out our regrets and burned them as we gave thanks for the blessings we had.

A few months before, I would have scoffed, but falling in love with Van had softened me.

I was thankful for my love for him.

He had been nothing more than accommodating, helping me with things that would send other men to the hills.

When I tried to tell him I didn't want him to see me in such a state, he reminded me he had seen me throw up on at least two occasions and still thought I was the most beautiful woman in the world.

He stayed with me as I gave my statement to the police, where I outlined every moment of the attack. It was hard for him to hear, but he didn't make a sound, holding my hand as I spoke.

I admitted to the catfishing account but left out the email hacking and other illegal portions.

The police didn't seem too interested in Cory's claims that I ruined his life, particularly because the IRS had opened up their case against him.

As I stood on the beach, flames licked my paper, and my words charred into nothing along with my doubts and fears.

After the equinox ritual, Autumn drove me to the bar to meet up with Van and his coworkers for a special Sunday trivia night.

As I sat beside him, Van laced an arm around my waist, pulling me close, and dragged the glass of my favorite cider over to me.

The host, Dr. Factoid, in a neon yellow bowler cap, got up to the microphone, carrying a stack of cards. "Alright, beardos and weirdos, we have another round of trivia, starting with this first question. For five points, what is the least popular flavor of Laffy Taffy?"

I smirked at Van as I wrote the answer.

By the time I had returned to his house, the ten sticks of banana taffy were gone. He told me later that he stress-ate them over a single day.

"What is the longest-running Aaron Sorkin show?" Dr. Factoid asked.

Putting down my cider, I glanced at Van. "This game is too easy, right?"

He laughed, penciling in the answer.

The host flipped another card. "In knitting, what does PSSO mean?"

I almost laughed.

Around us, people furrowed their brows, whispering to one another, while I wrote my anser.

"Hood Canal is not a true canal but a what?"

I had always been good at trivia, but it was as if these questions were made for me.

When we got the last question about the penalties of illegal trespassing, I glanced over at Van. "Did you do something?"

He frowned, but the casual expression couldn't hide the humor in his eyes.

"Me?"

"Seriously?" I nudged him. "I can't believe you fixed the questions for bar trivia."

"How would I do that, Sunshine? Who would spend hours researching to come up with questions that are perfectly in tuned to our interests and relationship and then track the host down at his day job, in Illahee where he works in IT, and pay him a few hundred bucks to switch the questions?"

Heat flooded my cheeks, and I couldn't bite back the smile blooming over my face.

Leaning forward, I rested a hand on his cheek.

Since I got out, he'd been so gentle with me. While there have been a lot of little pecks and hand-holding, his touch has been tender, tentative, even. Enough of that.

I kissed him in the middle of that dingy dive bar, with its peeling marbled contact-papered tabletop.

He held my cheek delicately as if I were a bubble about to burst, but I didn't allow it.

I deepened our kiss, my tongue tracing the seam of his lips.

It had been a long month without this. The need pulsed between us as he matched my kisses with his own.

His shouting coworkers, announcing we had won with a perfect score, interrupted us.

No surprise there.

Beside us, Eldon leaned forward, his arm around Savvy's shoulder. "You two should go grab the prize. You answered all the questions, anyway."

Van and I grinned at each other. With my thumb, I wiped the spot of pink lipstick lingering on his mouth. "As sweet as that is, I think we've both won, don't you?"

Van's smile widened.

"Absolutely." Clapping Eldon on the shoulder, he shook his head. "You two take it. We have other plans."

We walked through the house and straight out the back door into the garden.

In the middle of the lawn, Van had set a large picnic blanket, with a bottle of my favorite rosé on ice and little cakes. On the edge of the fabric were trios of battery-operated tea lights.

I covered my mouth at the sight. "Van, I—"

Taking my hand, he helped me sit before lowering himself beside me. He poured the rosé into one of the teacups from the cabinet.

He had insisted I use them as often as possible, even making a stray comment about them belonging to me.

I popped one of the little cakes in my mouth, the taste exploding across my taste buds. "I didn't know the bakery made mini lemon rose cakes."

He grinned at me. "They don't, normally. I put in a special request for them."

A swelling sensation filled my chest at the words. All these little gestures, the care, and details he created for me. My eyes prickled with tears. That was a new thing from the attack. I was rawer at first, crying over music lyrics and sad books.

But then, being in the safety of Van's arms, with the help of my friends and family, fulfilling it all made it easier to be vulnerable with him.

For the first time in my adult life, I could be soft. Before, I existed behind a shield, never showing my tenderness. But with Van, I grew stronger. And, in that strength, I could move on. Never forgiving, I wasn't a completely different woman. But I could let go, and eventually, I knew that bad day would be a passing memory I could easily forget.

I still considered myself a badass and went back to work with the same attention to detail and management style. If I felt someone needed to be called out, I was more than willing to do it. But in the confines of my relationship with Van, I could let go of that. He had seen me at my worst: the petty, the sick, and the mean.

And he loved me.

After setting down my finished glass of rosé, I got on my hands and knees to climb on his lap.

As nice as the kiss we had in the bar was. I could tell he was holding back with me. I would need to set the tone for the night.

My sundress rode up my thighs as I straddled him, nothing but my thin underwear and his shorts dividing us.

This kiss was hard, demanding, even, as my tongue delved into his mouth.

I rubbed my center along his ridge.

He pulled back, lust but also a hesitancy clouding his eyes. "Are you sure? I don't want to hurt you."

I softened, laying a hand on his cheek. "You could never hurt me. Donovan Logan, you healed me."

The softness of love in his eyes hardened to steely desire.

"Truly."

"Truly."

And with that, we kissed, his hands under my dress and pulling my panties to the side.

I slipped my fingers between us, unbuttoning him and pulling his cock free. I stroked down his length once, twice, and he gasped against my lips.

He put me on my back, the soft scratch of the blanket under my bare shoulders.

My underwear and his shirt was flung to some far reach of the garden and then my dress was over my head.

In the silver moonlight, Van braced himself over me, the hard muscles of his arms holding me in his grip.

His mouth left mine, kissing my jaw, before his tongue slid to my breasts.

A pulse thrummed inside me, demanding more.

"No more," I gasped out as his teeth scrape against my nipple. "I need you inside me. I need to feel you."

It had been weeks of chaste kisses and lingering glances. The mere brush of his hand against my clit was sending me close.

He didn't need any more encouragement. His cock sank into me, and I cried out.

The pace was frenzied. We had been apart for far too long to take our time.

Wrapping my legs around his waist, I brought him deeper and then crashed, stars filling my eyes as he exploded inside me.

The neighbors might've heard—hell, even the whole neighborhood—but as he thrust inside me, I couldn't care.

Together, we came down, limbs heavy and heated.

Still inside me, he kissed my neck, careful not to press on the bruises.

My fingers danced over the muscles of his back as we caught our breath.

Content with the moment, we lay there for what could have been an hour or five minutes.

As if it were heavy, he picked his head up from my chest and looked up at me. Brushing the hair from my face, he cupped my cheek before giving me a languid kiss.

"That wasn't part of my plan. Give me about two minutes, and we're going to make love."

My eyes drifted shut at the remark, a smile playing on my lips as we sank into the soft grass, the scent of midnight roses in the air.

Acknowledgements

Thank you to

Kate McWilliams for letting me borrow the terrible baby-voice analogy. Sorry you went through that trauma bestie.

Laura Mowery, Dillon Bancroft, Shannon Nikole, MJ Marino, and Greta Rose West.

My little brother, Andy for imparting all your bar trivia related knowledge. I know we're still salty about the time we got second place on Breaking Bad night, but you're number one to me.

My beta reader, Cassidy for being the first reader and encouraging me to go crazier.

My husband for not only being my favorite banana Laffy Taffy lover, but for telling me that a Datsun 280Z would be a very cool car.

Despite my (embarrassingly) extensive research, I could not find a definitive answer to which laffy taffy flavor was the least popular by sales. For the purpose of this story, I'm sticking with my answer of banana, (which is often ranked at the top for taste ironically) Forgive this egregious error if I am wrong.

About the Author

Linnea March is a contemporary romance author who writes steamy stories about self-confident women and the rugged men who love them. She lives somewhere in the wilds of the Pacific Northwest with her husband, their two boys, and a plump dog. After fifteen years of teaching early childhood education, she put down the googly eyes and picked up a pen. When not writing, she can be found reading her way through an ever-growing pile of books while drinking copious amounts of coffee. She proudly refuses to use umbrellas.

Wren's Winter

A missed turn, the wrong doorstep, and the right guy?

What was meant to be a romantic retreat in the picturesque town of Icicle Creek with her boyfriend becomes an unexpected solo adventure for Wren Alexander. Newly single, she arrives on the wintry mountain armed with romance novels, canned wine, and a passion for the unexpected. Fate intercedes when a missed turn, an accidental doorstep, and an encounter with a grumpy yet irresistibly handsome neighbor challenges all her ideas of what this trip could be.

Adrian Winter, grappling with the weight of managing his grandparents' cabin after a heartbreaking loss, is taken aback by the arrival of the radiant Wren on his doorstep. Despite leaving his playboy days behind, Wren's presence sparks a resurgence of emotions, prompting him to question the depths of his heart.

As reality comes to their door, they find themselves losing the battle against their feelings. Amidst a snowstorm, a couple of canine escapades, and an unexpected plunge into a river, Wren and Adrian discover that love often appears when least expected—even on the wrong front porch. Now, they must decide if their connection is strong enough to weather all that life throws their way.

Faultless Notion
They didn't mean to get married.

Eloise Dunning ran far from her small town in the Pacific Northwest to Los Angeles with little more than the clothes on her back and a dream of being a singer-songwriter. Now she is a personal assistant to the rock band, Prevalent Notion, and leaving her songbook in the bottom of her bag.

Keller Grant is everything a rock star should be. Sinfully attractive, an enigmatic artist with a dark past, and an immensely talented drummer. He loves the revolving door of women in each city, creating music with his bandmates in Prevalent Notion, and teasing an uptight Eloise.

The night before the band kicks off their American Tour, Eloise and Keller wake up in each other's arms with wedding bands on their fingers. Forced by the record label to maintain the marriage for the public, they face a hungry press, rabid fans, and jealousy from all sides.
As they get the world to believe in their facade, they find that, maybe, this marriage doesn't feel like a performance.